A
KILLER
CHOICE

TOM HUNT

ORION

First published in Great Britain in 2019 by Orion Fiction,
an imprint of The Orion Publishing Group Ltd.,
Carmelite House, 50 Victoria Embankment
London EC4Y 0DZ

An Hachette UK Company

1 3 5 7 9 10 8 6 4 2

A CIP catalogue record for this book is
available from the British Library.

ISBN (Trade Paperback) 9781409192275
ISBN (eBook) 9781409192299

Printed and bound in Great Britain by
Clays Ltd, Elcograf S.p.A

www.orionbooks.co.uk

To my two favourite people,
Mom and Dad

1

TWENTY MINUTES AFTER RECEIVING THE WORST PHONE CALL OF HIS LIFE, Gary Foster pulled his Corolla into the parking lot of McCann Medical Center. He followed the signs directing him to the emergency room and came to a stop in an open stall, slamming on the brakes hard enough to momentarily lock his seat belt.

He turned off the car.

Threw open the car door.

Sprinted to the ER entrance.

Inside, three women in green scrubs stood behind the check-in counter. Gary stared at them for a moment, heart thundering in his chest, every muscle in his thirty-nine-year-old body tight with tension.

"Someone just called me about my wife," he said.

The oldest of the group, a woman with cropped black hair who looked to be in her fifties, stepped out from behind the counter. She asked for Gary's name, then identified herself as Abby Fredrickson, the caller. Gary followed her to an empty nearby waiting area and sat down next to her.

"Right now, we don't know much more than what I told you on the phone," Abby said. She lightly touched Gary's knee. "Your wife was at Town Shoppe Mall. Apparently, she just collapsed and started convulsing. Someone called nine-one-one and she was brought here by an ambulance. She was conscious when she arrived and she's undergoing tests right now."

Gary slowly shook his head. Not even a half hour ago, he'd received the call. He'd been working at the outdoor-clothing retailer he owned with his brother, Rod—just a normal afternoon at the store, spent putting away inventory and helping the occasional customer—when his cell phone rang, displaying a local 989 Michigan number, one he didn't recognize. Pure terror had settled over him like a suffocating blanket as he listened to the story of his wife's—Beth's—sudden collapse. After the call, he drove straight to McCann Medical Center.

"What . . ." Gary said. The word trailed off. He swallowed and felt his Adam's apple bob in his throat. "What happened?"

"Beth collapsed at the ma—"

"I know," he said. "But why?"

Abby shook her head and shrugged. "We'll know more after the testing."

"Can I see her?"

"She's having a CT scan right now. You can see her once she's finished. It should only be a few minutes."

Gary opened his mouth but no words came. He ran a hand

through his thinning brown hair and massaged his temples, pausing for a moment to compose himself.

He just wanted to be alone, wanted to absorb this horrific news in private. But there was one final question he needed to ask, one question he had to have an answer to.

"Abby?" Gary said. He paused, glanced down at his hands, unable to look her in the eye. "The doctors know Beth is pregnant, right?"

"Yes," she said. "They noticed the baby bump right away."

"Is the baby . . ."

"We don't know. We'll know more soon. I'm sorry."

Gary slumped down farther in the chair and exhaled. He could not comprehend how his life had been upended in such a short amount of time. "Let me know when you hear from the doctors," he said.

"Of course. Please come get me if you have more questions," Abby said. She walked back to the check-in counter.

Gary stared out the window at the light snowflakes lazily falling in the parking lot, accumulating on the pavement, sprinkling the windshields of parked cars with an early-March dusting. He saw his reflection in the glass; his face was numb with fatigue, his eyes distant. It was the expression of a man who'd had his soul crushed, the look of a man who could do nothing but helplessly wait to find out whether the unthinkable had happened.

GARY WAITED AN AGONIZING FIVE MINUTES UNTIL A DOCTOR WEARING GREEN scrubs approached him. He had black hair, and the short sleeves on the scrubs revealed small, wiry forearms. Not young, but young for a doctor—mid-thirties or so.

"Gary, I'm Dr. Simpson," he said, shaking Gary's hand. "I'm the ER doc on duty."

Gary followed Dr. Simpson through a set of double doors. Down a long, dark hallway. After fifteen seconds that felt more like fifteen minutes, Dr. Simpson stopped in front of an open door, Patient Room 121, and motioned for Gary to enter. Gary said a silent prayer—the third prayer he'd said since receiving the phone call—and stepped inside.

It was a small room with beige walls and no windows. An anatomy poster depicting the muscles of the human body was taped on the wall above a small desk. In the middle of the room was a hospital bed, elevated at a slight incline. Sitting on the edge of the bed, her legs crossed and hands resting in her lap, was his wife.

Beth.

She wore a loose hospital gown that covered her petite, ramrod-straight body. Her light brunette hair was pulled back into a ponytail, revealing the delicate features of her face. Gary rushed to the bed, leaned over, and hugged her.

"It's so great to see you," she whispered.

Blinking back tears, Gary ran his hands over her hair and rubbed her back through the thin fabric of the gown. He held her for a moment longer, then sat down on the bed beside her.

Dr. Simpson pulled a stool from under the desk and dragged it over to them. "What have you been told so far, Gary?" he asked as he sat down.

Gary reached over and grabbed Beth's hand, squeezed hard. "All I know is that Beth collapsed and was rushed here."

"She was fully conscious and cognizant when she arrived," Dr. Simpson said. "After a few tests determined she was in no immediate danger, we performed an ultrasound. Your baby boy's heart rate is strong and within the expected limits, and everything on the ultrasound looked fine. He wasn't harmed in the fall."

Gary looked down at the basketball-sized bump protruding against Beth's hospital gown. Only six months ago, they'd found out about the pregnancy. After years of failed attempts, they'd accepted that starting a family through traditional means just wasn't going to happen. They'd started looking into adoption, possibly from China. But when Gary returned home from a long day at the store last September and Beth greeted him by handing him a positive pregnancy test, they'd danced around and celebrated like teenagers. It had been the most surprising, euphoric moment of their marriage.

"Our goal now is to figure out why this happened," Dr. Simpson continued. "Blood pressure will often rise and fall dramatically during pregnancy, and that can cause light-headedness, even fainting. But this was more than a dizzy spell. According to witnesses, Beth's entire body was convulsing when she collapsed. To try to learn what caused this, we'd like to perform a few more tests and scans."

Gary looked over at Beth. She stared back and slowly nodded her head—clearly, she'd already been told all of this.

"I'm sorry, but the only advice I can give you now is to stay positive until we have some answers," Dr. Simpson said. "We'll expedite Beth's results and should know more in a few hours."

Gary closed his eyes. Paused. Took a moment to let it all sink in.

"I realize this is a lot to hear," Dr. Simpson said. "Do you have any questions for me?"

Gary opened his eyes and blankly stared at Dr. Simpson. Questions? Only about a million of them.

A S GARY FOSTER AND HIS WIFE WAITED IN THE HOSPITAL, A MAN HALFWAY across the city nervously paced around the sales floor of a pawnshop named Solid Gold Pawn. He walked back and forth, back and forth, from the windows covered with iron bars at the front of the shop to the checkout counter in the rear, passing shelves and glass display cases filled with watches, electronics, and other assorted merchandise. His legs were unsteady and his hands trembled with nerves. His mouth was downturned, absolute worry etched over his face. He had much to worry about. His entire life was caving in around him. And he had no idea what to do.

His name was Otto Brennan. He was in his mid-forties, but his unforgiving face made him look older. Laugh lines spiderwebbed from the corners of his cold, snakelike eyes, but the lines weren't from years of enjoying laughter and merriment with friends. A tight tan T-shirt revealed skinny, pasty white forearms covered in tattoos, a crisscross pattern of winding designs. His head was shaved completely bald.

More pacing. He moved with a slight hitch in his step, a limp that was a result of a bullet shattering his left kneecap when he was a teenager. Otto looked at the room surrounding him as he walked, as if the answer to all of his problems were resting on a shelf next to the display of photo equipment or hanging from the wall above the laptop computers.

But there was no answer anywhere. Just merchandise. Stacks and displays of stupid shit he'd purchased from customers over the years.

The pawnshop's front door rattled open and he snapped his head toward it, alarmed. A Hispanic guy in his twenties stood in the doorway. The sides of his head were shaved but the hair on top was braided in tight cornrows. Underneath one arm, he carried a black flat-screen television.

"Yo," the younger guy said. The pawnshop door shut behind him.

"Hey, Carlos," Otto said. His voice was scratchy, like his larynx was wrapped in sandpaper.

Otto walked behind the counter and sat down.

"I got a TV for sale," Carlos said, setting the TV on the countertop. "Heard this was a good place to sell it."

"How much you want for it?" Otto asked.

"How much you gonna offer?"

"I'll give you fifty bucks," Otto said, making the offer without even looking at the television.

"Shit, fifty bucks? It's worth a hell of a lot more than that."

"So make a counteroffer."

Carlos paused for a moment. He appeared to be a man deeply contemplating his offer, but Otto knew it was an act.

"I'll take two hundred thousand dollars for it," Carlos said. "Two hundred grand seems like a fair price to me."

Despite everything going on in his life, Otto reacted to Carlos's offer with a tight, restrained smile. He couldn't help it. He and Carlos took part in these phony negotiations every time Carlos showed up at Solid Gold Pawn with something to sell. By now, these exchanges were an old song with a familiar tune, something they did for their own amusement.

"Two hundred thousand dollars, you say?" Otto said, keeping it going.

"Yeah."

"Seems pretty pricey for a cheap-ass TV."

"The TV's worth every penny—believe me," Carlos said.

"Piece of shit probably doesn't even work."

"How about I carry this downstairs?" Carlos said, picking up the television. "You can inspect it down there, appreciate some of its finer details. See what makes it so valuable."

"Let's go," Otto said.

Otto walked over to a display of ten electric guitars hanging from the wall. He nudged the gray wainscoting next to the guitars and a hidden door slowly swung open, revealing a darkened wooden staircase that led down to the basement. He flipped a switch on the wall and a light at the base of the stairs flickered on.

They descended the stairs and reached a shadowy room roughly half the size of the sales floor above. It looked like a mini warehouse, with large cardboard boxes stacked on metal storage racks pushed against the walls. The boxes contained various items Otto had purchased for the pawnshop, the contents scrawled on the outside in Sharpie—video games, books, car stereos.

In the middle of the room was a stainless-steel table, as wide as a card table and twice as long. Carlos followed Otto over to it and set the television on top.

"Think I'll take a closer look at this fine piece of equipment," Otto said.

"Be my guest."

A toolbox rested on top of the metal table, right next to the television. Otto grabbed a hammer from inside and hefted it in his hand, feeling its weight.

"Take a step back," he said to Carlos.

Carlos did as requested.

Otto swung the hammer against the television screen, shattering it. He set down the hammer and snaked his hand past a few jagged shards of black glass that were still stuck in the frame. He grabbed a cellophane-wrapped package duct-taped inside the television and put it on the table. One by one, he lifted three more identical packages from inside.

"Told you the TV was worth two hundred grand," Carlos said. "Fresh from Xalisco. Four kilos of black tar heroin, straight Mexican Mud."

"This looks good," Otto said.

"Then let's get to it. I got places to go. Our cut of last month's profits plus the cost of this stuff is two hundred grand. Fork over the cash."

Otto paused. He looked at the four cellophane-wrapped packages lined up on the table, stared at them for a moment before looking back up at Carlos. "Listen," he said. "I don't got the cash."

Carlos's eyes hardened. The hint of a smile on his face vanished. His casual, joking demeanor was gone—this was business now, pure and simple.

"You don't got the cash?" Carlos said. Even his voice had changed—it sounded deeper, more menacing.

"Not right now."

"Is this some kinda joke?"

"No joke. I'm serious."

Carlos glared at him, the emotion completely drained from his face.

"What the fuck, Otto?"

"I'll have the money in a couple months."

"*A couple months?* Fuck that. What the hell am I supposed to tell De La Fuente?"

"Tell him exactly what I just told you. Something came up and I don't got the cash right now. I'll get it to him later."

Carlos pinched his nose and ran his hand along his jawline. "Are you out of your mind? You're gonna stiff De La Fuente?"

"I ain't stiffing him. Make sure he understands that. I'm just delaying payment for a few months. He'll get his money later."

"He's gonna go ballistic."

"I know," Otto said. He tried to speak coolly, but his voice quavered. "I need you to help me out here. Tell De La Fuente I'm good for this."

Carlos shook his head. "I'll do what I can, Otto. But this ain't no joke."

They walked across the basement and ascended the stairs, the creaking of the rotting wood underneath them the only sound in the stairwell. Back upstairs, Carlos turned around and faced Otto.

"So, what's up?" Carlos said. "Between you and me, what's going on?"

"Just some shit."

"Gotta be pretty serious to screw De La Fuente out of nearly two hundred grand. This is the head of the El Este cartel you're fucking with, bro. He didn't get to where he is by letting people pull shit like this on him."

"I got the situation under control," Otto said. He hoped that Carlos didn't detect the uncertainty in his voice. "It'll be over soon, and I'll have the cash then."

"For your sake, I hope so," Carlos said. "You may be the man who calls the shots in this shithole city, but you're nothing but a pissant to De La Fuente. He's got a thousand people just like you in every city you can think of. All you are is a steady source of income to him. If you can't be counted on for the cash, he'll replace your ass in a heartbeat."

Carlos left the pawnshop and stepped into his beat-to-shit pickup.

Once the truck had backed out of the stall, Otto locked the pawnshop front door. He walked back to the front counter and sat down.

He'd bought himself some time.

Now he had to somehow get out of this mess.

———

"I DON'T KNOW WHAT TO SAY," GARY SAID AFTER DR. SIMPSON HAD LEFT the room.

"There's nothing to say," Beth replied. "All we can do is wait. And pray. Pray that it's nothing serious."

She fluffed the pillow on the bed, lay back, and stared up at the ceiling. They'd asked Dr. Simpson endless questions, but he only repeated the same refrain: a few hours—they'd know more then.

"At least the little guy's fine," Beth said, running her hand over her belly.

She looked over at Gary, a feeble smile crossing her lips. She seemed so calm, so collected, almost as if she were unaffected by what happened. But that was Beth. She was a rock, always the strong one, the shoulder he'd leaned on so many times over the years.

"Do you have any idea why this happened?" Gary asked. He lay down next to Beth.

"I don't know. I barely remember anything. I was walking, felt a headache, then blackness. Next thing I knew, I was surrounded by people. Paramedics loaded me into an ambulance and brought me here."

A headache. Over the past few months, Beth had experienced a few headaches. Neither of them had paid much attention, figuring it was a side effect of the pregnancy.

"Do you think the headache has something to do with your fall?" Gary asked.

"Maybe. Maybe not."

"What—"

"Let's not talk about it," Beth said. "I don't want to think about this until we learn more."

THEY LEARNED MORE THREE HOURS LATER. THERE WAS A KNOCK ON THE patient-room door and a tall, slender doctor with a graying mustache entered the room. He carried an iPad in one hand, a black leather case protecting the screen.

"Gary, Beth, my name is Joseph Levy," he said. "I'm head of the Radiology department here."

They shook hands. Dr. Levy sat down in a chair across from them.

"I'd like to discuss a few things with you," he said. "Over the past couple of hours, we've performed an array of tests and scans to figure out what caused Beth's collapse. One of these scans was a CT scan to look at her brain. I'm afraid that it gave us some bad news."

Dr. Levy unlocked the iPad and flipped the device so the screen faced Gary and Beth. It displayed a scan of a human brain. Dr. Levy pointed at a dark, foggy mark toward the rear of the skull. It was roughly an inch long, shaped like a torpedo.

"I'm sorry to tell you this," he said. "The scan showed a growth on Beth's left temporal lobe. A brain tumor."

It took a moment for the statement to sink in. Gary felt his body lightly sway to the left, then to the right. He was grateful that he was sitting down—had he been standing, he was certain the weight of the news would've made him lose his balance.

"A brain tumor," Gary repeated. Not a question, but not really a statement, either. Just something to say to break the silence.

"Yes. Again, I'm very sorry."

Gary put an unsteady hand to his face and wondered if he was going to vomit. He turned to Beth. She stared at Dr. Levy. Blinked once. The corners of her mouth were turned down.

"Is it cancer?" Gary asked, turning to Dr. Levy.

"We don't know. We'll perform a biopsy to remove a small sample of the tissue, then send it to Pathology for analysis. Once we get her results back, we'll determine our next steps. It should be a few days."

Dr. Levy continued talking, but Gary was unable to process any more information. It was all too much. He looked at the screen of the iPad resting on the desk a few feet away. The screen hadn't yet gone into standby mode and the image of Beth's brain was still displayed. Gary glared at the foggy, inch-long tumor with confusion, nauseating anger. Something so small, and yet it could have such a huge impact on Beth's life, their son's life, Gary's life.

On everything.

2

GARY AND BETH DIDN'T TELL ANYONE ABOUT THE TUMOR IN THE DAYS that followed. They knew their friends would have questions—*How serious is this? What happens next? Will Beth be fine?*—and right now, they didn't have any answers. It seemed better to wait until they heard back from Pathology, wait until they knew more about Beth's condition, before telling their friends.

They hardly left the house at all as the time passed. Gary told Rod he wasn't coming into the store for a few days, and he and Beth did whatever they could to distract themselves. Watched a few British crime shows on Netflix. Played Scrabble. Crossed items off their to-do list to prepare for the baby.

No matter what they did, it was impossible for Gary to focus. All he could think about was the worst-case scenario: What if this was something serious? What would his life be like if he lost Beth?

Eighteen years they'd been together. Nearly half his life. A mutual friend had introduced them during their senior year at the University of Michigan, and the connection was instant. They were inseparable for that final year of college, not falling in love so much as dive-bombing into it like two full-throttle kamikaze pilots. After gradua-tion, Beth followed Gary when he found a job selling insurance in his hometown of River Falls, Michigan. Within a year, they were engaged. Within two, they were married.

They'd been through a lot in the nearly two decades since then. They'd helped each other through the deaths of both sets of parents. They'd dealt with a flooded house. They'd fantasized about moving somewhere exotic but had never gotten around to it. They'd made mistakes and come to understandings. They'd won. They'd lost. They'd binge-watched countless shows together. *Seinfeld. Criminal Minds. Dexter. Mad Men.*

Beth was the best person he knew. She made the good times bet-ter and the hard times easier—and there'd been plenty of both over the years. If he were to list the ten best moments of his life, every one of them involved Beth; if he were to list the ten worst moments of his life, Beth had been there to comfort him during each one. She was his soul mate, his best friend. Happily ever after had always seemed a foregone conclusion. A given.

THE CALL CAME AFTER THREE DAYS: THE PATHOLOGY RESULTS WERE IN. Gary and Beth returned to the hospital and waited in a room that looked nearly identical to the one they'd been in earlier. A few minutes in, there was a knock on the door and an older Asian doctor with wispy white hair entered. He introduced himself as Alan Narita, an oncologist. He sat down across from them and paused for a moment. Then, in a calm, even voice, he spent the next ten minutes explaining three things.

Brain cancer.

Stage IV.

Inoperable.

———

SITTING BEHIND THE COUNTER OF SOLID GOLD PAWN, OTTO STARED OUT the pawnshop's front window at the dirty piles of half-melted snow accumulated in the parking lot's cracked and uneven asphalt. He massaged his knee as he stared, working his fingers deep into the hardened tissue around the ligaments—cold weather, for some reason, always made his bad knee throb.

The pain had him in a shit mood. His mood worsened considerably when his phone rang and Carlos's name popped up on the screen. He'd spent the past few days dreading this call.

"You talk to De La Fuente?" Otto answered, getting straight to the point.

"Yeah. I finally did."

"And?"

"He's pissed," Carlos said. "He went apeshit when I told him."

Otto clenched his jaw, ground his molars together.

"I'll have the cash soon," Otto said. "De La Fuente's overreacting."

"What else is new? He overreacts to everything."

"So what's the bottom line? How do I get out of this?"

"Bottom line is this: I'll be back up in your area at the end of April. About six weeks from now. Have the cash then."

"Might need more time than that."

"Tough shit—you get six weeks," Carlos said. "That's two hundred thousand dollars. No IOUs. No excuses. Nothing but the cold, hard cash. If you don't have it, you're a dead man. That simple. De La Fuente don't play when it comes to money."

"I'll have it," Otto said. Better to agree now and figure it out later.

"One final thing," Carlos said. "De La Fuente wants you to know just how serious this is. Wants you to know exactly how he deals with people who owe him money. I just sent you a video. Watch it on your phone. Then call me back."

Otto ended the call and looked at his in-box. He had a message from Carlos—a hyperlink. Otto tapped the link and his phone's video player opened. An image of a dark, dingy room appeared on-screen. A shirtless man was chained to a wall in the room, his face beaten to a bloody, bruised pulp. His arms were extended from his body, restraints pinning his limp hands to the cement wall behind him. Nothing happened for a few seconds; then a second man wearing a black ski mask walked into the picture.

He carried a chainsaw.

The tied-up man began wildly screaming and pulling against the restraints. Chainsaw man slowly walked across the room. When he was a few feet away from the tied-up man, he yanked the chainsaw's pull cord and the motor fired up. He inched the whirring blade closer and closer to the tied-up man, who was hysterically crying.

Just as the chainsaw was about to rip into the side of the tied-up man's neck, Otto exited out of the video. He called Carlos back.

"You see the video?" Carlos answered.

"I saw enough."

"That poor bastard was a dealer from some shithole in Tennessee who owed De La Fuente just under sixty thousand dollars. If you don't have the cash when I visit, the same thing will happen to you. De La Fuente will decapitate your ass with a chainsaw. Understand me, Otto?"

"Yeah. I understand."

Carlos ended the call. Otto set down his phone. The call had brought on a headache that mirrored the dull pain in his knee.

He blew out a hard, frustrated sigh and closed his eyes. What a mess. What a complete fucking disaster. He'd been involved in the drug trade for more than twenty years, had operated Solid Gold Pawn as a front to launder his drug money for fifteen of those years, and he'd never been as royally fucked as he was now.

He couldn't get that video out of his mind. He'd never even met Miguel De La Fuente, the ghostly figure who ran the El Este cartel from the bowels of Mexico, but he'd heard enough stories from Carlos and other drug runners to know how ruthless he was. But it was one thing to hear stories; getting a firsthand look at De La Fuente's cold-bloodedness was entirely different. The video had left Otto rattled—and very few things in life rattled him.

The hell of it was, this problem with De La Fuente wasn't even his biggest concern at the moment. There was something else—rather, some*one* else—he had to take care of first.

———

I T WAS LIGHTLY SNOWING WHEN GARY AND BETH EXITED THE HOSPITAL AN hour after speaking with Dr. Narita. Beth slipped on her peacoat but left the front of it hanging open—over the past month, the swell of her belly had become too pronounced for her to button the coat.

She hooked her arm into Gary's for support as they trudged to their Corolla. Gary helped her into the car and brushed a thin layer of snow from the windshield with the sleeve of his jacket. He opened the driver's-side door and collapsed into the front seat. They both stared blankly out the windshield at the storm clouds scudding across the sky like evil spirits.

Neither of them had reacted much while Dr. Narita gave them the news. They just sat there, expressions of disbelief frozen on their faces, as Dr. Narita explained that Beth's tumor was classified as a glioblastoma, an extremely aggressive, hard-to-treat cancer. The tumor was too deep, too far developed, and in too sensitive of a location to perform surgery.

They asked about Beth's outlook, and Dr. Narita gave them some statistics. Grim, but they appreciated the honesty. The average length of life for people diagnosed with glioblastomas was eight to twelve months. Eight without treatment. Twelve with. Only a few survived longer than that.

Staring out the windshield now, the memory of the meeting still fresh in his mind, Gary slowly shook his head. "I refuse to believe this," he said. His voice didn't sound like his own.

He reached across the armrest and placed his hand on Beth's thigh. She turned to him and opened her mouth but didn't even get a word out before she burst into tears. She covered her face with her hands and deep sobs racked her body. She let go of her posture and collapsed forward in her seat.

Gary draped his arm around her and she buried her face in his shoulder. The sobs kept coming, unstoppable. She cried the way someone might heave after food poisoning—explosively, violently. He felt the shoulder of his shirt dampen with her hot tears. Her deep, sloppy breathing and incoherent sobs were the only noises in the car.

In all their years of marriage, Gary had never seen Beth cry like this. He could barely even remember the last time he'd seen her cry. She'd cried on the day they'd found out she was pregnant, six months ago. But those tears were tears of happiness. She'd cried on the day he proposed to her almost two decades ago, but those tears, too, were tears of happiness, tears of joy. She'd cried five years ago, when both her parents passed away within a three-month span, but those tears weren't like these. These tears were like a tsunami, a full-scale emotional breakdown the likes of which he'd never seen from his wife.

Face burrowed into Gary's shoulder, Beth's tears continued. She'd been brave as they'd listened to Dr. Narita, but the floodgates had now opened. Gary tried to hold back but it became too much. His eyes filled with tears and he started sobbing, too.

They stayed in the parking lot for a long time—no words, just tears.

Holding Beth in his arms, Gary looked at the slender willow stem of her neck, the tender curve of her skull. Inside that small, delicate cradle of bone was a mass of foreign cells that could end her life at any moment.

A time bomb that was ticking away.

3

GARY AND BETH FOSTER LIVED IN A RANCH HOUSE WITH TWO SMALL BED-rooms, an even smaller kitchen, and a living room filled with a sad ensemble of giveaways and Craigslist purchases. A starter home, the Realtor called the house fourteen years ago when they bought it. A house to live in for a few years, build up some equity, then sell to raise a family in a more spacious house.

More than a decade later, they still remained in their starter home.

On the morning after they returned home from the hospital, Gary and Beth sat at their kitchen table. Beth's chair was pushed back a few feet, the upper curve of her belly just visible over the tabletop. A Detroit Tigers mug filled with coffee was in front of Gary, a glass of orange juice in front of Beth, and bowls of Cheerios in front of them both. They were doing more looking at their breakfast than eating.

"Can you give me a ride at ten?" Beth asked. "I'm going to head to yoga class."

Gary glanced up from his Cheerios. "Yoga?"

"I think so," Beth said. "Not to work out. When it's over, I'm going to give the girls the news. I'm going to tell them about the brain tumor."

"You're ready?"

"Yeah. I thought about it all night, and I think it's time."

They'd planned on telling their close friends yesterday; instead, they spent the evening alone in the house, just the two of them, trying to make sense of it all.

When they weren't crying, they'd searched online for as much information as they could find. *Glioblastoma treatment. Brain-tumor remedies. Odds of glioblastoma survival.*

Everything they read only reiterated the depressing, dismal news Dr. Narita gave them earlier. The cancer spread fast. Eighty-five percent of people diagnosed with glioblastomas didn't make it a year. It was rare, extremely rare, for patients to survive longer than five years.

But the situation wasn't hopeless.

They'd found a blog from someone who had lived for twenty years since being diagnosed with a glioblastoma. A message board post from another survivor who was diagnosed ten years ago. Various articles about new treatments that doctors were encouraged by.

"I just don't know what to say at yoga class," Beth said. "How do you tell people about something like this?"

"Just be honest. Up-front. Direct."

"I suppose so. I have to tell everyone at some point. Might as well be now."

Beth carried her bowl of Cheerios over to the sink and rinsed it out. She gazed out the small window over the countertop, out at the front yard.

"It will be good to get out of the house," she said. "There's nothing to do here but sit around and feel sorry for myself. Think about things I don't want to think about."

———

OTTO SAT IN A DINER A FEW BLOCKS FROM HIS PAWNSHOP. THE INTERIOR of the diner was shabby and worn down, with a few old Coca-Cola signs and sun-faded pictures hanging from the walls. Long strips of duct tape were raggedly patched over the booths, covering cracks and rips in the vinyl upholstery. On a chalkboard behind the counter, the day's specials were written in neat cursive writing. *Open-face Turkey Sandwich. Cobb Salad. Minute Steak with Mashed Potatoes.*

Otto was the only person inside the diner other than the cook in the back and the waitress reading a paperback book behind the counter. A cup of coffee, bottom-of-the-barrel slop, rested on the table in front of him, steam rising from the cup.

He lifted the cup but set it back on the table without drinking from it. He pushed it aside so hard that some coffee sloshed out. Nervous—he was so damn nervous.

After Otto had waited for five minutes, a guy walked into the diner. The waitress set down her paperback and asked if he needed help, but he ignored her and headed to Otto's booth.

Otto watched him approach. The man was six and a half feet tall at least, with a gray ribbed T-shirt hugging tightly against a chest so massive it looked like he had a bulletproof vest concealed under his shirt. His arms were two thick and defined cannons dangling from his body. He was almost bald but not quite. His nose was a mangled, crooked mess.

He reached Otto's booth and sat down across from him. Otto nodded at the big guy.

"Thanks for coming, Champ," Otto said.

He wordlessly nodded back. His name was Robert Smith. He was a retired heavyweight boxer who'd transitioned into a life of crime after his career ended, doing dirty work for whoever hired him. As a boxer, he'd collected a few small purses, but his career ended before he competed for, let alone won, any sort of championship; he had the brute strength but not the intangibles to go far. Despite never having won anything noteworthy, he told people to call him Champ. And when a guy that big told you to do something, you did it.

"You wanted to talk about something?" Champ asked. His voice was so deep, the question sounded like the blaring of a foghorn.

"Yeah. Yeah, I did."

"So start talking."

"I got a problem I need you to take care of," Otto said.

"Figured as much."

"It's some pretty serious shit."

"It's all serious to me. You know I don't play."

Otto looked over his shoulder. Empty booths and tables all around. The waitress behind the counter was focused on her book.

"What I'm about to tell you remains between us, all right?" Otto said, turning back to Champ.

"No shit, it does," Champ said. "You don't have to tell me that."

"I know, I know. But I gotta make that perfectly clear. No one can know about this."

"My lips are sealed."

"Good. I'll get straight to it, then. There's someone who's making my life hell. I need you to kill him for me."

Champ's heavy eyes stared across the table. Otto had hired him for jobs before, mostly to talk some sense into dealers who were behind on payments. Usually, the mere sight of Champ was intimidating enough for the problem to be resolved. But things got ugly occasionally. Champ put one guy in a coma for two weeks. Another time, Champ used a baseball bat to break a guy's leg so severely, the bones had been damn near pulverized.

"Murder, huh?" Champ said. "This won't come cheap."

"I'm prepared to pay."

"Who's the target?"

Otto grabbed a manila envelope resting next to him on the booth. He removed an eight-by-eleven-inch sheet of paper and slid it across the table. Printed on the sheet was a black-and-white photocopy of a Michigan driver's license.

"Devon Peterson," Champ said, reading the name on the license. "What's the story with this guy?"

"It don't matter. I need him dead. I want you to do it. That's all you need to know."

"Devon Peterson. Name sounds familiar." Suddenly, Champ's dull eyes lit up. A spark of recognition. "Wait a sec. Shit, is this—"

"Yeah," Otto said. "It is."

"How'd you get messed up with this guy?"

"Long story. You gonna be able to help me out?"

Champ slid the sheet of paper back across the table. "I'm passing on this one," he said.

"You're passing? The hell you talking about?"

Only when the waitress set down her book and looked in their direction did Otto realize how loud his voice had been. Otto raised his hand to let her know they were fine. She eyed them for a second and returned to reading.

"What do you mean, you're passing on this?" Otto said, lowering his voice.

"I'm not fucking with this guy," Champ said.

"You turn into a Boy Scout overnight? You've never had a problem with shit like this before."

"This is different."

"How so?"

"Too much of a risk."

"It's no more risky than anything you've done for me in the past."

"That's bullshit and you know it."

"I got everything you need. I know where he lives. I know when he arrives home every night. I know—"

"Save your breath. I ain't doing this."

Otto's anger crystalized, becoming pure and diamond hard. He took in a deep breath through his nose, filling his nostrils with the stale smell of fried food and grease.

"You gotta help me out here. I'm desperate."

"The answer's no."

"Listen, I—"

Champ cut him off with the wave of a burly, calloused hand. "Look, homeboy, the police don't care if some low-life dealer gets murdered in a shit area of the city. A case like that, the investigation lasts for a few days and the cops move on to the next scumbag who gets killed. But if this guy"—he tapped the picture on the table—"shows up dead, the cops will care. They will look into it hard. And I ain't facing that type of heat for anyone. No way."

Champ lumbered out of the booth. "My mouth is shut," he said. "I ain't mentioning this to no one. But I don't want nothing to do with this."

With that, Champ walked across the diner floor. After he disappeared outside, Otto looked back at the photocopied driver's license and stared at it for a long time.

———

GARY DROPPED BETH OFF AT HER YOGA CLASS AND DROVE BACK ACROSS River Falls, through working-class neighborhoods filled with unremarkable houses. Unremarkable: a fitting description for the city of River Falls itself. It was a drive-through city in a fly-over state, a once-proud manufacturing city that had seen its population steadily decrease for each of the past five decades as auto plants and other businesses shuttered. With more than two hundred thousand residents, River Falls was still big enough to have a mall, an airport, and most major chain restaurants. But the mall was barely half-occupied. The airport had fewer than ten departures a day. And it had been years since a worthwhile new restaurant had opened.

He reached the downtown district, passing a few of the city's essential institutions—the post office, the fire department, the water plant. Half a mile later, he drove past the junior high building where Beth had taught art up until the beginning of the school year, when she lost her job in a budget cut that gutted the district. She'd served as a substitute teacher since then, working no more than a few days a month.

Gary finally arrived at the small red-brick development that housed his store, Ascension Outerwear. He stayed in his car for a moment, tried to think of how to break the news about Beth's condition to his brother. It was going to be difficult. In some ways, he was closer to Rod than he was to anyone else in his life, Beth included.

Ever since they were young, Rod had been his opposite in almost every way imaginable, and Gary always felt that the differences in their personalities were why they'd grown closer over the years instead of drifting apart like other siblings he knew. Rod was impulsive, spontaneous, carefree—everything Gary wasn't. After dropping out of college more than a decade ago, Rod had failed and flailed his way through life, jumping from job to job and wandering from state to state without ever finding any sort of path to pursue. He'd worked at a ski resort in Colorado, painted houses in New Mexico and Arizona, bartended at a casino in Vegas. There was even a stint in LA when he tried to become an actor.

To Gary, their relationship always felt more like a father-son relationship than a brotherly one. Rod was the rambunctious, immature child; Gary, the responsible, straitlaced parent who looked out for Rod, cared about him, worried about him constantly.

Gary stepped out of the car, still unsure of what to say to his brother. *Just be up-front, honest, direct*—the same advice he'd given Beth.

He walked up to Ascension Outerwear and opened the front door, stepping inside. It was a small, quaint store with narrow aisles crammed with outdoor equipment and clothing—sandals and waterproof boots displayed on acrylic shelving, hiking coats and shell jackets hanging on rolling garment racks, backpacks and hundreds of other items neatly organized on the white slat panels that covered the store's walls.

"Look at what the cat dragged in," Rod said from across the empty store.

"Hey, Rod."

Gary passed the single cash register on the front counter as he approached the shoe display, where Rod stood with a small pile of shoes on the ground beside him. At thirty-four, Rod was a few years younger than Gary but looked like a man-child who'd never outgrown his early twenties. His shaggy blond hair was uncombed, a tangled mess of curls. His eyes were wide and expressive, the eyes of an overactive teenager. He wore an untucked black polo over his khakis.

"Jesus, man," Rod said. "Where the hell have you been?"

"I had to deal with some things."

"So you just disappear? Stop showing up to the store for a few days? I could see me doing something like that. But you? I thought you were supposed to be the responsible one."

Rod chuckled. He grabbed a shoe off the ground and tossed it over to Gary, who caught it.

"I'm just busting your balls," Rod said. "You haven't missed anything. Wanna give me a hand, or is this too much excitement for you?"

"Actually, there's something I want to talk to you about," Gary said. He walked over and placed the shoe next to a few others displayed on a half-empty shelf. He took a deep breath—*Just be open, honest, direct*—and turned to face Rod.

"Look, there's no easy way to say this," Gary said. "That phone call I got the other day, when I disappeared? It was from the hospital. Beth collapsed while running some errands. At the hospital, they found that she has a brain tumor."

Rod stared back with a dazed, blank expression on his face. "A brain tumor?"

Gary nodded.

"My God. Is she going to be all right?"

"It's a pretty aggressive type of tumor. Hard to treat. The outlook isn't good." Gary cleared his throat. "But she's going to beat this. She can do it."

"Is the baby . . . ?"

"He's fine."

A silent moment passed. Rod's eyes welled with heavy, glistening tears.

"I can't believe this," he said.

"It's awful," Gary said. "There's no other spin you can put on it."

"How's Beth holding up?" Rod wiped at his eyes with the sleeve of his shirt.

"She's strong, man. Heck of a lot stronger than I'd be if I just found out I had a brain tumor."

"And you? How're you taking the news?"

"It's tough. I was twenty-one when I met her. I'm thirty-nine now. I don't even remember what my life was like without Beth in it. If I lost her . . ." He paused for a moment. "If I lost her, that'd be it for me. There'd be no coming back from that."

Rod walked over and hugged Gary tight. Gary could feel the raw emotion in his brother's embrace.

"I'm telling you this right now: I'm here for you guys," Rod said. He pulled away but looked Gary in the eye. "Whatever you need. Whatever you want. If you need someone to spend time with Beth, I'll do it. You need someone to run errands, I'm your man. Hell, if the doctors find a way to perform a brain transplant, I'll let them crack open my skull and donate mine to her."

A weak smile crossed Gary's lips.

"I'm serious," Rod said. "I owe you two everything. You guys have done so much for me over the years. Who drove me out to Colorado when I got that job at the ski resort all those years ago? You and Beth.

Who constantly loaned me money when I was trying to make it as an actor in LA? You and Beth. Who let me live with them when I moved back to River Falls—thirty years old, flat broke, no idea what to do with myself? You and Beth. Time and time again, my dumb ass has screwed up, and you and Beth were there for me. Hell, I wouldn't have even met Sarah if it wasn't for Beth, and Sarah's the best thing that ever happened to me."

Sarah was Rod's wife. *Wife*—no matter how many times he heard it, Gary still couldn't get used to the fact that Rod was married. Sarah owned the yoga studio where Beth took classes, and Beth had introduced her to Rod eighteen months earlier. No one had expected much—Sarah was sophisticated and mature, about as opposite from Rod as a person could be. Instead, in true Rod fashion, the relationship became a year-long whirlwind that culminated in a wedding six months ago.

Since meeting Sarah, Rod wasn't drinking nearly as much and stopped staying out with his buddies until the early-morning hours. He'd thrown himself into Ascension Outerwear, regularly putting in twelve-hour days. Rod had even read a few books about running an online business—the first books Gary had ever seen him read—and set up an eBay store and a few other online channels to sell product through.

Rod had changed. Maybe it was being married, maybe it was his devotion to the business, or maybe it was a combination of both. Seeing his transformation over the past year, Gary couldn't help but feel like the proud parent of a misfit son who was finally getting his life together.

"Whatever you need, Gary," Rod said. "Don't hesitate to ask."

"I might be a little busy. Might not be able to devote much time to the store."

"I can hold down the fort," Rod said. "Take off as much time as you need."

Rod hugged Gary tightly again. "This will have a happy ending for you guys. You and Beth are two of the best people I know. There's no way this won't have a happy ending."

4

FOUR WEEKS PASSED.

There are twenty-eight days in four weeks, six hundred seventy-two hours spread across those days, and for every hour of every day, it seemed like something was happening.

Friends visited constantly as word about Beth's condition spread—there were questions, tears, vows to help, more tears. A group from her yoga class showed up with pink shirts inscribed with TEAM BETH over a small cartoon caricature of Beth. She broke down crying upon seeing them.

Endless trips to the hospital. Countless discussions about what to do next. Specialists were consulted. Oncologists, neonatologists, obstetricians. The fetus, they determined, was developed enough that Beth could proceed with treatment.

Treatment began. Targeted radiation. Weekly IV chemotherapy. Some days were bad days—tiredness, vomiting, nausea. Other days were good days, times when Beth didn't even appear to be sick. She'd even substitute taught for a few days.

The month had been the most exhausting time of Gary's life, but as he sat on the living-room floor now, ten o'clock at night, Beth directly across from him, he was nowhere near tired. Wearing the same outfit he wore most evenings after his nightly shower—a pair of blue-plaid pajama bottoms and a faded Pearl Jam shirt from a concert he and Beth went to a decade ago—he stared at the Scrabble board on the floor between them.

"Jump," Beth said, placing her tiles on the board. "That's eight, nine, twelve, fifteen points."

Gary wrote down the score. They'd been playing Scrabble for as long as they'd been together, thousands of games over the years. It was a simple pleasure, but that was their relationship—one full of simple pleasures, a relationship defined by little moments. Chinese takeout instead of a five-star dinner; a night watching Netflix instead of an evening at the opera. Vacations spent hanging out, maybe making a day trip to Detroit, instead of something exotic.

"Grazed," Gary said, arranging a few tiles on the board. "Seventeen points."

"Not bad."

"Just glad I didn't get stuck with the Z like I always do."

Beth's eyes went from her tiles to the board, back to her tiles. Her cheeks had gotten puffier over the past weeks, her skin a little pallid, but the treatment hadn't changed her appearance too drastically. No major hair loss, just a small patch on the side of her skull where the radiation had been targeted. The biggest difference was that her belly had continued to grow. Thirty-four weeks along now. She'd had a few ultrasounds in the past month, and doctors said everything looked perfectly fine and healthy.

"*Queen*. Fourteen."

"*Wan* and *cow*. *Wan* is a double word. Twenty total."

The game continued, back and forth, steady like a pendulum, but Gary could barely concentrate. All he could think about was tomorrow.

Tomorrow. That's when they would meet with doctors to learn if Beth's treatment had shrunk the tumor or if it was still growing. Everything that had happened over the past month was leading up to that meeting. The last thing they wanted was to spend the evening sitting around and obsessing, so they'd decided to play Scrabble to distract themselves. They were already on their third game.

"Gary? Your turn again."

"Sorry," he said.

He stared at his tiles.

"Thinking about tomorrow?" Beth asked.

"Of course."

"You're not the only one."

She weakly smiled, not much behind it. Gary set his tiles to the side and scooted over to her. Put an arm around her and she snuggled in next to him. She traced her finger over the Pearl Jam logo on his chest.

"Things will work out, Beth," he said. "I'm positive."

He kissed her forehead and held her in his arms for a few seconds—a nice little moment—then scooted back over to his side of the board.

THAT NEXT MORNING, GARY HELD BETH'S HAND AS THEY DROVE ACROSS town. He was on edge—a mixture of anticipation and dread.

They arrived at the hospital. Waited. Went to a room. Waited some more. Talked to a nurse. More waiting.

After all that waiting, what happened next felt like it happened very quickly, in the blink of an eye.

A knock on the door. Gary's chest tightened.

Dr. Narita entered. His expression gave away nothing.

They exchanged greetings. Small talk for a second.

After a pause, Dr. Narita spoke two words that told the entire story: "I'm sorry."

THE TUMOR, HE EXPLAINED, WAS STILL GROWING; TREATMENT HADN'T AF-fected it. Gary and Beth took the news well. No tears. They weren't blindsided, like they'd been when they learned about the cancer—they knew the facts; they knew they were facing a long shot.

"Now that standard treatment has failed, we'll want to treat the tumor more aggressively," Dr. Narita said. "We have a few options. A different combination of chemotherapy drugs to slow the growth. Or radiosurgery—a one-shot high dose of radiation—might buy a little more time."

Gary fixated on the phrases Dr. Narita used. *Slow the growth. Buy a little more time.*

Nothing about eliminating the tumor.

Nothing about saving her life.

Dr. Narita also advised Beth to consider enrolling in a clinical trial. He explained that biotechnology and pharmaceutical companies tested new, unproven treatments during trials to gauge drugs' effectiveness.

"I've talked to some people and looked online. I've found a few trials that I'd like to discuss with you."

He opened a folder and fanned a few sheets of paper onto the desk.

"One in particular," Dr. Narita said, "looks encouraging."

5

ARLY THE NEXT MORNING, THE SUN STILL HOURS FROM RISING, BETH AND Gary set the laptop on the coffee table. When the screen indicated an incoming Skype call, they answered it. A blond, middle-aged woman introduced herself as Dr. Tobin. She told them a little about GOSKA, the German biotechnology firm she worked for, then got into the reason for the call—explaining more about the treatment her company was holding a trial for.

"All tumors are different, composed of various proteins and cell mutations—some we can identify; some we can't," she said in perfect English, with only a slight trace of an accent. "In Beth's case, one of the proteins identified was a rare gene that's present in a very small percentage of cancers. We've recently begun testing a treatment that specifically targets this protein."

Gary nodded. Yesterday, Dr. Narita had told them something

similar. After talking about a few clinical trials taking place in the US, he focused on the trial he felt could potentially help Beth the most: one offered by GOSKA. He'd helped them schedule a Skype call to learn more. With the time difference, they'd woken at three a.m. for a call with Dr. Tobin before her workday started.

"What have your test results been like so far?" Beth asked. She took notes on a pad of paper as the doctor continued talking.

"The results have been promising. We administered the treatment to fifty patients—twenty-five without the rare gene you have, twenty-five with it. The treatment had little effect on the patients without the gene, but in those with the gene, we observed reduced tumor-metabolic activity in about forty percent of the participants—their tumors stopped growing and, in some cases, shrank. We found no evidence of the tumor after treatment in four of the participants. We're now looking for candidates for an expanded second round of testing."

"And you think this treatment could help me?" Beth asked.

"We saw success treating patients with the gene present in your tumor during our first round of testing, so yes, I think there's a good chance it could. No guarantees, obviously. If the treatment is success-ful, you could be looking at an expectancy of years or decades instead of months."

Gary's heart jumped. Beth set her pen down and grabbed his hand, squeezing so hard that it hurt a little.

"I'd be eligible for this treatment?" Beth asked. "Even though we're not in Germany?"

"You'd have to apply, but I see no reason you wouldn't qualify. Your doctor sent over your files. To remain eligible, you'll have to stop all other treatments. No chemo or radiation. Other treatments interfere with the test results, make it difficult for us to measure the effectiveness of the treatment."

"What would the steps be to get started?" Beth asked.

"You're pregnant, correct?"

"Yes. Thirty-four weeks."

"We'd wait until you gave birth; then we'd begin treatment. The only potential obstacle would be the money. Your insurance won't cover an elective, experimental treatment abroad, so you'd have to pay for treatment yourselves, out of pocket."

"How costly is the treatment?"

"You'd be closely monitored for the trial, frequent check-ins, so you'd have to move near enough to come into our facility whenever needed. With travel, housing, and the treatment factored in, a total cost of two hundred thousand dollars would be a safe estimate."

Gary barely reacted to the number. It was irrelevant. Dr. Tobin could've added a zero to the end and he would've had the same reaction.

They needed a miracle, and here it was. That was all that mattered.

THE MOMENT THE SKYPE CALL ENDED, GARY TURNED TO BETH AND SMILED.

"This is it, Beth," he said.

She nodded. "I don't want to get my hopes up, but it sounds perfect."

"A forty-percent success rate. A nearly fifty-fifty chance."

"There's just—"

"The money."

"Yeah. Two hundred thousand dollars, Gary. That much money . . .

and there are no guarantees. That's more money than I can even fathom."

"We'll find it."

Though he had no idea where. *Sell some things?* Even if they sold everything they owned, it wouldn't raise much; for them, everything was hardly anything.

Do something with the house? It was worthless. He'd taken out a second mortgage when he opened Ascension Outerwear with Rod a year ago; the house was underwater.

A loan from the bank? He was at the bank on a weekly basis, kissing butt to make sure they didn't call in the loans he already owed for the business. The bank wouldn't lend them two hundred dollars, let alone two hundred thousand.

But they'd find the money. Somehow, they would. Gary was positive of it.

All they needed was a second miracle.

6

OTTO STOOD IN A DARKENED ALLEYWAY, THE DISTANT RISING SUN PROVIDing just enough light for him to see the features of the man in front of him. Bushy, unkempt beard. Brown nubs for teeth. Leathery skin streaked with filth and grime. He wore a ragged flannel with the buttons in the wrong holes and oversized jeans that were so dirty they looked black.

The Bum. That's how Otto referred to the guy. Didn't know the Bum's name because it didn't matter. The Bum had a purpose. Otto didn't need to know his name for that purpose.

"You got the shit on you?" the Bum asked in a slurred, barely understandable voice. "'Cause I ain't walking halfway across the neighborhood to get it when we're done."

"I got the drugs," Otto said. "I'll fork 'em over later. Once we're finished."

"Okay. Just take it easy this time. Last time fucking hurt."

Otto looked both ways down the alleyway. Empty. Dark. He grabbed a pair of latex gloves from his jacket pocket. He took off a green shamrock ring on his left hand and slipped it into the same pocket, then pulled the gloves over his hands. He stepped closer to the Bum so only a foot separated them.

Without hesitating, he cocked his fist back and decked the Bum, his knuckle smashing square against the Bum's right cheek. The moment the punch connected, the Bum stumbled backward and fell to the ground.

"Fuck," gasped the Bum, on his hands and knees. "Fuck me."

Otto stood there, breathing heavily. He felt the adrenaline course through his body, felt that satisfying rush he always got when his fist struck the Bum's face. It had been two decades since Otto last did drugs, but this was the exact sensation he remembered feeling when he was out of his mind on drugs—high as a skyscraper, flying like Superman.

His agreement with the Bum was simple: one hit for one hit. One punch for a packet of heroin. Whenever he needed to take out his frustration, Otto visited the Bum to rearrange the poor bastard's face. It was his version of yoga or meditation, his stress reliever. His escape.

"Thought you were gonna take it easy," the Bum said, still huddled on the ground. His cheek was red and had started to swell but there was no blood.

"Needed to let loose. The second one won't be as bad."

"Shit, the second one?"

Otto nodded.

"Fine," the Bum said. "Just . . . damn, man. Not so hard this time."

As he watched the Bum stagger onto his feet, Otto thought about the utter mess he was caught up in. The situation had only gotten worse over the past month. After Champ's dumb ass had turned him down, he'd spent a few weeks reaching out to other felons in the neighborhood who had reputations for taking care of problems—five of them in total. They'd all recognized the name Devon Peterson and turned Otto down. No way they were fucking with Devon, they'd said.

The situation looked more and more hopeless as time passed; only two weeks remained until Carlos would be back for the money.

And then last night, Otto found something.

He was spending a sleepless night pissing around on the Internet. Sometime in the wee hours, he'd seen the article online. The one about that lady with the brain tumor. The article gave him an idea. An idea of how to potentially get out of this mess. It was a desperate idea, but he was a desperate man.

Feeling so desperate pissed him off, stressed him out. That was why he was here, visiting the Bum—to release some of that stress.

Once the Bum stumbled over to him again, Otto reared back and put his full body weight behind his second punch. The blow caught the Bum square in the nose, the impact so solid that Otto felt a dull pain that radiated from his fingers down to his forearm.

The Bum collapsed to the ground. "Goddammit," he yelled, pawing at the blood trickling from his nose.

Standing over the Bum, Otto cracked his knuckles, his heart thundering, his breaths short and choppy. Normally, a punch, maybe two, was enough of a release. But not this morning. Not with everything going on.

Otto limped over to the Bum and jumped onto his chest. He pinned the Bum's bony arms to the ground with his knees and began punching away. Left, right, left, right—all of them to the Bum's face.

The Bum cried out but went silent after the fourth punch. Otto rained blows down as if the Bum were to blame for this entire mess and needed to be punished, as if he alone were the cause of it all.

Otto suddenly snapped out of it. He got up off the Bum and took a few steps backward. Blood covered the Bum's face, the collar of his flannel, his scraggly beard. He mumbled something incomprehensible, then curled onto his side and spit up some blood.

Jesus Christ, Otto thought. He'd completely lost it. That had never happened before. It was always a couple of punches and that was it. But this . . . this time he'd almost killed the Bum.

Otto grabbed a handful of small heroin bags from his jacket pocket, the fresh blood on his gloves leaving smudges on them. He tossed the packets onto the pavement around the Bum, then threw his gloves in a trash can. He had to get the hell out of here.

As he walked back across the neighborhood to Solid Gold Pawn, Otto felt himself start to calm down, slowly come off his high. Losing it like that had only showed just how desperate he was, how helpless he felt. It was either very smart or very stupid, what he was about to do. Maybe a little bit of both.

When he arrived back at the pawnshop, Otto pulled his phone from his pocket and dialed a number.

―――――

GARY SAT ON AN OFFICE CHAIR IN THE SECOND BEDROOM OF THEIR HOUSE, holding a much-needed cup of morning coffee, staring at his laptop. Displayed was an article on the Web site for the *River Falls Courier*, the city's only newspaper. PREGNANT AREA WOMAN BATTLES FOR HER LIFE, read the headline. Accompanying the article was a picture of Beth and Gary—smiling into the camera, Gary in a yellow tie and a light blue button-up shirt, Beth in a blue dress a few shades darker than Gary's shirt. It was the most recent picture they had together—taken at Rod's wedding six months earlier.

Even though he'd read the article five times already, Gary scrolled up and read it again. Yesterday, after their call with GOSKA, they'd met with one of Beth's friends who worked for the *Courier*. She'd agreed to write an article about their situation and post it on the paper's Web site. The article wasn't much—just a blurb, really, only a few paragraphs—but it gave a nice brief summary of everything that had happened thus far: the sudden discovery of Beth's tumor, the unsuccessful chemo and radiation, the treatment abroad that could help her, the daunting task of financing the treatment. The final line of the article included the address for a fund-raising site they'd set up the previous night, and encouraged anyone willing to help with the money to donate via the site.

Gary wanted to tape the article onto a few community bulletin boards throughout the city, so he clicked Print. As he waited for the gray inkjet monstrosity to spit out copies, he leaned back in his chair and looked around the room. They'd recently begun converting the second bedroom into a nursery, and various baby items were scattered about: an unassembled crib in a cardboard box, a few unopened cans of light blue paint, a secondhand stroller purchased online. Prints of Pooh Bear and Tigger hung from the wall. A collection of baby clothes that a friend donated was stacked in a neat pile next to a—

Gary's phone rang. He pulled it from his pocket. The caller ID read UNKNOWN.

"Hello?" he answered.

"Gary Foster?"

Male voice. It was rough and scratchy.

"This is Gary."

"I read about your wife," the voice said. "The tumor. I think I can help."

Gary straightened up in the chair.

"Thank you," he said. "Help in what way?"

"Let's not talk on the phone. You free to meet in an hour? At nine?"

"Certainly."

"You know Willow Park?"

"Yes."

"I'll meet you there. Just show up, and I'll recognize you."

"Thank you. My wife and I look forward to—"

"No wife."

"I'm sorry?"

"Come alone. You and me—that's it. We'll talk in an hour."

The line went dead.

———

GARY THOUGHT ABOUT WAKING BETH UP TO TELL HER ABOUT THE CALL but decided against it. Something about it felt . . . off, somehow— the caller's insistence on meeting alone, his refusal to go into detail over the phone, even the caller's scratchy voice had unnerved him. Gary hadn't had a chance to get the caller's name or find out how he'd found his phone number. He wanted to learn more before getting his—or Beth's—hopes up.

He wrote out a note for her—*Going into store. Back by lunch*—and set it on the kitchen table. Then he left.

―――――――

HE HAD SOME TIME TO KILL BEFORE THE MEETING IN WILLOW PARK, SO GARY decided to do exactly what he'd written on the note. He swung by Ascension Outerwear and parked out front. Inside, the store was empty except for Rod.

"Didn't think you were coming in today," Rod said.

"I wasn't planning on it. I'm on my way to a meeting right now, over in Willow Park. Figured I'd stop by. I miss much yesterday?"

"A few orders came in through our eBay store. More than five hundred bucks' worth of jackets, a couple pairs of boots. Had a few walk-in customers, too."

"Nice to hear some good news."

"Yeah, well, there's bad news, too."

"Seems like there always is. What is it now?"

"I got a phone call from a rep at Aero Distributors. They're suspending our account."

"Whoa, what? Aero is suspending our account?" Gary said. Aero Distributors was the wholesale distribution company where they purchased inventory for the store.

"Yeah. We owe them over ten grand. They said they're putting a hold on our account, effective immediately, until we pay it all off."

"They know that we're a new business, that we're still working out some kinks, getting our feet under us," Gary said. "And it's not like we're not paying them at all. We've been slowly paying off what we can. Little by little."

"It's not enough. We can't purchase anything from them until we pay our outstanding bills."

Gary sighed. Even with everything else going on, the news hit hard.

"Great," Gary said. "This is just great."

"Sorry to spring this on you," Rod said. "I know you have a million other things going on. But I don't know what the hell to do. Figured you might have a suggestion."

"Let me think about it."

"Don't. I'll figure it out. I'll sweet-talk the guy into an extension or something."

Gary nodded, but he was plenty worried. Their main supplier abruptly cutting them off like this was nothing short of a disaster. He'd hoped that there might be something they could do with the store to pay for Beth's treatment, even a portion of it, but if their main supplier was cutting them off and calling for all the money they owed, they might not even be able to keep the store open.

He looked out at the sales floor—at all of the aisles and displays of merchandise. He focused on a framed photo hanging from the wall on the edge of the room. It was a photograph of Gary and Rod, taken on the very first day of business at Ascension Outerwear. Beth had shown up hours before they opened and draped a thick blue ribbon across the entrance door, and the framed photograph captured Gary and Rod just after they'd cut the ribbon—Gary holding the sliced ribbon in his upraised hand, Rod brandishing the scissors, both with mile-wide smiles on their faces.

The picture was taken ten months earlier; it felt like a lifetime ago.

Opening the business was Rod's idea. Rod had always been a dreamer, and over the years Gary had heard his younger brother float many a mad idea. There was the bar he always vowed to open. The dirt bike track he talked about purchasing land for on the edge of town. The auto restoration garage that would service and sell vintage cars.

Rod had never actually followed through with any of these ideas—he was a dreamer, not a doer—and Gary always responded to Rod's grand business schemes in the same way one might respond to a child talking about becoming an astronaut one day: *Anything's possible. Maybe someday. You never know.*

But that had all changed around eighteen months ago, when Rod started talking about opening a retail store to sell outdoor clothing and accessories. Gary instantly fell in love with the idea. Even though River Falls had seen better days, its population was still nearly a quarter of a million people. The city was an outdoors community at heart, surrounded by campsites, forests, and hiking trails. And ever since the big-box sporting-goods store at the mall closed a year earlier, there wasn't a store in the area that sold outdoor clothing and accessories.

After talking it over with Beth (she wasn't yet pregnant, which would have certainly factored into his decision), Gary decided to quit his dead-end job in commercial real estate and go into business with Rod. They'd both gone all in—Gary emptied out his 401k, Rod borrowed money from friends, and they pooled together the inheritance money they'd received when their father passed away years earlier. After endless work and planning, they'd finally opened what they decided to call Ascension Outerwear ten months earlier.

Owning a small business had seemed like such a romantic notion at first, such an exciting prospect—being their own bosses, building a business from the ground up, immersed in the nonstop thrill of it all.

Instead, the days were tedious and the customers were almost nonexistent. Ascension Outerwear plowed through money at an alarming rate during its first ten months. They managed to survive, but Gary wondered if their main supplier cutting them off might prove to be the deathblow for the store. Not even a year in, and Ascension Outerwear might be—

Gary snapped out of it. What was he doing, distracting himself like this? Ascension Outerwear couldn't be his focus now. He'd leave everything to Rod, hope that Rod could charm Aero into getting an extension or find another distributor if it came to that.

Gary looked at his watch. Quarter till nine.

"I better get going," he said, stepping out from behind the counter.

"Listen, don't even think about this, Gary," Rod said. "You've got plenty else to worry about."

"We'll be fine, Rod. We'll get this straightened out."

AT A FEW MINUTES BEFORE NINE, GARY PULLED INTO THE PARKING LOT BESIDE Willow Park.

The park wasn't much to look at—a flat plane of land stretching for a half mile, the grass discolored and splotched with semi-melted snow, the trees with bare and haggard branches. An asphalt running path cut through the middle of the park, dead weeds erupting from fissures in the pavement.

Gary killed the engine and stepped out of the car. The only other people he saw were a few teenagers shooting hoops at the far end of the park. They were bundled up in hats and coats for protection from the mid-forties temperature. Everything was quiet except for the dribbling of the basketball and their occasional yells, just barely audible from this distance.

Unless the man who had called him an hour ago was one of the teenagers—unlikely—Gary had arrived first. He walked over to a wooden bench next to the parking lot. The bench's damp wood soaked through the seat of his jeans a few moments after he sat down.

He waited. Five minutes in, he noticed a man at the beginning of the running trail, about a quarter mile away. He was barely more than a small dot from this distance, but as he walked toward Gary, his features came into focus. He wore a dark puffy coat and baggy jeans. He didn't move smoothly; his left leg unsteadily hitched forward with every step. He was completely bald and looked to be around Gary's age—late thirties, early forties. In one hand, he carried a black duffel bag.

When the man reached the park bench, he stood a few feet from Gary and looked down at him. Up close, Gary could see finer details. The man had beady, intense eyes. A few scars and pockmarks dotted his complexion. His mouth was downturned into something that wasn't quite a scowl but was more than a frown.

It was the face of someone who'd lived a rough life.

"Are you the man I spoke with?" Gary asked.

The man nodded. He sat down next to Gary and placed the duffel bag on the ground.

"I'm sorry . . . I never got your name," Gary said.

The man didn't answer. He wordlessly looked out at the basketball game on the other side of the park, glanced behind him at the parking lot with only Gary's Corolla in it, looked to his left and right.

"Call me Shamrock," he said. In person, his voice was even rougher and scratchier than it was on the phone.

"Shamrock?"

"Yeah—luck of the Irish and all." He raised a worn, dirty index finger and showed off a shamrock ring. Three green clovers outlined in gold.

"Look, I'm gonna make this quick," Shamrock said. "I saw the article about your wife. I can help you. Two hundred thousand dollars, right?"

"I'm sorry?"

"That's what you need. Two hundred grand. Is that right?"

"Yes. That's correct."

"I'll give you all of it," Shamrock said.

Gary stared across the bench at Shamrock. On the other side of the park, one of the teenagers playing basketball yelled out something, his statement drawing hollow laughter from the rest of the group.

"I don't understand," Gary said.

"The entire amount," Shamrock said. "Two hundred thousand. Cash. I'll give it all to you. No need to pay me back."

Time passed. It could have been ages or the blink of an eye. A thick knot formed in Gary's stomach.

Slowly, piece by piece, everything began to materialize, like photography film developing into a visible image.

"Are you serious?" Gary asked.

"Yeah. I am."

"That money could save my wife's life."

"I know."

Numbness everywhere. Complete disorientation. Shamrock—whoever he was—didn't look like the type of person who would have that much money, but Gary was so astounded that he didn't care.

"I . . . I don't know what to say," Gary said. "Thank you. Thank you so much."

Shamrock nodded. He looked over his shoulder again. The Corolla was still the only car in the parking lot.

"If I give you the money, there's something I need in return," he said, turning back to Gary.

"Sure."

"If you turn me down, this stays between us. You tell anyone what I'm about to say to you and there's gonna be a big problem."

"Of course."

"Good."

Shamrock pulled a folded-up sheet of paper from his jacket pocket and handed it to Gary.

"Take a look," he said.

Gary unfolded the paper. It was an enlarged black-and-white copy of a Michigan driver's license. The photo on the license showed a man with a buzz cut and a meaty, emotionless face.

"Who is this?" Gary asked.

"His name is Devon Peterson. Name sound familiar to you?"

"No."

"Good."

Shamrock paused for a moment, staring out at the teenagers playing basketball. His eyes returned to Gary.

"Devon's a problem," he said, his gravelly voice low, barely audible. "A problem for me. A problem for lots of people. He's a bad guy who does a lot of bad things."

"What's this got to do with me?" Gary asked.

"I'd like you to take care of the problem for me."

"What do you mean? I don't understand."

"Sure you do. It's easy to understand. I'll give you the money you need. In exchange, you'll take care of Devon Peterson for me. You'll murder him."

Gary looked back down at the photocopied driver's license and noticed that his hands were slightly shaking. He stared at the license for a long moment. The silence built.

"Murder?" Gary finally said.

"Yeah."

"You can't be serious."

"I am."

Gary's ears droned with a steady, hissing pulse. "Why . . . Why me?"

"It has to be someone the police won't suspect. Someone with no connection to me; no connection to him. I've looked into you. Your record's spotless—not even a parking ticket. You're an honest guy who's had some bad luck lately."

Gary was too overwhelmed to form a word to break the hushed silence that fell over the park bench. He read the personal information on the license. Devon Joseph Peterson. Six foot three. Two hundred twenty pounds. Blue eyes. His date of birth meant he'd turned thirty-seven years old two months earlier. He lived at 517 Walton Street in River Falls.

Gary read over the details a second time, a third time. A full minute passed.

"I'm not a murderer," he said. "I've never even shot a gun."

"First time for everything." Shamrock smiled, revealing teeth no dentist had ever touched. They were sharp and pointy, like a rodent's.

"I can't do this," Gary said.

"You sure you wanna walk away from the offer of a lifetime?"

"I'm not a murderer," Gary repeated. He had no idea what else to say.

Shamrock grabbed his duffel bag from the ground and placed it on the bench between them.

"Look inside," he said.

Gary didn't move.

"Go ahead."

Gary unzipped the bag and stared into it.

Money. Everywhere. Half-inch-thick bundles of money held together by orange bands with $10,000 inscribed on them.

"My God," Gary whispered.

"That's everything you need," Shamrock said. "Two hundred grand. Right there, you're holding your wife's life in your hands."

Shamrock reached over and yanked the duffel bag away. He zipped it shut and stood up from the park bench.

"Think about it," he said to Gary. "I'll call in two days. Wednesday at noon. I'll need an answer then. You accept, I'll tell you what to do next. You decline, we go our separate ways. And you'll never speak about this to no one."

Gary stared up at Shamrock's weathered, sullen face. He was speechless, completely floored.

"It's an even trade," Shamrock said. "Your wife's life for Devon's life. I bet your wife is a great person. Devon ain't. I bet your wife is caring and loving. Devon ain't. He don't got a family—no kids, no wife, nothing like that. He's nothing but a scumbag. The world would be a better place without him."

Shamrock turned and walked back toward the running trail.

———

As HE SHUFFLED DOWN THE RUNNING PATH IN THE MIDDLE OF WILLOW Park, Otto was still trying to make sense of the meeting that had just taken place. When he'd first seen the article online, he'd dismissed the idea of approaching Gary Foster. Put something so important in the hands of some random guy? Some choirboy who'd probably piss himself at the sight of blood? It was an absurd idea.

But the sad fact of the matter was that it was no more absurd than his other options. Six people had turned him down over the past month, his go-to man, Champ, included, and if he kept asking around, word would start to spread around the neighborhood like wildfire. Wouldn't take long for the whole hood to hear that he was looking for someone to off Devon Peterson. And the more people who knew about this, the more likely it was to blow up in his face. The next time some dirtbag was arrested and needed a bargaining chip for a reduced sentence, guess what card they'd play? *That murder, Devon Peterson— I know who was behind it. I know who paid to have him killed.*

No, the more he thought about it, approaching this guy, this Gary Foster, wasn't the worst idea. Someone with no connection to him. No connection to Devon. No criminal background. Someone the police would never suspect.

Looked like an organized person, too. Methodical. Probably owned a bunch of file folders and shit. The type of guy who'd plan things out, not make a mistake.

He'd never shot a gun before, but, really, what did that matter? You pointed it, pulled the trigger, and it went bang. It wasn't rocket science.

Of course, there were no guarantees. Otto was certain that Gary would look into Devon Peterson's life, and when he discovered Devon's identity, that could influence his decision. There was still the chance that Gary could turn him down.

But he'd worry about that if it came to it. He reached the end of the running path and walked west on Spring Street, the street that bordered Willow Park. He still had a ways to go—he didn't want Gary to see his car, so he'd left it at a McDonald's five blocks from the park.

Otto looked over his shoulder one final time. Far across the park, Gary Foster still sat on the bench. All alone. Just a man and his thoughts.

This crazy idea, Otto thought, *just might be crazy enough to work out.*

———

GARY STARED OUT AT THE EMPTINESS OF WILLOW PARK. THE TEENAGERS playing basketball had disappeared and not a single person had shown up since then. A light breeze blew through the skeletal trees in the distance, their swaying branches the only movement in the park.

Gary had spent most of the past hour suspended in a dreamlike state that was equal parts complete astonishment and abject confusion. His mind was a muddled mess, swirling with questions, grasping for understanding. He had difficulty believing that the offer was real, that it wasn't some sort of sick prank.

But it was real.

Commit murder to save Beth.

Once his disbelief wore off, he'd taken a sound, rational look at the offer. He'd examined it from every angle, obsessed over it. After carefully thinking about everything for what seemed like an eternity, he'd reached a decision.

He would decline the offer.

In the end, the only thing that mattered was that he was incapable of murder. No matter the circumstances, no matter the stakes, no matter what was on the line, he didn't have it in him to commit such an atrocity. There was simply no way. If he had some way to contact Shamrock, he'd call him at this very moment and decline the offer. Get it over with now instead of waiting for him to call in a few days. Just be done with it.

He stood up from the park bench and walked over to his car, still the only one in the small parking lot. Before stepping inside, he gave himself one last opportunity, one final moment, to reconsider.

If he accepted the offer, there would be nothing to worry about.

They could pay for Beth's treatment right now.

Everything could be taken care of.

But the words rang hollow. He simply could not murder someone. He was a decent, honest, moral person who was incapable of taking the life of another human being. And that was that.

His decision was final.

7

WHEN HE ARRIVED BACK HOME, THE LIVING ROOM WAS PACKED WITH ten women from Beth's yoga class. All of them wore their pink Team Beth shirts. Gary greeted everyone and grabbed his own pink shirt from the bedroom. He put it on and sat down at the edge of the room, next to Beth.

"I didn't realize we were having visitors," he said.

"I didn't, either," Beth said. "The doorbell rang this morning, I answered it, and this crew was waiting outside."

Gary recognized a few of them, but the only name he knew was that of Sarah, Rod's wife, the owner of the yoga studio. She sat on the couch, head held high, her short black hair fashioned in a tousled bob. The odd couple, Beth always called Sarah and Rod. The Beauty and the Beast. Sarah was confident and poised, the polar opposite of Rod, the grown child who'd won her over with nothing more than his juvenile charm.

"How was the store?" Beth asked.

"The store?" He'd forgotten all about the note he'd written for Beth before he left. "Nothing special. It was fine."

"With Rod in charge, I'm surprised the place isn't trashed," Sarah said. "I don't think Rod has ever once cleaned up after himself since we started living together. I feel like I'm married to a teenager sometimes."

Beth smiled. "Oh, he never cleaned up after himself when he lived with us, either. Months after he moved out, I was still discovering his dirty laundry all over the house. I can't tell you how many pairs of his socks I found crammed under our couch cushions."

"At least it wasn't his boxers."

Laughter all around.

"We were just talking, Gary," one of them—something with an M; Melanie? Mary?—said. "Talking about this treatment in Germany."

"It's a miracle. At least, we hope so."

"We're here to help," Something with an M said. "Do anything we can to raise the money."

"Speaking of . . ." Beth said.

She pulled her phone from her pocket and looked at the Kickstarter-style fund-raising page they'd set up last night. Beth's picture was at the top of the screen—her smile full and wide, her head slightly tilted to the side, her hand placed over her belly. The title SAVE BETH FOSTER was under the photograph. In the middle of the page was a short summary of her story. Farther down on the page was a horizontal thermometer stick with notches in ten-thousand-dollar increments.

GOAL: $200,000 read the inscription on the right side of the thermometer.

CURRENTLY AT: $2,237 read the inscription on the left side of the thermometer.

"There's more than when I last checked," Beth said. "People must have seen the article this morning."

"That's great."

"It's a start; that's all it is. Truly great news would be if someone showed up and just handed us a bag with all the money."

Everyone except Gary chuckled.

They spent an hour brainstorming names of people who might be able to help with the money. When they finished, they had a list that numbered well over a hundred people. Friends from the community. Old acquaintances. Former coworkers.

"If we cast the net wide, there's a chance," Beth said. "Get a couple thousand dollars from some people, a couple hundred from others, and the money could add up."

ALMOST SIX HOURS LATER, GARY AND BETH SAT IN THE LIVING ROOM, STILL in their pink Team Beth shirts. Of the group of friends, only Sarah remained.

The laptop was set up on the coffee table, displaying the fundraising site.

GOAL: $200,000 read the inscription on the right side of the thermometer.

CURRENTLY AT: $8,417 read the inscription on the left side of the thermometer.

They all three stared at the screen, their faces grim.

"It's better than nothing," Gary said. Even to himself, the words sounded insincere.

The day had been long. Beth's yoga friends had stayed at the house all afternoon, making phone calls, sending off texts, posting the link to the fund-raising site on social media. Doing everything they could to raise money.

After all that work, they didn't even have ten thousand dollars to show for it.

"It's frustrating," Beth said. "I want to be angry, but who's there to be angry at? Those who could help with the money did what they were able to. Those who couldn't just didn't have any money."

Gary nodded. Most people he'd talked to were polite, apologetic, genuinely sorry they couldn't do more. They offered to help by cooking dinner, by praying, by offering any sort of moral support needed. But they couldn't help with money and that was the only thing that mattered. He had spoken to at least fifteen people who'd been left unemployed when the Lorimer Brake Pads manufacturing plant closed last year and devastated the local job market. How could they expect people to help if they could barely make their mortgage payments or put food on the table?

"We'll find the money," Gary said. "It's still early."

There was no reaction from either woman, no enthusiastic rallying cry or passionate words of encouragement. Not that Gary expected anything. They both looked drained, totally spent.

AFTER SARAH LEFT, BETH AND GARY SAT DOWN TO EAT DINNER. BEFORE THEY started, Beth closed her eyes and massaged her temples.

"I have a headache," she said.

A headache. The word always caused a pang of fearful uncertainty. Beth had gotten headaches on and off during her treatment. And every time, Gary felt that knot in the pit of his stomach, that helpless feeling of not knowing how serious it was.

"Bad one?" he asked.

Beth winced. Kept her eyes closed for a moment.

"I'll be fine," she said. "I just need to lie down. Today has been exhausting."

Gary helped her out of her chair and led her into the bedroom. She curled up on her side of the bed and Gary tucked her in. He leaned over and kissed her forehead.

"We can go to the hospital if you need to," he said.

She weakly shook her head in response.

BETH STAYED IN BED ALL EVENING. GARY CHECKED UP ON HER PERIODICALLY. He offered to bring her soup but she declined. A glass of water he'd set on the bedside table remained untouched.

Later in the night, after she'd fallen asleep, Gary walked into the baby's soon-to-be bedroom and sat down at the computer. He opened the Internet browser and typed *Devon Peterson* into the search bar.

He paused before hitting Enter.

He told himself it was harmless to search for more information about Devon Peterson, the man Shamrock wanted him to murder. Simple curiosity—that's all this was. Nothing more than that.

He knew that was a lie.

They had barely anything to show for an entire day spent reaching out to friends. Only now that they'd started to try to raise the money did Gary realize just how difficult it would be. Two hundred thousand dollars: it was an enormous, mind-boggling figure.

All day long, as the twenty- and fifty-dollar donations and apologies for not giving more piled up, the offer had lingered in the back of his mind. Right now, the voice in Gary's mind said, he could take care of everything. He could have the money they needed for the treatment.

He owed it to Beth, he owed it to himself, owed it to their unborn son to reconsider the offer. His earlier decision to decline was made in the heat of the moment, immediately after his meeting with Shamrock. He wasn't thinking straight at the time—the sheer shock at being presented with such an unbelievable offer had clouded his judgment, made it impossible to look at everything objectively.

He'd spent an hour considering the offer then. An hour was nothing. No, for a decision with so much at stake, he had to take his time. He had to examine all of the facts and put far more than an hour's worth of thought into his decision.

First up: He wanted to learn more about Devon Peterson.

He wanted to learn who he was.

He wanted to learn what he did.

He wanted to learn why someone was willing to pay an enormous amount of money for his murder.

Gary tapped Enter on the keyboard. A moment later, the search results appeared. Text links filled the lower half of the screen but Gary focused on the thumbnail photos above the links.

The first photograph was small, yet he immediately recognized Devon Peterson's fleshy, thick face and buzz-cut hair. It was a head shot that looked similar to the picture on the photocopied driver's license, maybe a few years more recent. In it, Devon wore a black short-sleeve button-up shirt that was skintight against his large frame, hugging against his chest and riding up on his large, burly arms. Even though the photo was a thumbnail, Gary could see the gold badge pinned to the chest of his shirt.

The horrifying reality instantly became clear.

Devon Peterson was a police officer.

8

GARY STARED AT THE SCREEN IN STUNNED SILENCE.

A police officer.

Murder a police officer.

Right then, right there, he almost walked away. Murder was wrong on every level, but there was something particularly sinister about murdering a police officer.

Gary was about to shut down the computer when something caught his eye. The first text link, near the top of the page—the preview text grabbed his attention. He clicked on the link and a news article from a decade ago appeared on-screen.

SHOP OWNER RECANTS STORY; COPS WILL NOT FACE DISCIPLINE

DETROIT, MI—A convenience-store owner who accused two Detroit police officers of extortion and assault has dropped the charges.

Luis Aceveda, owner of Pronto Grocery, filed a complaint last month accusing officers Devon Peterson, 27, and David Ashcraft, 31, of using violence and threats to intimidate him into paying nearly $10,000 over a three-month period. Aceveda claimed the officers beat him with a nightstick and vandalized windows in his business to bully him.

Yesterday, Aceveda withdrew his accusation. He apologized for the misunderstanding, claiming he had misidentified the officers.

Neither officer will face disciplinary action.

Gary clicked the back arrow. He quickly scanned more search results, finding a few more articles detailing Devon Peterson's trouble with the law when he was a police officer in Detroit. The words blurred together as he scrolled past one article *(Multiple harassment claims were filed against Peterson, but an internal investigation found that no wrongdoing took place)*, past another *(A state arbitrator ruled that Peterson should be suspended with pay for one week and undergo anger management counseling as a result of his part in the assault).*

Gary found a longer article from a few years back, much more detailed than the other ones.

FOUR DETROIT OFFICERS TO STEP DOWN

DETROIT, MI— Detroit Police Chief Joe Antonio announced that four officers found not guilty of corruption charges will resign from the force, effective immediately.

Last month, Jacob Quinn, Perry Montgomery, David Ashcraft, and Devon Peterson—all narcotics officers—were brought to trial for corruption charges. Over the course of five years, the officers were accused of stealing more than $250,000 from suspects and businesses in the neighborhoods they patrolled. The lawsuit alleged that officers took cash, expensive watches, and kilograms of cocaine, in addition to strong-arming witnesses into recanting testimonies through intimidation and physical abuse.

A few of the allegations from the indictment are below:

—On multiple occasions, the officers used excessive force on persons who were not resisting arrest, including striking a suspect in the face with the butt of a pistol and beating handcuffed suspects.

—Montgomery planted drugs on a suspect and charged him with possession of crack cocaine, then conspired with Peterson and Ashcraft to write a report that cleared him of wrongdoing.

—Peterson and Quinn pocketed more than forty thousand dollars in cash during a drug bust, then tortured a suspect with a Taser when he threatened to testify against the officers.

After a trial that garnered headlines, the officers were found not guilty of all charges. Widespread protests and public outcry resulted in the officers' resignations.

Gary clicked on a link toward the bottom of the screen.

NEW RIVER FALLS COP HAS CHECKERED HISTORY

RIVER FALLS, MI—Police leaders have announced the hiring of a new police officer with a controversial past.

Devon Peterson, 35, was accused of corruption and unlawful activity during his tenure as a narcotics officer in Detroit. These past troubles did not deter River Falls Police Chief Darren Roselin from hiring Peterson to fill a vacant officer position last week.

"We know all about the allegations that were brought up against Officer Peterson," Roselin said. "He was found innocent in a court of law."

Roselin pointed to two factors that played a part in Peterson's hiring.

"Officer Peterson was one of the most decorated officers on the force in Detroit," Roselin said. "He brought down some major players in an extremely drug-infested and violent neighborhood."

The second factor was a depleted workforce in the River Falls PD.

"Our department is terribly understaffed," Roselin said. "The city is budgeted for 311 officers and operated with only 247 for most of last year. Thirteen officers have either left the force or retired since then. Not enough officers creates innumerable problems for our police force and the community we serve."

Roselin worked with Peterson in Detroit for six years before coming to River Falls, but the police chief insists their previous relationship has nothing to do with Peterson's hiring.

"Officer Peterson was hired because he's a tenacious, hard-nosed cop," Roselin said. "That's what our city needs, particularly some of the lower-income areas Devon will be assigned to."

Despite the police chief's words, some government leaders have questioned the decision to hire Peterson. Roselin insists that the new officer will be watched closely.

"We have a very elaborate accountability system in place for all officers to ensure they are performing their job with integrity," he said. "Officer Peterson, like all of our officers, will be monitored closely."

Gary turned off the computer.

ACROSS TOWN, OTTO SLOUCHED OVER THE COUNTER OF SOLID GOLD PAWN. He reached over and rifled around in a drawer until he found a package of Rolaids. He tore back the packaging and popped a few into his mouth. Indigestion, knee pain—fuck, he was getting old.

Just as the Rolaids began to combat the boil of sour acid in his stomach, he saw a pair of headlights pull into the pawnshop parking lot and come to a stop. A shadowy figure emerged from the car. A moment later, the pawnshop's front door opened. Devon Peterson, fucking Devon, stepped into the shop. The queasiness in Otto's stomach flared back to life.

Devon ducked his head as he walked inside, his large frame taking up nearly the entire doorway. He was a big bastard. Not that much smaller than Champ, but Devon was doughier, not as defined.

Devon stood inside the entrance for a moment, aviator sunglasses on even though it was nighttime, chest puffed out like he was hot shit in his officer's uniform. His lips were curled into a cocky smile. It was the smile of a man who knew he was in total control.

"Just your friendly neighborhood officer stopping in to say hi," Devon said.

He removed his sunglasses and casually walked over to the counter. In no rush. He looked at the assorted merchandise on the shelves as he walked. He stopped at a bin with some old 45s in it and lifted a Lynyrd Skynyrd record out. He looked at it for a moment.

"Highway robbery, what you charge for some of the shit in this place," Devon said, throwing the album back onto the table. "Fifty fuckin' bucks for a Skynyrd record? And it ain't even the good one, the one with 'Sweet Home Alabama' on it."

"What do you want, Devon?" Otto said.

"That's Officer Peterson to you," Devon said, that smile crossing his lips again. The smile of power, of dominance.

He took a step toward Otto. Took another.

"I'm checking to see about the money we talked about," Devon said.

"What about it?"

"You gonna have it in a couple weeks?"

"I think so."

Devon reached the counter. The smile was gone; his expression was stone. The tendons in his neck were tight with angry tension. Otto, nearly a foot shorter than Devon, craned his neck to hold eye contact.

"You think so? What the hell kinda answer is that?"

"Takes time to round up that type of cash. I told you that."

"And I told *you* I'd give you time," Devon said. "I'd give you two months. Deadline'll be in a couple weeks. You gonna have the cash then or not?"

"Yeah. I should."

Devon leaned in over the counter, so close that his face was only inches from Otto's. Otto could hear him breathing and smell the sour stink of his breath. He felt like he was staring down an angry bull at point-blank range.

"You don't sound very confident," Devon said.

"I'll have it."

"You're positive?"

"Yeah, I'm pos—"

Quick as a snakebite, Devon swung his hand and slapped Otto on the side of the face with an open palm. Otto staggered backward and his bad knee buckled under him. He fell against a fifteen-inch flat-screen computer monitor on a shelf. The monitor toppled over and fell to the ground, the screen shattering, the frame splitting in two.

"Don't fuck with me, boy," Devon said. "Don't give me this 'I think so' shit."

Hunched over, Otto brought an unsteady hand up to his face. He rubbed his cheek. The soft tissue stung, burned horribly.

"I'll be back at the end of the month, and I want the cash then," Devon said. "You don't have it and there'll be no love taps next time. I'll use a closed fist and bash your face in. And that'll be the least of your problems."

With that, Devon trudged back across the pawnshop floor and exited through the front door.

As he watched the headlights pull away, Otto felt hot, humiliating anger flood into his body. A slap! He couldn't believe it. A slap, like Devon viewed him as nothing more than some petulant child. He would've preferred a punch, would've preferred it if Devon had reared back and leveled him with a right hook. At least a punch showed respect.

So furious he was practically shaking, Otto opened a small cupboard and grabbed a dustpan and broom. He leaned over the shattered mess from the computer monitor and swept the broken pieces of glass and plastic into a small pile, catching dust balls and other bits of dirt. He swept with forceful sweeps, slamming the broom bristles into the ground.

It had been only a month since everything had gone to shit. A month ago—that's when Devon Peterson had walked into Solid Gold Pawn for the first time. Police officers stopped by the pawnshop on occasion to look for electronics and other items that had gone missing in home break-ins, and Otto always got a perverse sense of enjoyment from seeing them walk around to check the serial numbers of electronics, completely unaware that the pawnshop was just a bullshit business used to launder money from one of the major drug-smuggling rings in the city.

But it hadn't taken Otto long to realize that the officer who stopped in last month had something more on his mind than stolen merchandise. After walking through the door, Devon had walked straight up to the front counter, leaned in close, and looked Otto in the eye.

"I know your secret," Devon said.

Those four simple words had caused dark, constricting fear to seize Otto's heart. He'd numbly stared back at Devon, too shocked to respond.

"Me and you, we're gonna become friends," Devon said, that arrogant smile spreading across his face. "Real good friends."

From there, Devon had explained everything. Someone had spilled their guts and told him about the drug trafficking, the money laundering, Otto's whole damn operation.

"And now it's simple," Devon said. "My little birdie tells me you got around two hundred grand stashed away to pay for tomorrow's delivery. I want it all."

Otto's jaw quivered. Jesus Christ. The delivery—Devon knew about the delivery. Carlos, his smuggler from Mexico, was arriving tomorrow with the newest quarterly drug delivery from De La Fuente. Two hundred grand in cash was set aside downstairs to pay Carlos— a hundred grand for De La Fuente's cut of last quarter's sales; a hundred grand for payment of this quarter's supply.

"Delivery? I don't know what you're talking about," Otto said.

"Bullshit. I'm told the cash is probably downstairs. In the basement."

"This place don't got a basement."

Devon walked over to the electric-guitar display. He sized up the wall, then rammed his forearm against it. The door hidden among the wall paneling swung open.

74

"No basement, huh?" Devon said, smirking. "Come on. Let's go."

Otto didn't move.

"Last chance, boy," Devon said. "You don't wanna play ball, I'll arrest you on suspicion, get a warrant, and we'll tear this place apart. I'm sure we'll find plenty—enough to send your ass to prison for a long time."

His mind swimming, Otto stepped out from behind the counter. He couldn't believe any of this. Devon had him by the balls—and he was squeezing, hard.

Otto walked down the staircase, Devon behind him. In the basement, on the table in the middle of the room, there it was: the cash. Two hundred grand. Set aside to pay Carlos tomorrow.

Devon grabbed the stack of bills and they walked back upstairs.

Before leaving, Devon turned back to Otto.

"I'll be back next month," Devon said. "I want two hundred grand more then."

Otto's head nearly exploded. "You're out of your mind," he said.

Paying two hundred thousand dollars more to Devon would damn near clean him out completely. He wasn't Tony Montana, and River Falls, Michigan, sure as shit wasn't Miami. Lately, he'd barely been selling product for much above cost.

To pay Devon two hundred grand more, he'd have to empty out his bank accounts. Sell off everything he could. He'd hardly have anything left.

"I can't do it," Otto said. "Two hundred grand more—that's not possible."

"Find a way."

"I can't—"

"Figure it out."

Otto clenched his jaw. Being bullied like this, it infuriated him.

"At least give me more time," he said. "I'm not bullshitting you here. Only way I could possibly come up with this type of cash is if I get more time."

"I'll give you two months, then. That's when I'll return. If you don't have the cash, your ass is going to prison. That simple."

That was it. Devon left the pawnshop.

Otto clenched his jaw and gripped the broom even tighter, thinking back to that fateful day, just over a month ago. He still couldn't believe that everything he'd built was close to crumbling. If he somehow got out of this mess, he'd put everything he had into finding the gutless fucker who'd snitched to Devon. He'd make the rat bastard pay, whoever he was. He would—

He forced the broom bristles into the floor with such force that the wooden handle snapped in two. He slammed the splintered handle to the ground.

Fuck it. He'd clean it up later.

He looked out at the pawnshop sales floor and shook his head. Problems. So many problems.

Problem: That corrupt bastard Devon had already taken two hundred thousand dollars from him, and would be taking that same amount in two months.

Problem: He owed De La Fuente two hundred grand—and De La Fuente would shove the power of the El Este cartel up his ass if he didn't pay.

But the real problem was that he only had enough money to pay one of them. He'd scraped and clawed to round up the two hundred thousand dollars; that money was every last bit of his cash. He had a few assets beyond that but nothing worth much of a shit.

The situation was a shit storm. If he paid Devon, he wouldn't be able to pay De La Fuente. If he paid De La Fuente, he couldn't pay Devon. And he couldn't just disappear or go on the run; too many loose ends. He'd be lucky to last a few weeks with a drug kingpin and a corrupt cop on his ass, no matter where he went.

But now, Otto thought, there may be a way out of it. Pay De La Fuente. Eliminate Devon. That would take care of all his problems.

9

BETH WAS ALREADY AWAKE WHEN GARY WALKED INTO THE KITCHEN THE next morning. She sat at the kitchen table, wearing a pair of yoga pants and a white T-shirt with a smorgasbord of cartoony junk food screen-printed on the front—an ice cream cone, a pizza, a slice of pie. Written across the belly of the shirt was the inscription IT'S NOT FOR ME . . . IT'S FOR THE BABY.

"Feeling better?" Gary asked.

Beth nodded. "Much. No headache at all."

Gary sat down next to her, his entire body weary. Sleep had come in fits and starts last night; the few hours of rest he'd gotten had no effect.

On the table in front of Beth were two sheets of paper with names printed on them, one right after another, in Beth's perfect penmanship.

"More people to reach out to?" Gary said.

Beth nodded. "I've been working on this all morning. I've got a list for you, and a list for me."

They ate breakfast and chatted. Beth really did seem fine, totally different from last night. Her headaches were always so unpredictable—debilitating one moment, nonexistent the next. Usually, it only took a few hours of rest for a headache to pass.

When they finished breakfast, Gary grabbed his list and stood up from the table.

"I'll be in the baby's room, calling people," he said. "Maybe I'll catch a few before they head to work."

"Be sure to tell them about the Web site, send them the link," Beth said. "If they can't help with money, see if they can post the link to Facebook, e-mail it to friends. Spread the word any way they can."

"I will," Gary said. "Come get me if you need anything."

Gary walked into the baby's room and shut the door behind him. He sat at the computer desk and set down the sheet of paper, pushing it off to the side.

He wasn't making any phone calls. Not now, at least. It seemed pointless to try to painstakingly piece the money together, fifty dollars at a time, when they could have it all at once if he agreed to Shamrock's offer. Tomorrow at noon, the phone call would arrive. In just over twenty-four hours, he'd have to make the biggest decision of his life.

Commit murder to save Beth.

The initial shock of discovering that Devon Peterson was a police officer wore off once he read about everything else Devon was involved in—the assaults, the corruption, the illegal activities. Cop or not, Devon Peterson was clearly a bad person.

For the entire night, as he lay awake in bed, Gary thought about it all. Did it matter that Devon Peterson was a bad person? Perhaps.

It certainly made it easier to rationalize the murder. Beth was a good person. Devon was a bad person. Wouldn't killing a bad person to save a good person be somewhat justifiable? Not in the eyes of the law, of course. But in his own mind, could he justify killing a bad, immoral person for a chance at saving a good, kind person—a good, kind person whom he loved and who happened to be pregnant with his first child?

It was a question he'd have to answer soon. Gary told himself that right here, right now, he would sit at this computer desk, think long and hard about that question, and figure out his answer.

However long it took, he wouldn't leave the room until he had an answer.

SIX HOURS LATER, GARY LEFT THE ROOM. HE DIDN'T HAVE AN ANSWER.

He shuffled down the hallway, his shoulders slouched, his eyes glazed over, his hair jutting from his scalp in uncontrolled tufts. In the living room, Beth sat on the green vinyl sofa that served as the centerpiece of their meager furnishings. The bulk of her pregnant body was curled onto one half of the couch. A small television was turned to a late-afternoon talk show but the volume was muted.

"You're alive," she said.

Gary nodded. He'd taken only a couple of breaks all day, once to greet some of Beth's friends who visited, and once to eat lunch with her. The total isolation in the nursery had turned his weariness into something more, a zombielike exhaustion. All day, he'd thought about what his answer would be when Shamrock called. He still had absolutely no idea what he'd say.

"Did you have any luck making phone calls?" Beth asked.

"What?"

"Calling around, asking people to help us with money—was anyone able to donate anything?"

"Mostly dead ends," Gary said. He hadn't so much as glanced at the sheet of names in the past six hours.

"Same here. A lot of answers that began with, 'I wish we could, but . . .'"

She brought her phone to life and showed him the fund-raising page.

Goal: $200,000
Currently at: $12,185

"Almost six hours on the phone, dozens of phone calls, and that's all I have to show for it," Beth said. "I felt like a telemarketer. When one person turned me down, I called the next person on the list. When that called ended, I called the next person. And on and on, all day."

Beth's phone rang and she left the room to answer it. She returned after a minute.

"That was Sarah," she said. "She and Rod want to take us out to dinner tonight. Dagnostino's—your favorite."

"Tonight? I can't."

Time was ticking away. The tension was mounting, the pressure building. Tomorrow at noon would arrive in the blink of an eye.

"Why not?" Beth said

"I just can't. We have phone calls to make."

"That's what I told her, too, but she insisted that we needed a break. And you know what? I agree with her. We've been cooped up in the house all day. Dagnostino's is a five-minute drive, and dinner will take less than an hour. We'll be back here by seven and we can make more phone calls then."

Gary didn't respond. *Maybe,* he decided, *Beth is right.* Maybe stepping away and getting out of the house would clear his mind.

"Okay," he said. "Let's meet up with them."

10

AT JUST AFTER SIX, GARY AND BETH WALKED INTO DAGNOSTINO'S PIZZA. Thirty tables were arranged around the restaurant floor, covered in red-and-white-checkered tablecloths. Half were occupied with families or couples on dates.

They sat down across from Rod and Sarah in a corner booth. A waitress arrived with menus and took their drink orders—waters for the ladies, Budweisers for Gary and Rod. The waitress smiled and walked away.

"I want to make a rule for dinner," Beth said before anyone could grab a menu. "Tonight, from right now until we finish eating, I don't want to talk about everything that's going on with me. Not a word about the tumor, the treatment—none of it. For the past few days, that's all I've talked about, all I've thought about. And tonight, just for the next hour, I want to forget it all and have a nice, normal night out like we've had in the past. Okay?"

They all nodded.

"Good," she said.

"WHAT ABOUT OSCAR?" BETH ASKED.

She looked around the table for a response, at Gary next to her, at Sarah and Rod across from them. A circular tray of pizza with a few slices remaining rested on the table in front of them. The restaurant had gotten busier since they arrived; nearly every table was full. Warbled conversation surrounded them.

"Oscar?" Rod said.

"Yeah," Beth said. "Oscar Foster. I like it."

Beth took a pen and wrote the name on a napkin, adding it to a list that already numbered more than ten names. The evening had started out with stilted and awkward conversation—it was as if they'd become so used to talking about Beth's illness that they'd forgotten how to have a discussion about anything else.

But after ten minutes, Beth said that she wanted to decide on a name for the baby, something they'd been putting off for months. The conversation immediately picked up; they'd spent the past fifteen minutes discussing baby names while stuffing their faces with pizza.

"Oscar Foster," Sarah said. "Oh, I love that."

"It's got a nice ring to it, right?"

"Hold up, hold up," Rod said, taking a chunk out of the folded-up slice of pizza in his hand. "Oscar? Like the guy from the Muppets?"

"Oscar's from *Sesame Street*, not *The Muppet Show*," Beth said.

"But he's the one who lives in a trash can, right?"

"Yeah."

"So you want to name your kid after a furry green monster who lives in a trash can? Yeah, like that kid won't get bullied in school."

Rod laughed. A small smile crossed Beth's lips.

"If you're going to name him after a *Sesame Street* character, go with Ernie," Rod went on. "Grover, maybe. Even Elmo would be better than naming your kid after some creep who spends all his time in a trash can."

Beth chuckled and threw a wadded-up napkin at Rod. He laughed as he dodged out of the way.

No reaction to the conversation registered on Gary's face. He sat in the booth, his expression blank. A pizza slice missing a single small bite rested on a plate in front of him, next to a pint of beer that he'd taken two sips from. He stared down at the food, distracted and nervous. Antsy. He was so damn antsy.

He picked up the slice and took a small nibble. He normally loved the pizza from Dagnostino's, but it tasted like cardboard tonight.

"Gary?"

He looked at Beth.

"What?"

"I said, 'What do you think of Oscar?'"

"Sure. It's fine."

Beth's eyes stayed on him.

"Is everything all right with you?"

"Yeah," he said.

"You seem distracted."

"I've got a lot on my mind."

"Remember what I said. Forget about the tumor, the treatment, all of that until dinner is over."

"Right."

The conversation picked back up. Gary listened but he caught only bits and pieces. Everyone universally hated the named Freddie. Everyone liked the name Jonah.

As everyone voiced their opinion on the name Jeremy, Gary stood up from the table.

"I need to use the restroom," he said.

He walked across the restaurant floor to the men's room in back. The bathroom consisted of a row of urinals and two toilet stalls, all unoccupied. Gary turned on the sink and splashed some cold water on his face. Eyes closed, he remained huddled over the sink, droplets of water dripping off his face into the basin.

He wondered what it would feel like to murder another human being. It was something he had thought about all day. What would that feel like, to end another man's life, to know that the world was less one person because of Gary Foster?

It was unbelievable that he was even contemplating such a question.

Gary pulled a few paper towels from a dispenser and patted his face dry. He paced around the small bathroom as he thought about it all, paced back and forth, his footsteps tapping on the bathroom tile. Questions and worries tumbled around his mind like clothes in a dryer.

Did he honestly want to get involved in this? Was it madness to even consider this offer? Shamrock wanted a police officer murdered. Normal, upstanding people aren't willing to pay tremendous amounts of money for the murder of a police officer. Wasn't it utter foolishness to even consider putting himself in the middle of a situation like this?

The bathroom door flew open, startling him. Rod stuck his head inside.

"Yo, Gar. You all right in here?"

"I'm fine."

"I thought you might've fallen into the toilet."

Gary glanced at his watch. He was shocked to see that he'd been in the bathroom for almost fifteen minutes.

"It's nothing. I'm fine."

"Then let's head back. The ladies are asking about you."

Gary didn't move. "Hold on for a second," he said. "I want to ask you a question."

"What about?" Rod asked.

"Actually, it's not a question. More like a hypothetical situation."

"Can we do this at the table? I've had three slices but I'm still starving."

"This'll only take a second."

Rod walked into the bathroom and let the door shut behind him. He'd gotten dressed up for the evening—by Rod standards, at least—in a pair of Chuck Taylors and a light blue shirt tucked into worn jeans. His shaggy blond hair was slicked to the side.

"What would you do if you were in my shoes?" Gary asked.

"What do you mean?"

"Let's say Sarah's the one who's sick. Her life is at risk and there's a treatment that could help her. How far would you go to save her?"

"What kinda question is that?"

"A hypothetical one. Just humor me. How far would you go?"

Rod shrugged.

"I'd do whatever it takes. Obviously."

"Would you do something illegal?" Gary said.

"Of course."

"Of course? Just like that? No need to think about it?"

"Nope. She's the love of my life. I'd do anything to save her."

"Even something really illegal? Like terribly, horribly illegal?"

"Like what? Robbing a bank?"

"Sure. Robbing a bank. Say a guy comes to you, asks you to rob a bank for him, and lets you keep the money you'd need to save her if you agree. You'd do that?"

"Hell, yes, I would."

"What if you got caught? You could go to jail for a long time."

"True. But what if I decided not to do it and something happened to Sarah? What if I had a chance to save her, I turned down that chance, and I lost her? The guilt would kill me. Knowing that I had the opportunity to save her but didn't take it—it'd haunt me for the rest of my life."

Gary thought about Rod's response for a moment. He didn't know what type of answer he was expecting from Rod, but it wasn't that. The response intrigued Gary.

"Why do you ask?" Rod said.

"No real reason."

"Seems like a weird question."

"Just forget it, Rod. It's nothing."

"I know what it is," Rod said. "You're thinking of robbing a bank, right? Asking me to be your driver?" Rod smiled.

"That's it," Gary said, giving a halfhearted smile in return. "We can be the next Bonnie and Clyde."

That ended the conversation. Gary was glad to see it end. He had no idea why he'd even posed the question to Rod. It was a stupid thing to do. It wasn't going to clear up anything. The decision was his and his alone.

"Come on," Rod said. "Let's go. That pizza ain't gonna eat itself."

Gary followed Rod out of the bathroom and back across the restaurant floor.

"Everything okay?" Beth said as they sat down at the booth.

"I'm fine," Gary said.

Beth looked down at the napkin in front of her. A few of the names had been crossed off.

"We narrowed it down to four finalists while you were gone," Beth said. "Stephen, Tyson, Oscar, and James, but we'd call him Jimmy. What do you think?"

She looked across the table.

"Obviously, this is your decision," Sarah said. "But I'm partial to Tyson."

"Tyson," Rod said. "Although I'm tempted to vote Oscar, just to make the kid's life miserable."

Beth smiled. She turned to Gary.

"And you?" she said.

"Tyson," Gary said. "I like Tyson."

"That's what I was thinking, too."

Beth suddenly reached down and felt her belly. She grabbed Gary's hand and placed it next to hers.

"Feel that?" she said.

Gary felt the baby kicking. It was like an erratic heartbeat, two firm thrusts and a softer one.

"That must mean he likes his name," Beth said. "Little Tyson likes his new name."

THEY FINISHED THE PIZZA AND ROD PAID THE CHECK. SARAH STOPPED THEM just as they stood up to leave.

"Hold up," she said. "Before we go, Rod and I have something we want to discuss."

Rod looked over at Sarah and smiled. She set her hand on top of Rod's on the table.

"There's a reason we asked you to dinner," Rod said. "We've got something we want to say. I know you said you didn't want to talk about your sickness and everything else. But we're going to break your rule, just for a moment."

"When I heard about your tumor, I was crushed," Sarah said, staring at Beth. "We both were. We still are. I still remember that first day you walked into my yoga studio, looking like a lost little puppy dog. You told me you'd never done yoga in your life but wanted to try. The entire time, you were stumbling and flailing around, barely able to keep your balance. Remember when you fell and almost toppled over an entire row of people?"

Both Beth and Sarah smiled at the memory.

"Yeah. I remember."

"I thought for sure I'd never see you again," Sarah said. "But a couple days later, you came back. Then you came back again. And again. Ever since then, getting to know you has been such a blessing. You're my best friend—I've never told you that before, but you are. You're one of the nicest, most genuine people I know. It's not fair for something like this to happen to someone so great."

Both women looked like they were about to cry.

"This whole thing sucks," Rod said. "That's all there is to it. Sarah and I wanted to do something for you."

Sarah reached under the table. Gary heard a zipper being unzipped—her purse. A moment later, she placed a small folded piece of paper on the table in front of Beth.

"This is for you," Sarah said.

Beth picked up the piece of paper and unfolded it. Gary leaned sideways and looked over her shoulder.

It was a light blue check with Rod and Sarah's names and address in the corner. In Rod's sloppy chicken-scratch handwriting, the check was made out to Gary and Beth Foster in the amount of twelve thousand dollars.

"My God," Beth whispered.

Gary stared at the check. He closed his eyes, paused for a moment to compose himself. He knew that it had to be practically everything that Rod and Sarah had in the bank.

Beth looked up from the check, tears in her eyes.

"I don't know what to say," she said.

"You don't have to say anything," Sarah said. "We want to do this."

"If we could do more, we would," Rod said. "This is everything we had left over from our wedding, plus some money from Sarah's yoga studio that we had saved."

"I promise we'll pay you back. Someday, we'll pay you back."

"That's the last thing we're worried about right now," Sarah said. "We're not losing you. No way."

Gary still hadn't said anything; the donation was so genuine and heartfelt that he was completely speechless.

"Thank you," Beth said. "Both of you, thank you so much."

"We'll do whatever we can to help," Rod said. "Anything at all."

———

SHIRTLESS, HIS TATTED-UP ARMS AND CHEST ON FULL DISPLAY, OTTO stared into a bathroom mirror as he ran a disposable razor over the gleaming dome of his bald head. He pulled the razor from the back of his skull to the front, feeling a prickle as the razor shaved away barely there stubble. He didn't use water or shaving cream when he shaved. Just the razor. It scraped rough against his skin but he was used to the feeling.

For the past twenty years, shaving his head was the final thing he did before going to bed. Never missed a day—no exceptions. He knew if he went a day without shaving his head, his red hair would start to grow back. It wouldn't be much, just a fraction of an inch, but it'd be enough. He'd still be able to see it, and he never wanted to see his red hair again.

He hated his red hair because it reminded him of who he used to be. Reminded him of the kid with the flaming red hair who spent his youth in and out of foster homes after his father disappeared and his mother died of a drug overdose before he turned five. Reminded him of the kid who got the shit kicked out of him constantly, the kid who was an easy target because he was a loner with fiery crimson hair, the outsider who was too skinny and afraid to stand up for himself.

His red hair reminded him of the kid who said *Fuck it* at age fourteen and dropped out of school, the kid who soon discovered cocaine, then discovered how to smoke it, then discovered how to mix it with heroin, then discovered that potent mixture was a quick and easy way to royally fuck up one's life.

It reminded him of the kid who was a junkie living on the streets at eighteen, the kid who turned to robbery to finance his addiction, the kid who went to prison at twenty because a store clerk remembered seeing a flash of red hair on the strung-out piece of trash who robbed him at gunpoint, and the police who patrolled the neighborhood knew full well there was just one homeless junkie with red hair in the neighborhood.

Prison was where it all changed. Growing up in the rough section of River Falls, he'd been around gangbangers his entire life, but he'd never encountered animals like those in prison. They were hard-core motherfuckers from Detroit, prison lifers who were merciless with the few whites who were locked up, but even more so with the only red-headed white guy in the place. That flaming hair made him stand out in a world he didn't want to stand out in, made anonymity impossible in a world where anonymity was the only way to survive.

The red hair. It always came back to the red fucking hair.

He finally shaved it all off after a month in prison. He still remembered seeing his reflection for the first time. How different he looked. His left eye was swollen shut from getting his ass kicked earlier in the day, and his face was peppered with half-healed scars and bruises from other encounters during his first month in prison, but it was the bald head that stood out.

Everything changed that day. *He* changed. His flaming red hair was like a weight he'd carried around his entire life, a Kick Me sign on his back that he'd managed to slip free of. Prison was still hell, but it was easier to fade into the background without his red hair making him stand out.

When he was released after four years, he was a different man. His eyes, never the kindest, were more hardened. His pasty skin was weathered, tough. He was covered in tattoos done by a prison tattoo artist—his forearms, arms, his chest.

And the red hair was gone.

For the two decades since then, he shaved every night. Never wanted to see another red hair again. Standing at the mirror now, he finished shaving his head, then ran the razor over his cheeks. He winced slightly when the razor passed over the still-sore spot where that fuckface Devon had slapped him.

He leaned in close to the mirror and stared at his eyebrows. They were still black, with no traces of red; the dye he'd colored them with last week hadn't started to grow out. He looked at his chest, his stomach, his legs, inspected it all for any hair. Nothing. He got the rest of his body waxed every month, and no hair had started to grow back yet.

As he lay down in bed after shaving, he thought of tomorrow. He'd make the phone call to Gary Foster at noon. It wasn't an exaggeration to say that it was the most important phone call of his life.

He still couldn't believe that everything had come to this. If Gary turned him down, he'd have the choice of fucking over De La Fuente and having his head taken off by a chainsaw or fucking over Devon and heading back to prison. He could get involved and kill Devon himself, but that had the potential to be the worst outcome of all. His bad knee made running difficult; quickly escaping after the crime would be nearly impossible. If someone spotted him limping away or the cops took his ass down, he'd be looking at prison for the rest of his life. And not just that, but prison as a cop killer. He knew exactly what life in prison would be like for a cop killer. It'd make his last stint in prison look like a day at the spa.

He needed Gary Foster. Depended on him.

Tomorrow he'd have his answer.

11

WHEN HE AWOKE THAT NEXT MORNING, GARY HAD A BACKACHE, A STOM-achache, and a headache. He turned to one side and saw that he was alone in bed. He glanced at the digital clock on their bedside table. Seven thirty. The phone call from Shamrock would come at noon, in only a few hours.

Gary threw on his bathrobe and walked down the hallway. He found Beth sitting on the living-room sofa, holding a bowl of granola. A thick hardbound book was open on her lap.

"Why are you having breakfast in here?" he asked.

"I'm looking at this," she said. She put down her granola and held up the book. *Our Wedding* was written on the cover in gold script.

"Our wedding album?" Gary asked.

"I'm hoping it will jog my memory and remind me of a few long-lost friends who can donate some money. Some people from our past who I'd forgotten about. Sixteen years is a long time."

"I haven't looked at this album in forever," Gary said.

Beth opened the album and pointed at a picture. "Look at this one," she said.

The picture was of Gary and Beth standing in the middle of their wedding party, Gary in his black tux, Beth in her flowing white wedding dress. Gary and his four groomsmen were on the left, Beth and her four bridesmaids on the right. Everyone looked impossibly young.

"Talk about a blast from the past," Gary said.

"Check out Rod," Beth said, smiling. In the wedding party picture, Rod stood next to Gary, eighteen years old, with a goofy, youthful smile on his face. His blond hair was even longer than it currently was, down past his shoulders. He looked like a drummer for an 80s rock band.

Gary smiled; he couldn't help it. "I forgot how long his hair used to be."

"And this guy," Beth said, chuckling as she pointed at a member of the wedding party with a helmet of gelled-up hair with blond frosted tips. "What was his name?"

"Denny Willis."

"That's right."

Gary sat down on the couch beside Beth. With the book balanced on her lap, she flipped a few more pages. Past various pictures from their wedding day—the happiest day of Gary's life.

Gary slipping the ring on Beth's finger, both of them smiling.

Gary and Beth standing in front of a stained-glass window in the church.

Gary and Beth holding hands next to a flower garden.

Gary and Beth stepping into a limo after the wedding, the crowd of people surrounding them frozen in midcheer.

"This is a nice picture," Beth said, stopping at one. In it, Beth and Gary stood with Beth's parents on the left side, Gary's on the right side.

"It is," Gary said. It was one of the only pictures they had with both sets of parents.

Beth turned a few more pages. She stopped at a picture of her standing next to two girls in dresses.

"Pamela Kerpius, Lesley Thompson—I haven't even thought about either of them in years," she said, grabbing a pen and writing down their names. "I'll track down their phone numbers, try to contact them later."

More pages, more pictures. When she reached the end of the album, she set it on the coffee table and grabbed a different album from the small storage area underneath. She set it on her lap and opened it.

Gary numbly stared at the album as pictures flew past, endless memories from their nearly two decades together.

Gary and Beth at a Cubs game during a trip to Chicago.

Gary and Beth apple picking with a group of friends at an orchard in upstate Michigan one summer.

Gary and Beth bundled up in hats and gloves at a Michigan homecoming football game a few years ago.

There was hardly anything exciting or exotic in the pages. They didn't have the money to afford the luxuries, but even if they did, Gary didn't think they'd find them appealing. They could have fun anywhere. Doing anything. A friend once told Gary that true love happens when you're just hanging out. That you can have fun with anyone at Disney World or while staying at five-star resorts around the world, but true love was when you found someone you just enjoyed being with, even if you weren't doing much.

It was, Gary thought, the perfect description of his relationship with Beth.

Beth flipped the page and started laughing the moment she saw the picture displayed.

"Remember that?" she asked.

"Yeah. I do."

The picture was from a trip to Florida for their tenth anniversary, the closest thing to a true vacation they'd ever taken. In the picture, the two of them stood on the beach, a bright cloudless sky behind them. By their feet, a large mound of wet sand was lumped together.

"We spent all morning making that sand castle on the beach," Beth said. "And right as we were almost done, that wave came in and wiped it out completely."

Gary remembered exactly what had happened next, how they'd looked at each other in shock for a moment before busting out in uncontrollable laughter.

Beth continued turning more pages—memories, so many memories—but Gary wasn't paying any attention. He was staring at Beth.

Everything surrounding her slowed down, faded to black, like a movie. All he could see was her face staring down at the picture album. She bit her lower lip in concentration, something she always did when she focused, a little tic Gary always found cute.

Beth. The girl he'd shared a lifetime of memories with. The girl he was about to begin a family with. The girl who was his wife, his best friend, his everything.

All night long, as he'd turned this way and that in bed, Gary thought about what Rod said during their dinner at Dagnostino's. How he'd do anything at all, without a moment's hesitation, to save Sarah if she were the one who was sick. How the guilt would cripple him for the rest of his life if he lost Sarah and hadn't done everything in his power to save her.

Gary thought about those words now. How would he feel if he declined this offer and Beth collapsed next month? What if he lost her? Lost the baby? Lost them both? Could he ever live with himself if something like that happened?

Even with Rod and Sarah's heartfelt donation, they still didn't have a fraction of the money they needed. Beth had checked the fundraising site the moment they'd arrived back home last night. They hadn't even cracked $16,000. Combined with the money from Rod and Sarah, they were still shy of $30,000. And they'd already contacted virtually every single person they knew.

It was clearer and clearer to Gary that this offer—this one unbelievable offer—was his chance. His chance to save Beth's life.

———

THE PHONE CALL CAME AT NOON, RIGHT ON THE DOT.
Seated in the living room, Gary grabbed his ringing phone from his pocket. The word UNKNOWN was displayed. He hurried down the hallway and arrived in the baby's room before the phone rang a third time.

"Hello?" Gary said.

"I'm calling for your answer." Shamrock. Gary instantly recognized his scratchy voice, his direct, even tone.

Even though he knew his answer, Gary hesitated for a moment.

"Well?"

"I'll do it," Gary said.

"Smart man," Shamrock said. "Listen carefully. Go to the storage facility at Thirteenth and Jefferson. It's called Michigan Mini Storage. Head to locker one fifty-one. The combination's six, twenty-four, fifteen."

"Wait a minute," Gary said. He rummaged through some papers on the desk and found a pen. He asked Shamrock to repeat the information and he wrote it down.

"There's a gun inside the locker. A nine milli. The clip's full. It's a big-boy gun, so take it somewhere and shoot it a few times to get a feel for it. It ain't as easy as it looks in the movies.

"There's also ten thousand bucks in the locker. The money's a down payment. A show of good faith. Once I hear that everything's taken care of, I'll put the rest of the cash in the same locker. Understand?"

"Yes."

"This goes down tomorrow, okay? He gets home at eleven at night. His address is on the copy of his ID that I gave you. You still have it?"

"Yes," Gary said. "But this has to happen tomorrow?"

"That a problem?"

"It's so soon."

"Should I find someone else?"

"No, I'll do it," Gary said, surprising himself by how quickly he responded.

"Repeat everything I've just said."

"Thirteenth and Jefferson, Michigan Mini Storage, locker one fifty-one, combination six, twenty-four, fifteen." Gary read off the sheet of paper. "Tomorrow. Eleven p.m."

"Good. Got any questions?"

"How do I contact you if something unexpected comes up?"

"If that happens, I'll contact you. It better not come to that."

It better not come to that. The words ran an icy finger down Gary's spine.

"Any other questions?"

"No," Gary said.

"Good. And one last thing."

Shamrock paused.

"Don't fuck this up."

He hung up the phone.

GARY WAITED UNTIL IT WAS DARK TO DRIVE TO MICHIGAN MINI STORAGE. IT was a large, long structure with a uniform row of blue overhead-garage doors stretching along one side. He turned into the empty parking lot and slowly drove past the doors until he reached the one marked 151.

Leaving the car idling, he walked over to the door and spun the dial on a black padlock attached to the front. It took five attempts before he could steady his trembling hands enough to enter the combination. When the lock finally disengaged, he slipped it off and pulled the door upward.

The storage unit was a small room, around eight feet by eight feet. A brown paper bag rested on the ground in the middle of the room. Gary grabbed the bag and reattached the padlock before returning to his car.

The moment he sat down, he opened the paper bag. There were two items inside. The first was a half-inch-thick bundle of hundred-dollar bills, the money held together with a small orange band with $10,000 printed on it.

The second was a black handgun.

He stared at the gun resting at the bottom of the bag. The sight of it repulsed him, terrified him. It looked like a coiled snake, hiding in the shadows, ready to spring from the bag and lash out.

Gary reached into the bag and, using only his thumb and forefinger, picked up the gun by the barrel. He opened the glove compartment with his free hand, placed the gun inside, and quickly shut the door.

He drove out of the parking lot and headed for home.

THERE WAS STILL TIME TO BACK OUT.

That's what Gary thought about for the rest of the night. As he ate dinner with Beth and listened to her tell a story about yoga class, as he finished nibbling at his food while Beth talked about the phone calls she'd made earlier in the day, as he watched some television with Beth during the evening, that's what ran through his mind.

There was still time to back out.

He hadn't done anything wrong yet. Hadn't done anything illegal. Couldn't be charged with a crime. That would all change soon, but right now, before it all happened, he could back out. All he'd have to do was return the money and the gun to the storage locker. He even remembered the combination: 6, 24, 15. Shamrock would probably be furious, but there was nothing he could do.

Gary told himself that if he changed his mind, it wouldn't be over. He could focus on raising the money for the Germany trial. Maybe find a long-lost friend who had a bunch of money lying around, something like that. If he backed out right now, there was still a chance that they could find the money for the Germany treatment. . . .

But that's all it was. A chance. A long shot. Could he leave something so important, Beth's very life, to chance?

Gary thought about it more—while taking a shower, while stoically pacing around the house before bed, while enduring what seemed like his hundredth consecutive sleepless night. And the more he thought about it, the more he began to realize something.

He realized that this wasn't just about saving Beth.

This was about saving himself.

It was about saving himself from a lifetime of loneliness. Saving himself from the total devastation he would feel without Beth. Saving himself from the crushing emptiness of living in a world where everything would remind him of her—the house, the car, the bed they'd slept in, little things like the cups they'd drank from and the TV they'd binge-watched so many TV shows on.

Gary liked his life, didn't want to see it obliterated if he lost Beth. Didn't want to hit the Reset button and start from scratch as he approached forty.

Lying in bed, he continued to think about it all, but there wasn't much to think about. Even though Gary knew he could still back out, there was no chance he would.

12

GARY WOKE UP EARLY ON THE DAY HE'D MURDER SOMEONE FOR THE FIRST time in his life. The morning sun, just rising, cast a light through the bedroom's only window. Beth rested on her back beside him, still sleeping.

Gary gingerly walked over to his dresser, grabbed a T-shirt and jeans, and put them on. As he shut the dresser drawer, it creaked slightly. In bed, Beth rustled awake.

"Where are you going?" she whispered.

"Running some errands," Gary said. "Just go back to sleep."

Beth curled onto her side of the bed and closed her eyes.

GARY DROVE A FEW MILES PAST THE CITY LIMITS, TURNED ONTO A GRAVEL road, and continued on until he was in the countryside. No nearby houses, no major highways, no other cars—perfect for what he was about to do. He parked on the side of the road, took another look around to make sure he was alone, and opened the glove compartment.

There it was. The gun he would use to end someone's life tonight. Looking at the gun and knowing its potential was a powerful, scary feeling.

Gary grabbed the gun and carried it over to an oak tree on the edge of the road. The tree's gnarled, thick trunk was covered with dusty residue from the gravel road. A few crows were perched high up in the bare branches.

When he was ten feet from the tree, Gary stopped walking. He took in a deep breath of cold air through his nostrils and pointed the gun at the tree trunk. He grasped the gun with one hand, his fingers holding the grip in the exact position instructed by the article he'd read on the Internet last night.

Once he was ready, he looked down the sights at the tree trunk. Stared at it. Concentrated. And squeezed the trigger.

A lot happened all at once.

A high-pitched, sharp crack—much louder than he'd expected—ripped through the tranquil morning. The crows resting on the tree branches squawked loudly and took flight.

The recoil of the weapon made the gun jump in Gary's hand, sending the shot waywardly off to the side of the tree trunk. The kickback was so intense that he felt the vibration in his hand, his arm, even up through his shoulder.

Little puffs of smoke filtered out from the barrel and the hard, coppery scent of gunpowder filled the air.

Gary stood there for a few seconds, waiting for the ringing in his ears and the tingling in his arm to pass. Once he was ready, he gripped the gun tighter, flexing the muscles in his arm to steady it. He stared at the tree trunk and pulled the trigger. He missed again, but it felt more comfortable. The recoil didn't seem as intense. The sound not as loud.

He took a few steps closer to the tree, just over five feet away now. He pulled the trigger twice, anticipating the recoil and sound. Both shots hit the trunk, sending a few small chunks of bark splintering off.

He carried the gun back to the car. That was enough. He'd come here to familiarize himself with the weapon as best he could, and he'd done just that.

One less thing to worry about for tonight, but there was plenty else.

TWENTY MINUTES LATER, GARY PULLED THE COROLLA OFF OF I-84 AT THE exit for Stephens Street. He turned left at the base of the off-ramp.

The neighborhood he entered was nice and quaint. The houses up and down the street were similar, each one built on a lot with a medium-sized yard out front. A few of the houses had For Sale signs in the yard. A park with dense trees along the perimeter bordered one edge of the neighborhood, stretching on for almost five blocks.

He drove for two blocks on Stephens and took a right on Walton Street. His head was on a swivel as he drove down Walton Street, taking in as many details of the neighborhood as possible, making mental notes about anything that stood out.

His heart pounded heavily as he reached the 500 block of Walton Street. He slowed his car—not enough to appear suspicious but enough to allow him to observe his surroundings.

He drove past 501 Walton. 505 Walton. Drove past a few more houses until he reached 517 Walton.

The address on Devon Peterson's driver's license.

The site for tonight's murder.

It was a white house with a small front porch. A single-car garage was off to the side, and a cement walkway led from the side entrance of the garage to the porch. Next to the walkway was a cluster of two-foot-high bushes.

After Gary passed the house, he continued on for five blocks and made a U-turn. He drove back through the neighborhood, Devon Peterson's house on his right side now. Once again, he mentally noted as many details of the house and surrounding area as he could.

A few blocks past 517 Walton, Gary headed back to the interstate. Two passes through the neighborhood was enough. Any more than that seemed risky.

———

BETH WAS AWAKE WHEN HE ARRIVED HOME. SHE STOOD AT THE KITCHEN counter, wearing a white bathrobe cinched loosely over the bump of her stomach.

"I'll be in the baby's room, making some phone calls," Gary said, walking past her.

"Tyson's room," she said.

"What?"

"Tyson's room. Not the baby's room. He has a name now, remember?"

"Right. I'll be in there, calling people."

In Tyson's room, Gary walked over to the desk and grabbed a pencil and pad of paper. He sketched out a diagram of Devon Peterson's neighborhood, drawing quickly so he could include all the details while they were still fresh in his mind.

The park that stretched along the east end of the neighborhood.

The streets that intersected with Walton.

The layout of the front yard of Devon Peterson's house.

The shortest route back to the interstate.

He mapped out the houses he could remember and indicated which houses had For Sale signs in the front yard—houses that were most likely vacant, information that could prove to be useful.

Once he finished sketching, he started planning for the night: what time he'd arrive in the neighborhood, where he'd hide while waiting for Devon, the escape route he'd take to minimize the risk of being spotted by someone.

He reviewed this plan over and over again, committing every last detail to memory, then put together a solid, organized blueprint for the night. It was an exhaustively researched, finely tuned plan with total attention to detail.

Despite his planning, he worried about the endless things that could go wrong. An observant neighbor could spot him. He could injure an ankle, take a nasty fall. Devon could arrive home before eleven o'clock, or after, or not at all. The gun could malfunction. His aim could be off. His car could fail to start or get stuck as he escaped.

All it would take, he knew, was one mistake, one slipup or unexpected twist, for everything to veer out of control.

13

THE DAY PASSED QUICKLY. HE ATE LUNCH WITH BETH, CARRIED ON A CON-
versation as best he could. Drove her to yoga class, which left him
alone in the house for a while.

When six p.m. arrived, Gary crumpled up the diagram he'd sketched
and threw it in the garbage in Tyson's room. It was no longer needed. He
had the neighborhood and the surrounding area committed to memory.

In the living room, he sat down on the couch next to Beth.

"How'd it go?" she said.

"Long day."

"Same here. Made a lot of phone calls. Not much luck."

She showed him the fund-raising page on her smartphone. Just
under eighteen thousand dollars total raised.

He put an arm around her, and she leaned into his body. Gary
kissed the top of her head.

"I'm going to throw something in the microwave for dinner," she said. "You feel like lasagna or mac and cheese?"

"Actually, it'll just be you and Tyson for dinner. I have to run to the store and take care of some business."

"Think it'll be a late night?"

"It might be. There's a lot to do to get ready for spring."

He placed one hand on Beth's stomach, running his fingers over her baby bump. Holding Beth and Tyson in his arms, Gary allowed himself to forget about the murder for a moment. Forget that he'd be ending the life of another human being in a matter of hours. Forget that he was more scared than he'd ever been before.

For just this moment, he wanted to forget about tonight and hold Beth and Tyson in his arms.

———

A FEW SHORT HOURS LATER, GARY LOOSELY GRIPPED THE COROLLA'S steering wheel as the car, its lights out, drifted to a stop in a thicket of pine trees. He shut off the engine and silence enveloped him. As his eyes slowly adjusted to the darkness, the trees clustered around him came into focus—maples, oaks, buckeyes, sycamores. They surrounded the car, rising tall against the blackness of the night sky.

Gary remained in the front seat, his hands on the steering wheel, as though the decision to stay or drive off was still unresolved in his mind. He appeared to be a man deep in thought, but there was nothing left to think about. He had a plan. All that was left was to execute it.

He grabbed a plain black cap off the passenger's seat and pulled the bill down over his forehead. He'd taken the hat and a heavy black coat from the shelves of Ascension Outerwear earlier. They were the two most inconspicuous-looking items in the store, perfect for blending into the night. He slipped on a pair of black gloves—also taken from the store—and grabbed the handgun from the glove compartment. He carefully placed the gun in the pocket of his coat, the barrel pointed downward, and exited the car, lightly shutting the door behind him.

Bundled in his coat, Gary walked through the heavily wooded area. It looked like a forest preserve, but it was just the park that stretched for blocks along the edge of Devon Peterson's neighborhood. After five minutes, Gary slipped through a cluster of bushes and exited onto the street that bordered the park. This was the 800 block of Fredricks Street. Less than three blocks from Devon Peterson's house.

When he reached the intersection of Walton and Fredricks, he turned left onto Walton. Everything was just as Gary had sketched it, exactly as he remembered it. There were seven houses on each side of the block, all of them dark and shadowy. Devon Peterson's house was on the left side of the street, third house from the end. Gary approached the house—walking briskly, no hesitation in his movements—and slipped behind a thick, shaggy bush in the front yard.

The bush was big enough to conceal him entirely. The detached garage was roughly ten feet in front of him. The small cement walkway that led from the garage's side door to the house's front entrance passed directly beside the bush.

Gary focused on the street in front of the house, waiting for Devon Peterson's car to arrive. His gloved right hand rested in his coat pocket, brushing up against the gun. He adjusted the bill of the hat, pulling it down farther.

Time passed. Eleven came and went. Eleven ten. He tried to focus, but all he could think about was everything that could go wrong when the moment arrived. Ignoring these thoughts was impossible; the words settled into his mind like tiny seeds, sprouting pale shoots of doubt. He envisioned the gun snagging on his coat pocket, his shoes slipping on the damp grass, the gun not firing, or firing wide or high or low.

Stay focused, he told himself. *Stay focused on the task at hand. Don't think about anything else.*

More time passed. The neighborhood remained silent and dark as a tomb. Gary moved his head from side to side and back to loosen his neck. He flexed his toes and ran some muscle tension through his calves, his thighs, his back, his shoulders.

And then a car appeared at the end of the street. It was only a pair of headlights at first, two beams cutting through the darkness. As they approached the house, the red and blue strobe lights on top of the car and the River Falls PD insignia on the side slowly became visible.

The sight of the police cruiser sent Gary's heart into overdrive. He crouched down lower behind the bush, a cheetah preparing to pounce.

The cruiser slowed a few feet from the house's driveway, the rear brake lights casting a low red illumination behind it. As the car turned into the driveway, the tires lightly crunched on the asphalt. A moment later, the automatic garage door opened with a rattling noise that cut through the tranquillity of the night.

The cruiser was fifteen feet from the bush concealing Gary, so close that he could see Devon in the driver's seat, staring straight ahead at the rising garage door. Once the door was fully open, Devon pulled the cruiser into the garage. The door rattled again as it closed shut behind the car.

Gary's hand tightened around the gun. He pulled it from his coat pocket and rested his index finger on the trigger. Inside the garage, he heard the car's engine go silent. Immediately after that, the car door opened, then slammed shut.

Gary focused on the garage's side door, only a few feet away. He breathed in and out, faster and faster, working himself up, making himself practically hyperventilate. Seconds ticked away in his head.

The doorknob jangled in place and the garage's side door swung open. A shadowy figure emerged. Even in the darkness, Gary could make out Devon's burly face and buzz-cut hair, his tree-trunk arms.

Devon shut the door behind him and stepped onto the small cement walkway. He walked toward the house. He was only five feet away, close enough that Gary could hear the soles of his shoes on the cement. Gary gripped the gun tighter. Suddenly, there was no heartbeat in his chest, just total and complete silence.

Gary sprang from behind the shadow of the bush. Devon's head swiveled toward the sudden movement, but before he could react, Gary raised the gun and pulled the trigger's metal tongue. The gun fired.

The gunshot was incredibly loud in the serene night, sounding even louder than the shots he'd fired in the country earlier. The bullet ripped a hole in Devon's uniform right above his stomach, exposing a small piece of white undershirt that immediately darkened with blood.

Devon staggered backward and pawed at the stomach wound. When he moved his hand away, the palm was covered in blood that looked completely black in the dark night. Devon stumbled backward another step. He stared at Gary.

"You motherfucker," he hissed. He coughed, and a few droplets of blood splattered onto the edge of his mouth. "I'm a cop, you motherfucker."

Devon collapsed to his knees, throwing one hand out to brace his fall. His other hand still pushed against his stomach, blood pulsing from the wound and covering his hand. Gary looked down at this man dying right before his eyes, the life slowly draining out of him and the—

Devon's left hand. Gary suddenly noticed his left hand. Devon had moved the hand to the gun holstered on his belt. He fumbled at the gun, trying to unclasp it.

Gary took two quick steps toward Devon and aimed the gun at his head. He pulled the trigger, but just as the gun fired, Devon jerked his head to the side. The bullet hit him in the lower jaw, breaking it so that it hung from his head like a broken ventriloquist's dummy. His tongue was severed and a river of blood poured from his mouth, oozing onto his police uniform. A frightening, gurgling scream emerged from his throat. His left hand continued to fumble at the gun holstered on his belt.

Gary took another step toward Devon, at point-blank range now. His hands were slick with sweat inside the gloves, trembling. He held the gun so the barrel was pointed directly in the middle of Devon's face, only inches away.

He pulled the trigger a final time and Devon Peterson's face exploded.

———

HIS ESCAPE PLAN WENT WRONG FROM THE START.

Gary had mentally prepared himself for the moment as best he could, but he was not at all ready for the kind of ugliness produced by his final squeeze of the trigger. Devon Peterson's body lay on the blood-soaked pavement, the middle of his face nothing more than a gaping bloody wound. His lifeless eyes stared out into the night sky, unblinking. Bone shards and chunks of brain were splattered onto the sidewalk behind his head.

Gary stood above the body, the gun still pointed downward. The scene in front of him was the most horrific, awful sight he'd ever seen . . . yet he couldn't look away. He stared at Devon's destroyed face as if in a trance. The blood. The carnage. It was everywhere. It was like a bomb had gone off inside Devon's skull. It—

Through his peripheral vision, Gary saw the porch light flash on outside the house next door. He instinctively glanced in that direction. A man looked out the house's front window, a phone to his ear, staring in the direction of Devon's house. His eyes locked with Gary's for a brief moment, and the man quickly ducked behind the window frame.

Across the street, the porch light of another house flashed on, illuminating the darkened street. Two houses down, another light came on.

Gary spun away from the dead body and sprinted toward the backyard of Devon Peterson's house. Still holding the gun, he pumped his arms like pistons as he tore past the garage. Gary turned left, cutting across the backyard of the house next door.

He could barely see a few feet in front of him but he ran as fast as he could through the darkness. His footing was unsteady on the damp grass.

Another house light came on.

Another.

He reached the end of the block. Hustled across the road. For no reason other than to stop running in a straight line, he abruptly turned right and zigged through one yard, then zagged through another. He slipped on the wet grass, fell to the ground, and instantly sprang back up. Cut through a few more yards; crossed another road. He came to an abrupt stop at an intersection.

He was completely lost. He'd had his entire route back to his car planned out—two blocks north, two blocks east, then run a few blocks through the park to his concealed car—but he'd gotten spooked and simply started running around the neighborhood like a maniac. He had no idea where he was in relation to his car. He was—

Gary heard a police siren.

The sound was still distant, but it was definitely a police siren, rising and falling in cycles.

In a blind panic, he looked up at the street sign at the end of the block. The intersection of Van Nuys and Byron. He'd mapped out Devon Peterson's entire neighborhood but he didn't recognize either of the street names. He looked around at his darkened surroundings. Looked for some sort of landmark or sign pointing him in the right direction. Something. Anything.

And then he spotted it. In the distance, he could just barely see the tops of a cluster of pine trees against the night sky, rising above the neighborhood. The park where he'd left his car. It seemed impossibly far away. He'd been sprinting away from the park.

He instantly took off toward the treetops. He cut across a backyard and scaled a privacy fence, hurling himself over the top. The police siren continued to sound. It was closer, no longer in the distance, close enough and loud enough for Gary to determine that there wasn't a single siren but two or three, maybe more.

His surroundings flashed by in a blur as he continued on for a block, then another. His shoes slapped into the soggy ground. The trees were closer but he was running slower now, purely on fumes and fear. Adrenaline had given way to absolute exhaustion.

He reached a front yard at the exact moment a cop car turned onto the street a few houses away. The car's tires squealed as it took the turn and headed straight toward him. Blue and red strobe lights flashed off of cobblestone driveways and the sides of houses.

Gary jumped behind a tree and stood still, completely motionless. If the cops spotted him, that would be it. He was too tired to outrun them. There would be no last stand. If they'd seen the shadowy figure that ducked behind the tree, they would catch him. It was that simple.

The siren grew earsplittingly loud as the cruiser raced toward him. Closer. Closer. Without slowing, the cruiser zoomed past him and turned left at the end of the street. Gary stepped out from behind the tree. He hurried over to the thicket of pine trees across the street and slipped past some shrubbery. Police sirens—some distant, some close—sounded around him as he trudged through the park.

When he reached his car, he scrambled inside, throwing the gun down on the passenger's seat. He rammed the key into the ignition and fired up the engine. Headlights out, he inched the car toward the edge of the road and looked both ways. The road was clear. Mere blocks away, he could see the police car lights flashing red and blue kaleidoscopic pulses into the night sky.

Gary pulled the car onto the road and turned on the headlights. His heart racing, his eyes constantly scanning the road, he drove in the opposite direction from Devon Peterson's house. A mile later, he reached the on-ramp for I-84. He pulled his car onto the highway and drove away, forcing himself to observe the speed limit.

———

IT WAS ALMOST MIDNIGHT BY THE TIME GARY PULLED THE COROLLA INTO an empty parking stall in front of Ascension Outerwear. He exited the car and crept up to the front door. It took three tries before he could steady his shaking hand enough to insert the key into the lock.

Inside, the store was dark, even darker than the night. Leaving the lights off, Gary fumbled around behind the counter until he found a large plastic sack. He walked down the main aisle and stepped into the small bathroom in the rear of the store. He needed to clean himself up before returning home to Beth.

He stripped naked and crammed everything into the sack—his coat, his shirt, his pants, his socks, and his shoes. He set the gun and car keys off to the side.

Gary looked at himself in the mirror above the sink, his face only inches from the reflection. There were small droplets of Devon's blood dotting his face like freckles. Stuck to his cheek was a bloody chunk of pink tissue the size of a dime. A bloody lump of muscle or skin.

Gary forced back the bile rising in his throat and turned on the faucet. He cupped his hands underneath and splashed water onto his face. He pumped the liquid soap dispenser mounted above the sink and furiously scrubbed away at his cheeks and forehead. The bloody chunk of tissue fell into the sink basin; it was small enough to be carried down the drain by the rushing water. After patting himself dry with some paper towels, he looked at himself in the mirror, studied his face, gazed into his eyes.

It had been close.

He'd come so very close to getting caught. He'd been spotted by neighbors, nearly seen by the police. On the interstate, he saw three separate police cars speeding opposite him, toward the scene of the crime. Every few seconds his eyes darted to the rearview mirror, certain that he would see one of the cruisers making a U-turn and speeding up behind him in pursuit. He'd been so spooked that he almost crashed twice on the drive to Ascension Outerwear.

Gary walked back to the sales floor and put on a T-shirt and a pair of sweatpants he took off a shelf. He grabbed the gun from the bathroom and carried it into the back room. The east wall of the back room was nothing more than an unpainted sheet of plywood hammered over a layer of insulation. He pulled back a corner of the plywood and stuffed the gun behind the insulation. It was as good of a hiding spot as any. Simply throwing the gun in a garbage receptacle or down a sewer grate seemed too risky, too prone to being randomly discovered by someone. Plus, he hadn't wanted to stop even for a minute when driving away from the crime scene; he wanted to get far, far away, as quickly as possible. In a few weeks, once the lakes in the area thawed from the late winter freeze, he'd find one to throw the gun into.

He set the plywood back in place and walked over to the small desk in the middle of the room. His cell phone and wallet rested on top of the desk, in the same place he'd put them before leaving for Devon Peterson's house. He grabbed his phone and brought the screen to life. He had a text from Beth, sent an hour ago:

Heading to bed. Hope you're not working too hard xoxo.

He typed out a message:

Sorry. Phone was on silent. Still up?

Yeah. Tired. But I can't sleep ☹

Heading home now.

DRIVING HOME, GARY'S PHONE RANG. UNKNOWN, READ THE SCREEN. HE ANswered it.

"Well?" Shamrock. Gary recognized the voice instantly.

"It's done," Gary said.

The line went dead.

14

BACK HOME, GARY GINGERLY WALKED DOWN THE HALLWAY AND LOOKED in on Beth. She was awake—lying on her back, bedside light on, reading a book: *Your Baby's First 90 Days*.

"Hey," he said.

"Hey."

"Still can't sleep?"

"Nope. Tyson's kicking like the Karate Kid."

"Let me jump in the shower and I'll come to bed." Even though he'd washed up at the store, he didn't feel clean. He didn't want to even be in the same room as Beth until he had a shower.

He carried the sack of clothes down to the basement and threw them into the washer. He added detergent and turned on the machine. After he washed the clothes, he figured he'd donate them to Goodwill or find some other way to get rid of them. He never wanted to see them again.

He returned upstairs and stepped into the shower. He bristled at the water cascading over his body—cold for the first few seconds, then warmer once the water heater kicked in. He closed his eyes as the water pattered against his face, his chest.

He poured shampoo into his hair and scrubbed so frantically that his scalp hurt.

He ran a bar of soap over his body until all that remained was a small sliver that he washed down the drain.

When he finished with the soap, Gary shut off the shower and toweled himself dry. He threw on a pair of boxers and his Pearl Jam shirt and lay down in bed next to Beth.

He put an arm around her. She set her book to the side and turned her table lamp off.

It was only with an extreme amount of effort that Gary finally fell asleep.

GARY WOKE AT SIX THE NEXT MORNING—ARM STILL AROUND BETH, HER HEAD resting against his chest.

He slowly inched away from her and stood up out of bed. The muscles in his thighs instantly screamed in pain. The full-bore sprint through the neighborhood had ruined them last night.

Last night.

He could see everything about the night in vivid detail, but it didn't feel real. It was as if the murder were a scene in a movie, something he'd watched someone else do—not something he'd done himself.

Gary hobbled across the bedroom, the soreness in his legs slowly becoming manageable as the muscles stretched out and blood began circulating.

He went to the bathroom and took another shower. Soaped. Shampooed. This time, he stood under the steady stream of water for half an hour, as if there were a chance he could wash away every single remnant of last night, including the memory of it, if he stayed under the water long enough.

Once the hot water ran out, Gary shut off the shower and toweled himself dry. He dressed in clean clothes and walked out into the kitchen. A bowl of oatmeal rested on the counter. Beth sat at the kitchen table, staring at a small thirteen-inch television that rested on a shelf beside her. He walked over and kissed the top of her head.

"Morning," she said.

"Morning."

"I made that oatmeal for you earlier," she said. "You might want to warm it up. It's been sitting out for a while. I didn't realize your shower was going to take half an hour."

"Sorry, I got distracted," Gary said. He carried the bowl over to the microwave and placed it inside. He set the timer for twenty seconds.

"Did you hear what happened last night?" Beth asked. "There was a murder. A police officer was killed right in River Falls. That's all they've been talking about on the morning news."

A heavy lump formed in Gary's throat. He stared at the microwave's digital display, refusing to look at Beth, as it counted down to zero.

"A murder?" he said.

"Last night, right around midnight. It's terrible."

The microwave beeped and Gary grabbed the oatmeal. He carried it over to the table, though there was a part of him that wanted to avoid the television, wanted to stay far away from the news broadcast.

He sat down next to Beth. A commercial for a nail salon played on the television. When it finished, a close-up of an older local news anchor named John Francis appeared. A picture of Devon Peterson's face was shown in the upper right corner of the screen. The words OFFICER SLAIN were displayed under the photo.

"To recap our top story, a shocking murder occurred in River Falls last night," Francis said. "Devon Peterson, a two-year veteran of the River Falls Police Department, was returning home from his shift just before midnight when he was shot in the city's Pine Grove neighborhood. He was taken to McCann Medical Center, where he was pronounced dead on arrival from a gunshot wound to the head."

Francis began talking about the few details that had been released thus far: robbery had been ruled out as a motive, Officer Peterson was alone at the time of the shooting, detectives were still combing the neighborhood for evidence. As Gary listened to the anchor mechanically recite information from last night, he felt a tightness in his chest, a tightness that quickly spread throughout his body.

He couldn't believe that he was the killer, the monster, who had done this.

"Based on eyewitness accounts, detectives are looking for a white male, around six feet tall and a hundred eighty pounds, in his late thirties or early forties," Francis said. "Anyone with information is encouraged to contact the River Falls PD immediately."

Gary fidgeted in his chair. The description was vague, probably described half of the male population in River Falls . . . but it also perfectly described him.

He balled his hands into fists underneath the table and squeezed hard, trying to calm himself, even just a little, but the act did nothing. On-screen, Francis continued talking, recounting a mini biography of Devon Peterson's life.

Gary had seen enough—had seen too much, in fact. He wasn't ready for this, not at all.

"I'll be right back," he said to Beth, before leaving the kitchen.

GARY GRIPPED THE SIDES OF THE TOILET, BRACING HIMSELF AS HE HUNCHED over the porcelain bowl. He clenched his stomach and breathed in short, ragged gasps. He willed himself to vomit. *Just vomit and get it over with, dammit.*

But he couldn't produce anything more than a few coughs and dry heaves. When it became clear that nothing was going to come up, he stood and looked at himself in the mirror. His bloodshot eyes had dark bags under them. A few capillaries around his nose had burst. Two days of salt-and-pepper stubble dotted his cheeks.

He looked bad.

He felt worse.

The news broadcast had rocked him, affected him deeply. Up until this morning, everything had been far too frantic for him to reflect upon the murder—he'd been so focused on fleeing the scene and so charged up with adrenaline from nearly getting caught by the police that there had simply been no time for everything to sink in.

But the news broadcast made it real. It hammered home just how brutal and heinous his actions had been last night.

He had murdered another man. He had played God and ended a human being's life.

Gary splashed some water onto his face. Hunched over the sink, he stared down into the basin.

There was a light knock at the door. Beth peeked her head inside.

"You doing okay in here?" she asked.

"I'm fine," Gary said. "Just an upset stomach."

Beth stepped into the bathroom and placed her hands on his shoulders. She massaged her fingers into the muscles, giving him a back rub.

Gary closed his eyes. Just feeling her touch was soothing, relaxing. *Beth.*

He'd done this for her. He mustn't forget that. He'd ended a life . . . but he'd also potentially saved Beth's life. Gary told himself that he had been forced into extraordinary circumstances and did exactly what anyone would have done in his situation: traded the life of a bad, corrupt person for a chance to save the life of a good and sincere person, a good and sincere person who was pregnant with their first child.

Before the murder, that justification had seemed perfectly sound, but the words now felt hollow, unconvincing. No matter how he tried to rationalize it, nothing could change the fact that he'd committed the ultimate sin last night.

15

TWO HUNDRED MILES TO THE SOUTH, OTTO SAT AT A BAR IN O'HARE International Airport. Not even ten a.m., and he was the only customer. In front of him was his second drink of the morning, an old-fashioned made with rye whiskey.

He swiveled around on his barstool. A row of windows overlooked one of the airport runways. He looked out at the planes taxiing and taking off. In the distance, he saw the downtown skyscrapers rising high into the morning sky, although the only ones he recognized were the Hancock Center and the Sears Tower, or whatever the hell it was called now. Beyond that, hidden by the city's skyline, was the corridor of Lake Shore Drive, the chasm of Lake Michigan.

Chicago. Such a beautiful city, so much to see and do, but he hadn't had time to enjoy it. His trip was a functional one, a trip to give him a rock-solid alibi for the night of Devon Peterson's murder.

He doubted the police would connect him to the murder. But if they did, his ass was covered.

———

THE INKJET PRINTER WHINED AS IT SPIT OUT A SHEET OF PAPER. ONCE IT went silent, Gary grabbed the sheet from the paper tray and read the message typed on the front.

> Dear Mr. and Mrs. Foster,
>
> I heard about your situation and it broke my heart. I'd like to donate this money, two hundred thousand dollars cash, so you can pay for the treatment and medical care you require.
>
> This is an anonymous donation, and I would please ask that you respect my wish to keep my identity a secret.
>
> Thank you for understanding. My prayers are with you.
>
> Sincerely,
> Your White Knight

Standing in Tyson's bedroom, Gary slowly nodded. For the first time all day, he felt his spirits rising. He had the feeling that maybe, just maybe, everything would be all right.

The day had been rough, one of the hardest days of his life. He tried to forget about the murder, but it was impossible to move past the horror of what he'd done. Guilt and remorse had gnawed away at him like a ravenous parasite. As the day dragged on, those feelings only intensified. No matter how hard he tried, it was impossible to ignore the awful reality that the world was now less one human being because of him.

Then there was the paranoia about the police investigation—the crippling, debilitating paranoia that plagued him all day long. He'd been glued to his smartphone, obsessively checking local news sites every few minutes for any breaking news about the murder. His chest tightened every time he refreshed a page, certain that he'd see his picture with WANTED superimposed over it once the site loaded. Thus far, there was nothing new, but that did little to reassure him. The police could have plenty they hadn't made public yet.

Everything combined to wreak an all-out assault on his sanity. It left him wondering if he'd ever be able to live with what he'd done, ever be able to look at himself in the mirror again, ever be able to go back to a normal life.

But the money, Gary hoped, would be the lifesaver he needed. Halfway across town, there was $190,000 waiting for him in a storage locker—combined with the earlier down payment, they'd have all the money they needed. And the money, after all, was the reason he'd done what he'd done. The money gave them a chance to save Beth's life. The money would make this all worthwhile.

Gary read over the note a second time, a third time. It looked good. He knew that such a large sum of money would attract attention—not just from Beth and their close friends but from the media, maybe even from the authorities. He needed an explanation for the money, and decided that an anonymous donation was the easiest way to explain it. After getting the money, he would put it and the note in a nondescript paper bag and "discover" it resting on their doorstep when he returned home.

It was the best explanation he could come up with. Detailed

enough to sound legitimate, vague enough to make it nearly impossible for someone to disprove.

Gary folded the note and slid it into the pocket of his jeans. He walked out of Tyson's room into the hallway.

Beth was in the living room, holding her phone to her ear. She motioned Gary over.

"That would be great," she said into the phone. "Thank you. I appreciate this so much. . . . Yes, I'm looking forward to it."

She ended the call and smiled—a genuine smile.

"Who was it?" Gary asked.

"I think I have some good news. That was a lady from the local community center. She heard about everything that happened with me and wanted to talk about hosting a fund-raising dinner."

"That's great."

"We're meeting with her tomorrow. First thing in the morning." The smile stayed on her face. "*Finally*, some good news."

She talked a little more about the meeting and Gary listened, though he knew full well there was no need for the fund-raiser. They'd soon have all the money they needed, every last cent. He just liked seeing how enthusiastic she was. That enthusiasm had been missing during the gloom and doom of the past week.

When Beth finished talking about the fund-raiser, Gary hugged her and grabbed his keys off the living-room table.

"Where are you going?" she asked.

"I have to make a quick trip to the grocery store," he said. "Pick up some milk. Be back in ten minutes, tops."

And then, right before he left the room, because he couldn't resist:

"I think there's some more good news coming, Beth. I just have a feeling. A really good feeling."

———

GARY ARRIVED AT MICHIGAN MINI STORAGE AT JUST AFTER FIVE P.M. HE drove down the alleyway, past the long row of blue overhead doors, and brought his car to a stop in front of locker 151. He walked over to the door and grabbed the lock dangling from the front.

He stared at it, puzzled.

The lock had been changed.

Earlier, when he'd picked up the gun and the ten-thousand-dollar down payment, the lock had been a black padlock with a combination dial. But the padlock on the door now had no combination dial. It was a plain gray Master Lock with a hole on the bottom for a key . . . a key that Gary didn't have.

Gary stepped back and looked at the number painted on the front of the door. Number 151. He was at the right locker.

He got back in his car and made a loop around the building. Near the parking lot out front was a small office; he'd been too preoccupied to notice it last time he was there. Gary parked his car and exited. Through a window, he could see a college-age kid standing behind a desk inside.

The kid looked up when Gary opened the door. He was tall and lanky. Wispy light brown hairs covered his upper lip and cheeks. He wore a black Led Zeppelin T-shirt and distressed jeans.

"The lock on one fifty-one was changed," Gary said. "I need to access the locker."

"The lock was changed?"

"There was a black combination lock on the door a few days ago," Gary said. "Today there's a different lock."

"What number was it?"

"One fifty-one."

"One fifty-one, sure, yeah. You the guy I talked to on the phone?"

"The phone? No."

"You're not the guy who rented the locker?"

"No. Someone else rented it. They left a package inside for me and gave me the combination. I need to get the package, but the lock has been changed."

"Huh," the clerk said. "That's weird."

"What?"

"The guy who rented the locker called us and said he didn't need it anymore. Told us to cut off the lock and throw it away. So we did. That lock that's on there now is one of ours. We padlock every locker that's not being rented. Keeps out homeless people, squatters."

"When did this phone call come?"

"This morning. I changed the lock right after he called."

"What happened to the package that was inside the locker?"

"There wasn't one. It was empty."

Gary felt a sense of unease in his gut, a discomfort that bubbled to life like indigestion.

"Listen— What's your name?" he asked.

"Brian."

"Listen, Brian. You need to be honest with me. Was there anything inside the locker when you cleared it out?"

"Nope. Nothing."

"You have no idea how important this is. If you're lying to me—"

"I swear, I'm not. I don't know what you're getting at, man, but there wasn't a single thing in there when I opened it up."

Gary paused. Something was wrong. Something was gravely wrong.

"I need to see inside the locker," he said.

"You want to see the locker?"

"Please. I want to see for myself."

Brian shrugged. "It's not rented out now. No reason I can't show it to you." He grabbed a key ring with about twenty small copper keys on it.

"Follow me," he said.

They walked down the alleyway to locker 151. The entire walk, Gary felt his stomach doing somersaults, his mind tumbling backward and forward. Deep down, he knew what had happened. He tried to deny it, but deep down, he knew.

When they reached locker 151, Brian inserted a key into the lock and pulled it off. He grabbed the door's handle and yanked upward, sliding open the door.

The eight-foot-by-eight-foot room was dark—not pitch-black, but close to it. Just enough daylight crept inside for Gary to see the cement floor, the corrugated tin walls, the overhead lights hanging from the ceiling.

He could also see that the room was empty. His worst fear was confirmed. There was no package inside.

Gary stood on the edge of the room and stared inside for what seemed like a very long time. He looked around as if he didn't understand the sight in front of him. . . . But he understood it perfectly, of course. He knew exactly what had happened. There was no money, none at all.

"He screwed me," Gary said, his voice a whisper. "I can't believe it. He screwed me out of the money."

16

GARY GAVE UP TRYING TO SLEEP AT FOUR THIRTY THE NEXT MORNING. HE SHUT off the alarm two hours before it was scheduled to go off and slid out of bed quietly, so as not to wake Beth. He wanted to let her sleep— but even more than that, he didn't want her to know that he couldn't.

He threw on his robe and padded out of the bedroom. In the kitchen, he scooped ground coffee into the filter of the coffeemaker. As he waited for the coffee to brew, he thought. He had much to think about.

There was no money.

All evening, he'd thought about it. After leaving Michigan Mini Storage, he drove around the city for half an hour—stunned, over-whelmed, in total shock. Questions danced around in his mind like fireflies.

He couldn't believe he hadn't seen this coming. The time leading up to the murder had been such a rush that it never entered his mind that he could be cheated out of the money. He cursed himself. Looking back, it seemed so obvious; he should've anticipated something like this. He felt like such a fool.

When he had finally arrived home yesterday, Beth was deep in a phone call, so he slipped past her and disappeared into Tyson's room. Later, she asked him why his trip to the grocery store had taken almost an hour. He couldn't even remember what excuse he'd given her. They'd eaten dinner together but Gary couldn't remember anything about that, either—couldn't even remember what they ate. That night, he lay down in bed and closed his eyes but sleep didn't come.

The coffee machine beeped and he turned it off. He filled his Tigers mug and sat down at the counter. Staring into the mug, he thought about everything for the millionth time. He had murdered a man for no reason. He had ended a life with nothing to show for it. The murder hadn't been an even trade—kill a bad person, save a good person. It was just a senseless act of violence.

Now his next move was obvious. Somehow, he had to find the man who had hired him to perform the murder. Shamrock. That was the only logical next step. He'd have to find Shamrock and do whatever it took to get the money.

Somehow, Gary would find him and get the money he'd been cheated out of.

There was just one problem: Gary had no idea where to start looking.

THE MEETING AT WILLOW PARK, GARY DECIDED, WAS THE KEY. THE MEETING was brief, but it was the only time they'd met. If he was going to find out who Shamrock was, that was the place to start.

Gary tried to remember everything he could. Was there something distinctive, something that could be a clue into Shamrock's identity?

His appearance. He was about six feet tall. Mouth downturned into a snarl. Head totally shaved. He looked skinny, but the puffy coat he wore during the meeting concealed his upper body like a cloak and made it impossible to get an accurate look at his build.

What else? His voice—that scratchy, distinctive voice. If Gary heard that voice again, he'd recognize it.

Gary closed his eyes, replayed the meeting in his mind. There had to be something he was missing. Somewhere in that brief five-minute meeting, there had to be a clue as to who Shamrock was, how Gary could find him.

"You're up early."

Beth's voice startled him. She stood on the edge of the darkened kitchen. In her white bathrobe, she looked like a ghostly apparition hovering a few feet away.

"I couldn't sleep," Gary said.

"How long have you been awake?"

"I don't know. A few hours."

Beth grabbed a pillbox off the counter, shook out a prenatal vitamin, and took it with a glass of water. She poured herself a bowl of Cheerios, then opened the refrigerator door and stared inside for a moment. "No milk," she said.

"What?"

"There's no milk in the fridge. When you left the house yesterday, you said you were going to get milk."

"I forgot to pick it up."

"You forgot?"

"Yeah."

"Wasn't getting milk the only reason you went to the store?"

Her voice had an edge to it. Not a sharp one, but Gary detected just a little something more behind the words than her normal tone of voice.

Gary stared into his coffee mug. Hesitated for a moment as he thought of an excuse. "I ran into a few people at the store," he said. "Started talking, got distracted, and completely forgot the milk."

Beth's eyes lingered on him. He thought she was about to say something to him; instead, she shook her head. She closed the refrigerator door and poured the dry cereal back into the box. "Never mind," she said. "I'll just grab a few granola bars and eat them on the way."

"The way to where?"

She set the cereal box on the counter and stared at him. This time, a heavy sigh accompanied her look.

"Seriously, Gary? We're meeting the lady from the community center about a fund-raiser this morning. Were you not paying attention when I told you about it yesterday? Or when I spent all dinner talking about it?"

Of all days, he thought. He didn't want to talk to anyone. Didn't want to leave the house. He simply wanted to isolate himself from the outside world and figure out how he was going to find Shamrock and get the money.

But he couldn't send Beth to the meeting by herself. He could tell she was close to getting upset with him, and if he bailed on the meeting, it might send her over the edge.

"I'm sorry, Beth. The fund-raiser slipped my mind. I just—"

"Forgot? Like you forgot the milk?"

"Yeah." All of the lies he'd told Beth had come so effortlessly. He felt like he'd lied to her more in the past week than he'd lied to her previously in their entire marriage. It bothered him how easily he lied to her, as if it was a natural, normal thing to do.

"I'm sorry, Beth," he said. "I mean it."

Beth glared at him as she walked past. She headed back to the bedroom.

"It's in an hour," she said. "Please be ready."

———

OTTO STEPPED OUTSIDE OF SOLID GOLD PAWN, LOCKED THE DOOR, AND pulled a protective metal shutter down over the front window. He lumbered across the empty parking lot and headed down Washington Avenue, on his way to meet someone he hoped could answer a very important question for him.

He looked at the hopeless, decaying neighborhood around him as he walked. Used condoms and syringes in the trash-strewn streets. Boarded-up, graffiti-tagged buildings. Junkies on every park bench; nickel-and-dime dealers on every street corner. A true piece of shit, this neighborhood was.

He'd always wanted to get the hell out of this place. After getting released from prison two decades earlier, he'd come straight back to the old neighborhood because he had nowhere else to go, then started selling drugs because he didn't know what else to do. Business was good right from the start—he knew all the old junkies, the dealers, the tricks of the trade. The weekly drug testing mandated by his release kept him clean, made sure he didn't fall into the trap of abusing his own shit. His business grew quickly as his competition was either arrested or killed off; then he started doing serious damage when he hooked up with El Este.

He'd planned on slinging until something better came along, but nothing ever did. The years passed. Some were good, but lately, they were all bad. The same problems that affected the rest of the city trickled down to the drug trade, too. No one had money, no one had jobs, and people had abandoned the neighborhood in droves. All that was left were homeless derelicts and hard-core junkies. Dealers who had pushed his product for years were moving to Detroit, Chicago, or even farther away to escape the dried-up local scene.

More and more, he was thinking he should do the same thing. Get the hell out of here. Start over somewhere. After he took care of a few loose ends, maybe he'd do just that.

It took Otto ten minutes to reach the intersection of Washington and Clark. An old man leaning on a gnarled wooden cane stood at the intersection. He was frail and skinny, all sticks and bones. His skin was black as a struck match, lined with deep creases. Tufts of gray hair peeked out from the edges of a fedora.

"There he is," the old man said when he saw Otto. His voice was raspy, barely there.

"What's up, Gramps?"

"Nothing but the sky, big man. Ain't nothing up there but the sky."

Otto gave Gramps a fist bump. "You do some looking around like I wanted?" he asked.

Gramps stared at him with the eyes of a battle-weary soldier. "Sure did," he said.

"Got a name for me?"

"Sure do."

Otto smiled. His Devon Peterson problem was taken care of and he was positive that, by now, Gary Foster had discovered there was no money. That whole shit show was over, and Otto now had another focus: revenge. Pure and simple, he wanted revenge on the little canary who'd given his name to Devon and started this mess. When he arrived back from Chicago yesterday, he'd called up Terrence "Gramps" DeRozan, an old stalwart who served as the eyes and ears of the neighborhood. Knew everyone. Saw everything. He'd told Gramps to do some digging and find out if anyone in the neighborhood was tight with that cop who'd just been killed.

"So what've you got?" Otto asked.

"Devon Peterson, he was a bad one, all right. Came down here after he was canned from the PD in Detroit. Had dirt on the captain here, threatened to make it public—that's how he got hired. Least, that's the rumor. He was assigned to our neighborhood and started causin' trouble from the start. Planting drugs on people. Shaking down businesses. Them sorts of things. He—"

"I don't need his life story, Gramps. Was there anyone around here who was working with that bastard? Maybe feeding him info, shit like that. That's what I'm after."

Gramps nodded. The hand holding his cane trembled slightly, and Gramps grasped the cane with his other hand to steady it.

"Yeah, one name kept comin' up when I was chatting with folks," he said. "This cat's a tattoo artist. Owns a shop over on Westfield Ave. Man by the name of Scotty."

Scotty. The name stabbed like an ice pick. Otto numbly stared back at Gramps.

"Scotty?" he said.

"That's the name I kept hearin'. Gonzalez at the car wash saw Scotty in the backseat of Devon's cruiser three weeks ago. Crouched down real low, like he didn't want no one seein' him. My boy Chuck seen the same thing a couple days later. Rico on MLK Drive said he seen Devon in Scotty's tattoo shop three times over the past month."

Scotty. The name echoed in his mind. Otto couldn't believe it.

He'd figured one of the thirty-some dealers he sold product to had snitched to Devon. Figured Devon had one of his dealers by the balls and they'd given up the next man on the totem pole to get out of it. One of the dumb-fuck younger dealers who bought from him—that's who he'd assumed it was.

But Scotty? Scotty wasn't some young kid. Scotty had been buying from him for more than a decade. They were even kinda close. They always sat around and shot the shit when Scotty picked up product. The fucker had even inked a few of Otto's tattoos.

"Thanks, Gramps," Otto said. He wasn't pissed. That would come soon enough. Now he was just in shock.

Otto gave Gramps another fist pound.

"You need anything else, you just let me know," Gramps said.

"I'll take it from here."

———

"I READ ABOUT YOUR STORY IN THE NEWSPAPER. HEARTBREAKING. JUST heartbreaking."

Gary held Beth's hand as they walked a few steps behind Gloria Vanderfleet, the head of the local community center. She was an older lady but she moved with a spryness that belied her age. Gary and Beth struggled to keep pace as they followed her down a hallway that led to the banquet hall.

"We're more than happy to help you however we can," Gloria said. "That's the point of a community center. To be here for the community when they need us."

"We appreciate it," Beth said. "We appreciate it so much."

They walked on, down the long hallway. Gary's shoulders were slouched, his grip around Beth's hand limp. He continued to think back to the meeting in Willow Park—focusing on it, obsessing over it, searching for some sort of clue into Shamrock's identity. But nothing about the meeting stood out. He had been so astonished by the offer, so shocked and spellbound, that he could barely remember anything about the meeting at all.

Gloria stopped in front of a closed door at the end of the hallway. She unlocked the door and pushed it open. "This is our banquet hall," she said.

The room was a couple hundred feet wide and twice that long. Maroon linoleum floor. A ceiling made up of exposed wooden beams. The room was completely empty—no tables or chairs, no decorations on the walls.

"We host a variety of events here," Gloria said. "Wedding receptions. All sorts of parties—graduation parties, anniversary parties, even birthday parties occasionally. We've held fund-raisers in the past. Plenty of them. If you're interested, we'd love to provide you this space to host a fund-raising dinner."

"That would be perfect," Beth said.

"We'd require a cash deposit, but we'd be happy to waive the additional fees we normally charge to rent the facility. We provide the chairs and tables, the plates and silverware, the kitchen for preparation and storage of food. You'll have to set up and provide everything else. The food. The drinks. You'd have to clean up afterward, as well."

"Absolutely. This sounds wonderful."

"Did you have a particular date in mind?"

"As soon as possible," Beth said, glancing at Gary. "Within the next week or two would be ideal."

"That might be difficult. People typically book our facility months in advance. Open dates fill up quickly. Let me check our schedule."

As Gloria flipped through a small notebook, Gary thought about the phone calls he'd received from Shamrock. Perhaps there was some sort of clue there. There were three phone calls. The first call to arrange the initial meeting in Willow Park. The second to get Gary's answer. The third to confirm the job was done.

But nothing about the calls stood out. The number showed up as UNKNOWN all three times. Each call lasted for barely ten seconds.

No, the meeting in Willow Park was the key to uncovering Shamrock's identity. There had to be something there.

"This could be your lucky day," Gloria said, closing her notebook. "Three days from now, we were scheduled to have a bridal shower. A week ago, the wedding was called off. So we have that night open."

"Three days from now?"

"Yes. It would be a lot of work to put something together so quickly. And it doesn't leave you much time to spread the word about the fund-raiser. But the soonest opening we have after that is in two months."

"We'll take the one in three days," Beth said.

Gloria wrote something in her notebook. Gary looked around them, at the large, cavernous room.

"These fund-raisers you've held in the past. How much do people usually raise?" he asked. It was the first time he'd spoken since a brief greeting when they arrived.

"It all depends on the turnout," Gloria said. "One of the high school basketball teams held a fund-raiser recently and raised almost three thousand dollars."

"Three thousand dollars?" Gary said.

"Yes. How much were you looking to raise?"

"Much more than that," Beth said. "But every little bit helps."

"People sometimes raise more. If you spread the word, you never know who will show up."

Gloria talked about a few preparations to make before the fund-raiser but the words didn't even register with Gary. Three thousand dollars was nothing. Even ten times that was nothing. No, his only option was to find Shamrock. Find him and get the money.

Once again, Gary thought back to the meeting in Willow Park. Tried to remember something distinctive—a gesture, something Shamrock wore, an offhand remark.

But there was nothing.

"THREE DAYS, GARY. DO YOU THINK WE CAN DO IT?"

"What?"

"The fund-raiser's going to be in three days," Beth said, once they arrived back home from the community center. "There's so much to do before then."

They walked into the living room and sat down on the couch. Beth pulled her smartphone from her pocket and tapped the screen a few times. She turned it toward Gary. "This is everything that needs to be done," she said.

Beth had spent the entire drive home typing a to-do list into a notes app on her phone. More than thirty tasks were listed, ranging from *Buy napkins* to *Create event on Facebook*.

"Looks good," Gary said. He couldn't help but think how different everything could have been. Right now, they could have been celebrating, rejoicing that a miracle had occurred and they'd found the money for the Germany trial. At this very moment, they could've been planning out the details, preparing for the trip.

Instead, they were talking about a fund-raiser that wouldn't bring in a fraction of the money they needed.

"I'm sure it'll be just like everything I plan out," Beth said. "A few hours before the dinner begins, I'll realize a million things I've forgotten."

"Right."

"And we'll scramble to get everything together at the last minute."

"Uh-huh."

Beth turned off her smartphone and set it on the coffee table.

"Nice to see you're so enthusiastic about this, Gary."

Gary looked at her. She glared back, her eyes shooting daggers.

"Sorry," Gary said. "I'm excited. I am."

"Funny way of showing it."

Gary apologized again. "It's just . . . frustrating." He sighed. "This whole thing is so frustrating. Every bit of good news seems to come with bad news. Even this fund-raiser. We'll be lucky if this raises a few thousand dollars. We need so much more."

"I don't disagree. But raising the money a little bit at a time is our only option right now. And it's like Gloria said: you never know who will show up. It's a shot in the dark, but at least it's a shot."

"I know. I really am sorry." He leaned over and grabbed Beth's feet. Placed them in his lap and massaged her left foot, her right foot, working his fingers deep into the soles.

"Trying to get back on my good side?"

"Of course." He wasn't lying; for a second there, he'd really thought she was going to blow up at him.

On the coffee table, Gary's phone rang. Rod's name was displayed. He reached over and tapped Ignore.

Gary thought back to Willow Park as he massaged Beth's feet. For what seemed like the millionth time, he visualized the meeting and tried to recall something distinctive about Shamrock, anything at all.

His phone rang again. As before, it was Rod.

"Who keeps calling?" Beth asked.

"Rod. I don't feel like talking to him right now."

"Answer it. Tell him about the fund-raiser. Maybe he and Sarah could stop by, give us a hand with the planning."

Gary answered the call. "Rod, I—"

"Gary, man, you gotta come in here," Rod said.

"Come in where?"

"The store. Ascension Outerwear."

"Now? I can't, Rod. I'm busy."

"Doesn't matter. You gotta get here right now."

"I've got a million things going on, Rod. I'll try to swing by tomorrow, maybe the day after. We're planning a fund-raiser and—"

"There's a police detective here," Rod said. "He wants to talk to you."

Gary nearly dropped the phone. Rod kept talking, but Gary could hear nothing at all, nothing except his own blood—not a pounding in his ears so much as the feeling that all of the blood was draining from his head.

Gary set Beth's feet back on the ground and stood up from the couch. Somehow he did it without tumbling over. He walked into the hallway and lowered his voice.

"What are you talking about, Rod?" Gary said, a frantic whisper. "A police detective?"

"Yeah. He's got a few questions about some cop who was murdered the other night."

17

GARY STARED OUT THE WINDSHIELD AS HE DROVE TO ASCENSION OUTER-
wear, breathing in through his nose for a count of four, then ex-
haling for a count of four. It was a breathing exercise he'd read about
that was supposedly calming, but it did nothing to help his frayed
nerves. His jittery hands could barely grip the steering wheel. His
stomach was so tense it felt like it was trying to digest itself.

When he'd told Beth he was leaving to go to the store, she angrily
set her phone onto the coffee table and gave him a look, the same look
she'd given him when he'd forgotten about the fund-raiser earlier. He
told her there was an urgent problem with the store's computer system,
which was two-thirds true—definitely urgent, definitely a problem,
but it had nothing to do with computers—and left the house right as
she was about to confront him.

There was no time to worry about that now, though.

Focus. He had to focus. Focus on the fact that a police detective was waiting to talk with him about the murder he'd committed two nights ago.

After twenty minutes, he arrived at Ascension Outerwear. Rod's pickup was parked in one of the stalls out front. A few spots down was a black Crown Victoria with a large antenna mounted to the trunk hood. Clearly an unmarked police cruiser.

He pulled into one of the open stalls and walked up to the front door. Inside, Rod sat behind the front counter, wearing a pair of khakis and a black polo. On the other side of the counter was a tall and thin black man. He wore a gray blazer over a crisp button-up shirt tucked into a pair of jeans. His cheeks were clean-shaven, the jet-black hair on top of his head trimmed short. He stood ramrod straight— perfect posture, shoulders thrown back, head held high.

The badge clipped to his belt identified him as police, but he looked more like a prim-and-proper accountant or college professor.

"You must be Gary," he said, walking over.

Gary nodded.

"My name is Tony Whitley." Deep, commanding voice. "I'm a homicide detective with the River Falls PD." Whitley extended his hand and Gary shook it. They locked eyes. Whitley showed no emotion whatsoever. Strictly matter-of-fact.

"I had a few questions for you," Whitley said.

"About what?" Gary said. His voice sounded thin, higher-pitched than usual.

"A murder investigation."

"Here, take a seat, Gar," Rod said. He jumped off the stool behind the counter. Gary walked over and sat down. Whitley stood on the other side of the counter, staring at Gary.

"The investigation has to do with the murder of Devon Peterson," Whitley said. "Are you familiar with the case?"

"No," Gary said.

"You're not? You ever watch the nightly news? Read the newspapers? He's a cop who was murdered a few nights back."

Gary paused. Should he keep denying? Admit he was familiar with the case? Confess now and save everyone some time?

"I think I saw an article about the case," Gary said.

"I'm sure you did. It's been all over the news. We found some evidence at the crime scene we were hoping you could help us with."

Whitley grabbed a brown paper sack off the ground. He pulled an item from inside and set it on the glass counter.

It was a black baseball hat, encased in a clear plastic evidence bag. Gary immediately recognized it as the plain black hat he wore the night he murdered Devon Peterson. The hat he grabbed off the shelf at Ascension Outerwear on his way to the murder.

A large unswallowable mass formed in Gary's throat. He hadn't even realized the hat was missing.

"We found this hat two blocks away from the crime scene," Whitley said. "Devon's blood is splattered all over the outside of the hat. The assumption we're working under is that the murderer was wearing it on the night of the murder. He shot Devon, blood splattered onto the hat, and then it fell off when he was running away."

Whitley paused, as if he was waiting for a response from Gary. Gary stayed silent.

"This hat was one of the first pieces of evidence we found," Whitley said. "From the moment we found it, we thought it would be key to solving the case. We find a few hairs on the hat, maybe a DNA sample from whoever was wearing it, and boom: we're in business."

Gary's expression remained calm but his mind was a chaotic, overwhelmed mess. He couldn't believe he hadn't noticed that the hat had fallen off.

"There's no trace evidence on the hat, though," Whitley said. "No hair, no DNA. Nothing but Devon's blood splattered on the front. So we shifted our focus to try to find where the hat was purchased. We find that out, we can hopefully discover who bought it. And if we know who bought the hat, we could have our murderer. Or at the very least, something to work with.

"Now, this isn't the type of hat you can just go down to Walmart and buy. It's made by a company named Pangaea—a very obscure, high-end outerwear company. Pangaea doesn't sell their stuff at that many places. Long story short, we talked with a few people at Pangaea. They were able to track a code on the tag of the hat and put us in touch with the distribution company they sent the hat to. Aero Distributors was the name. Aero went through their records and found that this hat was part of an order that was sent to a business named Ascension Outerwear. A business right here in River Falls."

"I see," Gary said. He felt a lone droplet of sweat slide from his armpit down his rib cage.

Whitley looked at Rod, who stood on the edge of the discussion.

"So I drove over here and had Rod look into your purchase history. See who has bought one of these hats from your store. Turns out you haven't sold a single one of these hats since you've been in business, but your records show that one hat is missing. That hat was in stock after your last inventory two weeks ago. In other words, one hat disappeared sometime in the past two weeks."

Gary stared at the hat, unable to look at Whitley.

"So, that's what we have," Whitley said. "A hat that we're almost certain our murderer was wearing went missing from your store in the past two weeks. Now, we need your help. We need you to think back. Can you remember any customer who seemed suspicious? Someone who was looking at the hats, maybe? Anyone at all who could've stolen the hat?"

"A suspicious customer?" Gary said.

"Can you think of anyone?"

It took a moment for everything to click into place, for Gary to understand what was happening. But everything soon became crystal clear.

Whitley wasn't here to arrest him. He wasn't here to interrogate him about the murder. Whitley was here to talk with him. To get his assistance.

Whitley didn't suspect him at all.

Gary felt a relieved smile creep onto his face. He clenched his jaw, pushed the smile back.

"I can't remember anyone," Gary said.

"No one at all? You're sure?"

"Two weeks is a long time."

"Plus, Gary hasn't really been around here much," Rod said.

"My wife is sick," Gary said. "I've been focused on being with her."

"That's right," Whitley said. "I thought I recognized your name. I saw that article in the paper. She's pregnant, too, right?"

"Yeah."

"Boy, that's something awful. You have my best wishes."

"Thank you."

Whitley grabbed the plastic-encased hat off the counter and placed it back in the brown paper bag.

"I appreciate your guys' time," he said.

He pulled a business card from his inner jacket pocket and set it on the counter. "Call me if you think of anything."

"Of course," Gary said.

Just like that, it was over. The anxiety he'd felt for the past twenty minutes drifted from his body like an evil spirit being exorcised. He'd dodged a bullet. Done more than that, really—dodged a grenade that was dangerously close to obliterating his life. He was—

"If I can get those security tapes we talked about, I'll be on my way," Whitley said, turning toward Rod.

"No prob," Rod said. He walked toward the rear of the store. "Gimme a minute and I'll make a copy."

"Security tapes?" Gary asked.

"Rod mentioned that your security cameras might've captured someone taking the hat," Whitley said. "I want to take a look at the tapes, hopefully spot the guy we're looking for. Gonna be a pain looking through two weeks of security footage, but that's why God created junior detectives, right?"

The detective smiled, but Gary didn't return it. His heart skipped a beat. The security cameras—he'd forgotten all about them in the frenzied moments after the murder. The security footage would show him grabbing the black hat and black coat right before the murder. The security footage would show him arriving at the store after the murder, clad in all black. The security footage would show him cleaning Devon Peterson's blood off in the bathroom.

At the rear of the store, Rod disappeared past the double doors, into the back office. All he had to do was transfer the footage onto a USB flash drive and give it to the detective. The entire process would take less than a minute.

"Nice place you got here," Whitley said, staring out at the sales floor.

"Thank you," Gary stammered.

"How's business?"

"It's okay."

"Lots of businesses are struggling in the city. I'm ever in need of a new coat, I'll stop by, check out what you have. Do what I can to support the local economy."

"Great," Gary said, stepping out from behind the counter. "I'm going to check on Rod. Give him a hand. Sometimes he's not the best with technology."

"I know the type. In fact, I'm one of them. I'll wait here."

Gary moved as fast as he could without breaking into a sprint. When he reached the back office, Rod was at the desk, leaning over the computer with one hand resting on the mouse.

He glanced up at Gary. "I almost got it here," he said.

Gary shut the door behind him. He took three hurried steps toward Rod.

"Listen to me," Gary said. "Don't give the detective the footage from two nights ago."

"What are you talking about?"

"The security footage from two nights ago. Delete it. Don't give it to the detective."

"Why? Gary, what—"

Gary reached out and grabbed Rod's arm at the elbow. He squeezed.

"You just have to trust me," he said. "Delete the footage from two nights ago, and we can give him the rest."

"Gary, what the hell is going on?"

"I'll explain everything later. I know it sounds crazy, but you have to do this for me."

"This guy is a cop. I'm not deleting anything. I—"

"Just move out of the way," Gary said, his voice low but intense. He yanked the mouse from Rod's hand and shoved his brother to the side—not hard, but enough to force him back a few inches.

Their security-footage program was already displayed on the computer screen. It took Gary only a few clicks to delete the footage. He grabbed a flash drive with the logo for a construction company on it and plugged it into the USB port. A few more clicks and he transferred the footage from the past two weeks—sans the footage he'd just deleted—onto the drive.

"Let me handle this, Rod," Gary said, grabbing the flash drive after the data had transferred. "I'll explain later."

Rod stared back, his face blank.

"You have to trust me," Gary said. "Please."

"Fine."

Gary walked out to the sales floor, Rod a few steps behind. He handed Whitley the flash drive. "That's everything from the past two weeks," he said. "The batteries ran out in our camera two days ago, so we weren't able to record that day, unfortunately."

Whitley went silent for a moment. Gary thought he was going to start asking questions about the camera failing to record, but instead the detective slipped the flash drive into his pocket. "We'll take a look at what you have. See what we find."

With that, Whitley picked up the brown paper bag and walked through the front door, out into the parking lot.

A moment later, Gary watched through the window as the black Crown Victoria pulled away and disappeared down the street.

ONCE THE CAR WAS GONE, GARY CLOSED HIS EYES AND BREATHED OUT A massive lungful of air, feeling as if his entire body were deflating. He slowly inhaled and exhaled a few times.

"Start talking, Gary."

He turned around. Rod stood a few feet away, glaring at him, arms crossed over his chest.

"Don't worry about it, Rod," Gary said.

"Too late. I'm worried. You just had me lie to a cop."

"You didn't lie to him. I did."

"Doesn't matter. What the hell is going on?"

Gary walked toward the front door. The past twenty minutes had been the most harrowing, terrifying twenty minutes of his life, even worse than the stretch of time immediately after the murder. Now he just wanted to get out of here.

"Gary?" Rod said, following him.

"This doesn't concern you. Just forget about it."

"Forget about it? I'm not going to forget anything."

Gary arrived at the door. He didn't even have a chance to open it before Rod's hand reached over his shoulder and slammed against the door, blocking it shut. Gary turned around and looked at Rod.

"Gary, man, these answers don't cut it," Rod said, their faces only a few feet apart. "You just kept security footage from a police detective. I didn't stop you. If he finds out, both our asses are in deep shit. You're not leaving here until you tell me what's going on. You don't start talking, I'll call that detective back and tell him what you did."

Rod pulled his phone from his pocket.

"Just calm down. You have no idea what—"

"I'm not messing around," Rod said, bringing the phone's screen to life. He walked over to the counter and looked at the business card Whitley had left.

"Rod, don't—"

"I don't know what's going on, but I'm calling him. This is ridiculous. We lied to a police detective, Gary."

Rod tapped the screen a few times, his eyes darting from the phone to the business card.

"Fine," Gary said. He didn't want to drag Rod into this, but he could tell his brother meant every word of what he said. He was too shaken up to try to talk his way out of this; he couldn't think straight. All he could do was give Rod the truth.

Gary walked back to the counter and sat down on a stool. He despondently stared off for a moment, his eyes distant.

"Gary?" Rod said. "What is it?"

"I'm in trouble, Rod," Gary said. "Big trouble." He leaned forward and rested his elbows on the counter. "The murder the cop was here about? I'm the one who did it. I killed the guy. I'm the person the police are looking for."

Rod was silent. Then:

"What the hell are you talking about?"

"A few days ago, I got a call from a guy who wanted to meet with me. When we met, he said he'd give me the money we need for the Germany treatment. All two hundred thousand of it. In exchange for the money, I had to kill someone. That someone turned out to be that cop."

Gary shook his head.

"And I did it. I swear to God, Rod. I did it. I murdered a man."

The look on Rod's face was more than confusion. It was bafflement. Total bewilderment. "Are you joking?"

"I'm serious. I wore the hat the night I murdered him. I'm the one who grabbed it. The security footage would have shown me taking the hat, shown me arriving back here after the murder. That's why I had to delete the footage."

"Jesus, Gary."

"It gets even more unbelievable. I did it. I killed the guy. And then I got screwed out of the money."

"What?"

"The money. I went to pick it up yesterday and it wasn't there. The locker I was supposed to get it from is no longer rented. And I have no way of contacting the guy who screwed me. I don't know who he is, what his name is. Nothing."

Gary's heart rate had finally started to return to normal, but the total fear he'd felt during Whitley's visit still lingered.

"Gary?" Rod said.

"Yeah."

"Look at me."

Gary looked at his brother.

"Now tell me that you're not lying to me," Rod said.

"This is the truth, Rod. As incredible as it sounds, it's the truth."

"Jesus," Rod said. "So that night at the pizza place—this is why you were asking me what I'd do, how far I'd go to save Sarah?"

"Yeah. Kind of. I think my mind was already made up, to be honest. I just needed to talk to someone."

"I can't believe this."

"I can't, either," Gary said. "I can't believe any of it. I can't believe

Beth has a brain tumor. I can't believe I murdered someone. I can't believe a police detective was just here."

Gary slowly, sadly shook his head.

"None of this seems real."

———

"**WHAT'S GOING ON WITH YOU, GARY?**"

Beth hit him with the question the moment he arrived back home. She still sat on the couch, the same place she'd been when he left. She stared across the room at him, jaw clenched, her mouth a straight line.

"I'm sorry, Beth. Our inventory program was acting up."

"The inventory program?" Beth said.

"Rod doesn't know how to fix it. If I didn't do something, we could've had a big problem."

"We have a million things to do for the fund-raiser, and you're worried about the store's inventory system?"

She silently stared at him. The same look she'd given him earlier, when he'd forgotten about the fund-raiser. Suspicion. Distrust.

"Have you given up?" she said.

"Given up?"

"Given up on raising the money, the Germany trip, the treatment. Have you just decided that it's too much of a long shot? Just given up on trying to save me?"

"No. God, no. Of course not. That's ridiculous."

"Is it? Because lately, it kind of seems like you have. Just given up. You've been so distant. Preoccupied. Off in your own little world.

You're leaving the house to get milk and returning with no milk. You're forgetting about the fund-raiser after I spent hours talking about it." Her eyes started to glaze over. "And you're disappearing all of the time. Spending the entire evening at the store a few nights ago. Going to the store right now when we have a tight deadline for the fund-raiser. I realize the store's important. But is that really what you should be focusing on?"

The words stung like acid. He couldn't stand the idea of Beth thinking that he'd just given up on saving her. He wanted to tell her that the opposite was true, wanted to tell her that he still believed, that his belief had driven him to do things that he still found unfathomable.

For one moment, he thought about confessing everything. Telling her about the murder, about everything he'd done for her. He didn't want to involve her in this, but the idea of Beth thinking he'd just given up on her was enough to make him sick.

But he couldn't tell her the truth; he simply couldn't.

"I'm sorry, Beth," he said. "If I've seemed distant, I'm sorry. So much has happened, and it's just been difficult for me to handle it all. But I haven't given up. Not even close. I believe. I believe so strongly. This is going to have a happy ending. I'll do everything I can to make sure of that."

He walked over and put his arm around her, ran his hand along her back. "You know that you and Tyson are the two most important people in my life. You know that I'm here for you. No matter what, I'll be by your side."

"Okay. If I'm overreacting, I apologize."

"You're not overreacting. Not at all."

Beth wiped at her eyes. Her features had softened a little. But there was still that look on her face, that look of suspicion. That look like she didn't entirely know whether she believed him or not.

———

"Yo."

Otto looked up from behind the counter of Solid Gold Pawn just as Scotty stepped into the pawnshop, the door slamming shut behind him. Here he was. The greasy little rat who'd given him up and started this mess. At least, according to Gramps. Before declaring thermonuclear war on Scotty's ass, Otto wanted to make sure the info was legit.

"You wanted to talk about something?" Scotty said.

"Yeah, I got a couple questions for you."

Scotty strutted up to the counter with a street-tough, cocky swagger, shoulders rocking back and forth with every step. He had a scroungy goatee and tattoos everywhere—on his neck, his chest, even some sort of intricate tribal tattoo winding across the left half of his face. He wore a dirty gray hooded sweatshirt with the sleeves rolled up to his elbows, revealing even more tattoos on his forearms.

"What's good, O?" he said.

"Got some Mexican Mud with your name on it," Otto said to Scotty, staring at him across the counter. "Need a restock?"

"Not now."

"Been a while since you bought anything. You ain't getting your product from someone else, are you?"

"Nah, man. Just been slow. You know how it is. The city's going to shit, taking the drug scene right along with it."

"Ain't that the truth."

A newspaper rested on the countertop, placed off to the side like a prop in a play. Otto had purchased it earlier and set it out on the counter right before Scotty arrived. The newspaper was open to page three, folded back to an article in the middle of the page. NO NEW LEADS IN OFFICER MURDER INVESTIGATION, read the headline.

"You see this shit?" Otto said, tapping the article's headline.

Scotty glanced down. The moment he saw the article, his Adam's apple bobbed in his throat. A subtle reaction—but a telling one.

"Yeah, I heard about it," Scotty said, avoiding eye contact.

"A real tragedy, ain't it?"

"Sure is." Another tell: he blinked his eyes a few times.

"I'll miss the smell of bacon in the neighborhood," Otto said.

A ghost of a smile appeared on Scotty's tattooed face. His eyes stayed focused on the article, still avoiding eye contact with Otto.

The reactions were enough. They told him everything he needed to know. Scotty was the reason for his mess. This bastard was the one who turned him in. He was the one who snitched.

It infuriated Otto, but he managed to push down the feeling, burying it. The middle of the day wasn't the right time to get revenge. The sales floor of Solid Gold Pawn wasn't the right place to teach Scotty a lesson.

"You keep in touch," Otto said, grabbing the newspaper and tossing it behind the counter. "Lemme know when you need more product."

"Oh, for sure," Scotty said. He took a step toward the door. "You need any more ink, maybe a back tat or something, you just stop by my shop. You know you're welcome anytime, O. On the house."

"Think I'm good now," Otto said. "Maybe later." Otto nearly shook with restrained anger as he watched Scotty strut back to the pawnshop entrance and walk past the door.

The little bastard would pay. Would he ever.

Soon he would pay.

———

NIGHTMARES VISITED GARY THAT EVENING.

A lone still image of Devon Peterson's face appeared in his dreams on the night after Detective Whitley's visit. Devon's face looked exactly as it did immediately after Gary pulled the trigger the final time. The left side of his face was completely destroyed, nothing more than a giant bloody wound. Chunks of brain matter and tissue were splattered on the ground behind his skull. His short buzz-cut hair was matted with blood. His eyes stared out into nothingness.

Nothing happened—the body didn't come back to life and start chasing him or anything like that—but the close-up image of Devon's mangled face was horrifying enough to startle Gary awake.

His entire body was sticky with sweat and his heart beat crazily in his chest. He stared at the ceiling, waiting for the pounding to subside. The room was nearly pitch-black, the only illumination coming from the faint red glow of the alarm clock on the bedside table. Three forty-nine a.m.

The rest of the night was spent tossing and turning. Once he'd woken up Beth beside him and apologized. Sleep came in sporadic fits lasting no longer than ten or twenty minutes. Twice he was startled awake when the same image of Devon's mangled face flashed into his dreams.

When he finally got out of bed in the morning, Gary was so tired, it was as if he hadn't even slept at all.

18

POLICE LOOKING AT SLAIN OFFICER'S QUESTIONABLE PAST

RIVER FALLS, MI—The River Falls police officer who was murdered late Thursday night was accused of assault and other crimes while a member of the Detroit Metro Police Department. Detectives are looking into the possibility that this past criminal activity played a part in his murder.

Devon Peterson, 37, was shot repeatedly outside of his home in River Falls Thursday night, a murder that sent shock waves throughout the community. Prior to joining the River Falls PD, Peterson worked in the Detroit Metro Police Department, where he was accused of assaulting criminals, racial profiling, and other crimes, before ultimately resigning from the force.

Peterson's past, according to River Falls Police Chief Darren Roselin, could have played a part in his murder.

"That's just one of the many angles we're currently investigating," he said.

No arrests have been made in the murder, but Roselin insists that the investigation is progressing.

"We've talked to hundreds of people, both witnesses and suspects," he said. "We'll talk to as many as we need to until the case is solved."

In addition to looking at Peterson's past, Roselin acknowledged the possibility that Peterson had become involved in criminal activity while an officer in River Falls.

"We knew about Officer Peterson's previous accusations when he was hired," he said. "He was a model officer in the two years he was on the River Falls PD.

"Is it possible that he was involved in illegal activity that we didn't know about? Anything's possible. Considering how closely we watched him, it's unlikely, but it's an angle we're investigating. Right now, detectives are looking at everyone and everything."

GARY AND ROD WALKED ACROSS THE COMMUNITY CENTER'S BANQUET HALL to a large storage closet on the opposite side of the room. They each grabbed four folding chairs from a stack in the closet and began to set up the chairs around the room.

"You see that article in the newspaper this morning?" Rod said, unfolding a chair. He slid it under one of the thirty tables that they'd already placed around the hall.

"Yeah," Gary said. "I saw it."

"That's good for you, right? That the cops think it's someone he pissed off a long time ago who came back for revenge?"

"I guess so. That visit from the detective yesterday is still freaking me out, though. When he showed me the hat, I really thought it was over. I thought he was going to arrest me on the spot."

Gary unfolded the last of the four chairs. As they walked back to the closet to grab more, he looked around at the banquet hall. The fund-raising dinner for Beth would take place in two days, and the addition of tables and chairs was slowly transforming the room. They planned on working all day—Ascension Outerwear would remain closed for today, probably for the next few days.

Gary had hoped the manual labor would help him think straight. While it felt good—he'd even worked up a bit of a sweat—his mind was still a jumbled mess.

"You thought any more about the guy?" Rod asked as he grabbed more chairs.

"What's that?"

"The guy who screwed you. Have you thought any more about how to find him?"

"I've been thinking about it constantly."

"And?"

"I have no idea. I don't know the guy's name, who he is, where he lives—nothing."

They walked to an empty table and placed chairs around it. Rod wiped his forehead with the sleeve of his T-shirt, clearing away his mop of blond hair. Gary wasn't the only one who'd worked up a sweat.

"Think back to the meeting," Rod said. "The meeting you had with him when he made the offer. Take me through it, moment by moment. Tell me everything you remember."

"The meeting was scheduled for noon, and I arrived at the park five minutes early," Gary said. "I sat on a bench and waited. I was alone, other than a group of teenagers playing basketball on the other side of the park."

"Then what?"

"Right at noon, he appeared."

"Did he show up in a car? Did someone drop him off?"

Gary and Rod sat down in two of the folding chairs they'd just set up. They were alone in the large room—Beth and Sarah had left half an hour ago to pick up groceries for the fund-raiser—but they still kept their voices down.

"The guy was on foot when he arrived," Gary said. "He told me to call him Shamrock, showed me a green clover ring on his finger. Said he read the article about Beth's tumor and that he'd give me the money we need. In exchange, he said I had to murder someone." Gary's voice was flat. He was merely recounting facts. Ticking off the events for Rod, just as he'd done for himself countless times since finding the empty locker. "Shamrock handed me a copy of Devon Peterson's driver's license and told me that was who I had to kill. I was so shocked, I barely said anything. He had a duffel bag with him and he opened it up. There was money everywhere. Bundles and bundles of hundred-dollar bills. He closed the bag and said he'd call in a few days for my answer. Then he left. The entire meeting didn't even last five minutes."

"Describe the guy."

"Completely bald. Rough voice. He looked skinny but he was wearing a black puffy coat and baggy jeans so it was hard to tell."

"Did he choose to meet at Willow Park or did you?"

"He did."

"Why do you think he chose Willow Park? He could've chosen anywhere to meet."

"I have no idea. My best guess is that he chose it because it's right off of I-Eighty-four, easy access to the interstate."

"What about the cop? There has to be a reason he wanted the cop dead. Maybe the cop arrested him in the past, was investigating him now, something like that. You learn more about the cop, it could lead you to this guy."

"I thought about that, too. But I'm not going anywhere near that. This soon after the murder, I'm sure the police are looking into everything about Devon. I start asking around about him, the police might find out and wonder why I'm so interested. No way am I taking that risk."

"So how are you gonna find this Shamrock guy?"

"I have no idea. I don't even know if he lives in River Falls—he could live in Detroit, farther away than that. Even if he lives here, there are almost a quarter of a million people in this city. Having a vague description of what he looks like isn't enough. There's no way I could find him. Not unless I can narrow down the search somehow."

"There's gotta be something more," Rod said. "Some sort of clue."

"I don't know what it could be," Gary said. "I can't think of anything."

RIGHT BEFORE ELEVEN, GARY SUGGESTED THEY TAKE A BREAK. "ANY IDEA IF there's a TV around here?" he asked.

"Think I saw one in a side room when we walked in," Rod said.

"Let's go check it out. There's something I want to watch."

They found the room with the TV. Gary turned it to channel 7 just as the midday local-news broadcast was beginning. A female anchor talked about the lead story: Devon Peterson's funeral, which took place that morning.

"This is why you wanted to find the TV?" Rod asked. "To watch this?"

Gary nodded.

"Why?"

"I want to see if they report anything new about the investigation," Gary said.

He'd continued to obsessively check the Internet for updates—by now, he'd bookmarked ten sites on his phone that he looked at every hour. Occasionally, there was something new, like this morning's article about the police focusing the investigation on Devon's past, but most articles just rehashed the same information. The comments sections of the articles were usually more informative than the articles themselves, full of speculation and rumors. One anonymous poster claimed Devon was killed by a drug dealer, another said a fellow police officer pulled the trigger, and another insisted the police were about to arrest one of Devon's neighbors for the crime.

On the TV, the funeral report began with a few establishing shots—the closed casket, the pastor, a collection of flower bouquets. A younger female field reporter was talking, mentioning that there were no new developments in the investigation. That was what Gary had wanted to know, but he kept watching.

The report continued with various quick shots of attendees—a sea of grim and solemn faces, probably at least three hundred people.

People crying, dabbing their eyes with Kleenexes, others with their faces buried in their hands. A group of around fifty uniformed police officers sat up by the casket—most stared straight ahead with stony expressions. The report continued showing attendees, more tears, more grief, more heartache. Looking at this crowd of grieving people, Gary felt light-headed, nauseous. He tensed the muscles in his stomach, clenched his jaw to try to relax himself.

He'd done far more than murder a man when he pulled the trigger. He'd affected countless other lives, too. People who'd lost a friend, a coworker, a neighbor. People who'd attended high school with Devon, worked with him, known him from the local bar. People who would never talk to him again, hadn't even had a chance to say good-bye. Right on-screen, here were hundreds of people who'd come together to mourn, all because of what Gary had done. He—

"You look like you're gonna pass out," Rod said. He reached over to turn off the TV. "I think we've seen enough."

"Leave it on, Rod."

"They already said there's no update on the investigation."

"Doesn't matter. Leave it on."

"You're just punishing yourself, watching this."

Maybe he was. Maybe that was the real reason he wanted to tune in. Not to see if anything new was reported on the investigation, but to punish himself, to make sure the horror of what he'd done remained fresh in his mind. To make sure he didn't forget that he had done something reprehensible. To make sure it remained real.

IT TOOK ANOTHER TWO HOURS TO FINISH SETTING UP THE BANQUET-HALL seating area—thirty tables, two hundred forty folding chairs. Once they were done, Rod collapsed into a chair and exhaled heavily. "Shit, I am out of shape," he said.

Gary nodded, said nothing. They'd worked mostly in silence for the rest of the afternoon. A few times, Rod had attempted to start a conversation but it went nowhere. After watching the report from the funeral, Gary didn't feel like talking.

As they silently sat at the table, Beth and Sarah walked through the door. Their purses were slung over their shoulders and they each carried a few white plastic grocery sacks. They walked over to Gary and Rod and set the sacks on the table in front of them.

"Everything looks great," Beth said. Gary was pleased to see her in an upbeat mood today. Yesterday he'd spent all day planning out the fund-raiser with her after she'd confronted him, and her anger had faded as the day passed.

Beth gazed around the banquet hall. "It's actually starting to resemble a place that's hosting a dinner for hundreds of people in two days."

"It was a productive morning. How was the grocery store?"

"Good," Sarah said. "We decided on hot dogs. They're cheap. They're easy."

"I figure with Rod on the grill, we want to keep it as simple as possible," Beth said, smiling. "Even he can't screw up hot dogs."

"Low blow," Rod said. "Don't *ever* insult my grilling skills again, Beth."

Beth set her purse on the table and pulled out her smartphone. "We already have a ton of confirmed guests," she said. "And I only sent out the Evite this morning."

She showed the phone to Gary. Displayed was an event invite page with more than two hundred confirmed guests and hundreds more who hadn't responded yet.

"That's great," Gary said. He looked at the groceries. "Will this be enough food for that many people?"

"Oh, there are still plenty of sacks in the car. At least ten of them." Beth smiled. "You gentlemen aren't going to make the pregnant lady carry them all in, are you?"

"Come on, Rod," Gary said, standing up. "Let's grab them."

"Bring them into the kitchen," Beth said. "We'll start putting everything away."

Gary followed Rod outside to the Corolla. The backseat was crammed with grocery bags overflowing with two-liter bottles of soda, hot dog buns, chips, condiments.

"Hold on, Gary," Rod said. "Before we grab the groceries, there's something I wanna say to you."

"What's that?"

"I just want you to know I don't think any less of you," Rod said. "The murder—it doesn't make me look at you differently. I would've done the same thing in your shoes. Anyone would've."

"Thanks, Rod."

"I didn't get a chance to tell you that yesterday, so I wanted to tell you now. It should go without saying, but if it doesn't, I'll say it. You're my brother. I love you. I don't care what you do; those two things will always be true."

Gary opened his mouth to respond but his voice caught in his throat. He paused to get control of his emotions. The sincerity of Rod's words touched him deeply.

"I was wondering what that must have felt like, to find out your brother did something so horrible," Gary said. "I'm sure it was a shock to hear."

"You kidding? It shocked the living shit outta me." Rod briefly smiled, then turned serious again. "But what's done is done. You can't beat yourself up over this. When we watched that report on the funeral, you looked like a zombie. You've been acting like one all day, too, and that needs to stop. You think you're feeling down now? Think what you'll be like if you lose Beth. You gotta remember that you did this for her. This is still about her."

"Thanks, Rod," Gary said. "I appreciate it. I really do."

THEY STAYED AT THE COMMUNITY CENTER ALL AFTERNOON. AROUND SIX o'clock, they headed home. Five minutes after walking through the door, Beth collapsed.

She was in the kitchen, making pancakes, when it happened. Food cravings had been almost nonexistent during her pregnancy except for one thing: pancakes. At least a few times a week, she'd have a sudden desire for pancakes and Gary would make them for her. When they'd arrived back home from the community center, she'd told Gary she was hungry for pancakes. He offered to make them but she said she'd handle it and had gone straight to the kitchen to prepare them.

In the bathroom, Gary was getting ready for a shower. Just as he took off his shirt, he heard a noise from the kitchen. A dull, heavy thump that he could hear even through the closed bathroom door. The thump was instantly followed by the sound of something metal crashing to the ground.

Gary opened the bathroom door a crack.

"Beth?" he yelled out.

No response.

"Beth?"

Again, no answer. Gary put his shirt back on and stepped out of the bathroom. He walked down the hallway, yelling her name a third time. When she didn't respond, he picked up his pace, walking faster, almost at a sprint.

He reached the end of the hallway and turned into the kitchen. He froze. Beth's body lay on the ground, shaking with light convulsions, facedown on the white kitchen tile. Her legs and arms were contorted at awkward angles. A carton of eggs and a frying pan were on the floor. Cracked shells, egg yolks, and pancake mix were splattered everywhere.

"Oh, God, no," Gary whispered.

He sprinted over, dropped to his knees, and flipped over her body. Beth's eyes were closed. Her mouth lifelessly hung open. A few drops of egg yolk had splashed onto her cheeks. The hem of her shirt had risen up, exposing the underside of her belly.

He lifted Beth's head off the ground and leaned in so his face was just inches away.

"Beth? Beth, can you hear me?"

Her eyes remained closed. Her body continued to lightly convulse.

Gary grabbed his phone from his pocket and dialed 911.

19

GARY SAT IN A HOSPITAL ROOM, SLUMPED IN A CHAIR. THE LIGHTS IN THE room were off and the window blinds were closed. He stared at the bed in the middle of the room. Beth lay on it, her eyes shut, her body still and silent, the mound of her stomach covered with a thin white bedsheet pulled up to her chin. Diodes were taped to her temples. Thin plastic wires connected them to a monstrous machine next to her bed. A display monitor on the machine showed an ever-changing array of readouts and numbers that made no sense at all to him.

He'd arrived at the hospital with her more than four hours earlier. It was the same local hospital, McCann, she'd gone to the first time she collapsed. Upon arrival, doctors had immediately rushed Beth into an exam room while Gary sat in the waiting room. After two hours, the young, wiry doctor from their last visit to the ER, Dr. Simpson, approached Gary and told him that Beth and the baby were fine.

A sense of relief flooded over Gary, but it only lasted for a second before Dr. Simpson added that they'd been extremely lucky. Had they not gotten to the hospital so quickly, the outcome could have been different.

After delivering the news, Dr. Simpson led Gary to Beth's room. She offered up a weak smile, briefly spoke to him, then drifted to sleep. Grogginess from some medication they'd given her, Dr. Simpson explained. Gary had questions, but the doctor had few answers. Before leaving he said that specialists and other members of the medical team would arrive in the morning to discuss Beth's condition.

Gary had stayed at Beth's bedside since then. Pacing around the room. Searching for answers. Unable to calm down. Twice he broke down and cried.

He shifted his body in the chair but his eyes remained focused on Beth. Her chest rose and fell with her slow, steady breathing. Gary grabbed his smartphone from his pocket and tapped a button. The screen displayed the time: 10:51 p.m. He placed it back in his pocket.

"You awake?"

Gary looked at the doorway. Rod and Sarah stood there, nearly silhouetted in darkness.

"Yeah," Gary said, keeping his voice low. "I'm awake."

They walked inside. Sarah set two granola bars onto the table beside Gary.

"We figured you might be hungry," she said.

"Thanks."

Gary tore the wrapper from the first bar and threw it into the trash. He took a bite and slowly, methodically chewed. Rod and Sarah walked over to Beth's bed and stood beside it, looking down at her.

"How's she doing?" Rod whispered.

"Tough question. She survived. That's the main thing. But the doctor said it was a close call."

"Anything we can do?" Sarah asked.

"Did you find two hundred thousand dollars since we last talked?" Gary asked.

"Unfortunately, no."

"Then there's not much you can do."

Gary stared at Beth's motionless body, lying in bed, hooked up to the enormous machine. He'd been staring at her for the past four hours, all alone in her room, until he finally called Rod and Sarah to tell them what happened. They'd immediately driven over.

"I thought I was going to lose her," Gary said. His voice cracked with emotion; he cleared his throat and continued. "As I was waiting for the ambulance, her body was lightly shaking and convulsing. Her eyes were rolled back in her skull. I really thought I was going to lose her."

Gary stood up from the chair and walked over to the window. He peeked behind the blind and looked outside at the dark, still night sky.

"This is terrible, Gary," Rod said. "I don't know what to say."

Gary let the blind fall back into place. He didn't know what to say, either.

GARY SPENT THE NIGHT IN BETH'S ROOM, HIS BODY CRAMMED INTO THE small chair at her bedside, his head leaning against the chair's wooden backrest. It was painful and awkward, but he somehow had his best night of sleep in a week—the exhaustion and lack of sleep from the past few days finally catching up with him.

Beth was sitting up in bed when he awoke the next morning. Gary stood from the chair and hugged her, lightly rubbed her belly, held both Beth and Tyson in his arms for a long, blissful moment.

"How are you feeling?" he asked.

"Groggy," Beth said.

"Have you been up long?"

"About an hour. A nurse stopped by earlier. We talked for a while."

Gary's eyes stayed on Beth. Her unwashed hair was stringy and she looked completely worn-out, but seeing her awake was beautiful to him, so beautiful.

"You're staring at me," Beth said.

"Yeah," Gary said.

"I look like some sort of weird sci-fi robot with these diodes taped to my forehead, don't I?"

A small smile crossed her lips. Gary reached over and grabbed her hand.

"I was just thinking about yesterday. I was scared, Beth. I was so scared."

"I don't know what happened. I can't remember anything at all."

"You were in the kitchen, and I heard a noise. By the time I got there, you were on the ground. Your eyes were closed and your body was shaking. I called nine-one-one and it seemed to take forever for the ambulance to arrive."

Gary shook his head. In some ways, the fall yesterday had been so much more terrifying than her first collapse. He'd been blindsided by her first collapse, but he'd been right there for this second one. He'd had an up-close-and-personal view of almost everything.

There was a knock at their door. Dr. Narita—the older Asian doctor they'd met with previously—stood in the doorway, wearing a white lab coat.

He smiled warmly and walked into the room.

"It's great to see you awake, Beth," he said. "How are you feeling?"

"A little bit of a headache. Tired."

"That's to be expected." Dr. Narita pulled up a stool next to Beth's bed and sat down.

"There are a few things I'd like to discuss," he said. "First off, we were extremely fortunate last night. Your vitals were dangerously low when you arrived. The doctors on duty were able to get everything under control, but we'd like to perform a few brain scans and tests to see just how serious this is. Based on what we find, we'll determine whether you can be released from the hospital."

Gary looked at Beth. The expression on her face was the same sad, somber look of helplessness that she'd had in the car after her first collapse, right before she started sobbing uncontrollably. This time, no tears fell.

"We were supposed to hold a fund-raiser tomorrow night," Beth said. "A way to raise money for the Germany treatment. Can I still go?"

"You'll have to reschedule it, I'm afraid," Dr. Narita said. "I wouldn't feel comfortable releasing you until we know more."

Dr. Narita asked if they had any more questions. They had none.

"Very well," he said. "I'll be in touch once we've figured out a schedule for later today and tomorrow."

Dr. Narita stood up from his stool and left. The room was eerily silent. No machines beeping. No voices drifting in from the hallway. No sounds outside the window.

"The bad news never ends, does it?" Beth finally said. Her voice was weak but it cut through the silence.

Beth stared straight ahead, at the plain white wall near the base of her bed. There was a frail sadness in her eyes.

"When does the good news come?" she said. "That's what I want to know. When does the good news come?"

"It's coming, Beth."

Gary wanted to say something more, but he couldn't think of anything that he hadn't already said hundreds of times before. *Stay positive. Things will work out. This will have a happy ending.*

MOST OF BETH'S MAJOR SCANS AND TESTS WERE SCHEDULED FOR TOMOR-row, so there was little for them to do that afternoon. After an hour of sitting, mostly in silence, Gary had wandered around the hospital until he found a lounge area on the children's floor. It had taken him a minute of rummaging in a toy bin to find what he was looking for: a Scrabble game.

"*State,*" he said now, laying out his tiles. The board was set up on a tray they'd balanced on Beth's belly, stabilized by a few wadded-up blankets. Gary was curled on the bed down by her feet, just able to see the top of the board.

"*State?* You wasted an S on a five-point word?" Beth said.

He shrugged. It was impossible to concentrate. He'd hoped the game would offer a distraction, even a slight one, but it didn't. Everything was still so fresh in his mind: the image of Beth sprawled out on the kitchen floor, the terror that gripped his heart in that moment, the frantic drive to the hospital.

"*Pitch*, and the C turns *hunk* into *chunk*," Beth said, laying out her tiles. She counted up the total. "Twenty-six points."

They played on. It wasn't only the memory of Beth's collapse that distracted Gary; it was the uncertainty of what would happen next, too. It just felt like bad news was coming. Like things were only going to get worse.

The game dragged on. When it finally ended, Beth counted up their totals and looked at Gary.

"Two hundred ninety-seven to a hundred forty-one. Gary, I destroyed you."

"Wasn't my day, I guess."

Beth cleared the tiles off the board. "Another?" she said.

It was either that or sit in silence.

"Sure," Gary said.

ONCE THE EVENING ARRIVED AND BETH DRIFTED OFF TO SLEEP, GARY RE-turned home. A dank, putrid stench hit him the moment he stepped through the door. As he walked down the hallway, the smell intensi-fied, lingered heavily in the air. In the kitchen, the eggs and pancake mix Beth had knocked over when she fell were streaked across the counter and splattered all over the floor. The eggs had hardened into a pasty, coagulated mixture. It reeked horribly. Gary grabbed a bottle of cleaner from under the sink and tore off a handful of paper towels. He got down on his knees and sprayed some cleaner onto the mess on the floor, wincing at the strong stench of the eggs.

So many emotions weighed on him, each like a heavy stone—grief, anguish, exhaustion. Guilt, too. All day, he kept thinking that he was in some way to blame for Beth's collapse, as if it were some sort of punishment for the unspeakable thing he'd done. He had played God and ended a man's life—and this was God's way of reminding him who was really in charge.

It took twenty minutes to clean up the mess in the kitchen. When he finished, he called Gloria from the community center. He told her they had to cancel tomorrow's fund-raiser. After that, he called the grocery store and told a manager about their situation. Both phone calls went well—Gloria said she'd hold their deposit and work with them to reschedule at a later date; the store manager agreed to give them a full refund for the groceries Beth had purchased for the now-canceled fund-raiser—but Gary barely had any reaction. It all seemed so irrelevant. So meaningless.

After the calls, he showered and put on a clean pair of jeans and a sweatshirt. Right as he finished dressing, Rod called his cell.

"How's Beth?" Rod asked.

"Better than yesterday," Gary said. "She's awake now. We'll know more after she's done with testing tomorrow."

"You still at the hospital?"

"Not now. I'm home."

"Any chance you could step away?"

"I probably have an hour free. Why?"

"I've been doing some thinking. I know how we can find him."

"Who?"

"The guy who cheated you out of the money. I think I know how to find him."

20

AFTER THEIR FATHER PASSED AWAY, GARY AND ROD INHERITED THE HOME they'd grown up in, a small two-story house about two miles from where Gary and Beth lived. Initially, the plan was to sell the house and split the proceeds evenly. But after talking with Beth, Gary decided to simply let Rod have it outright. At the time, Rod had just returned to River Falls after his failed stint in LA and was living in Gary and Beth's second bedroom.

Gary's gift to Rod was done partially out of the goodness of his heart, partially because he knew selling a decades-old house in a working-class neighborhood would be a nightmare in the local real estate market, but mostly because Rod was starting to wear out his welcome with them. He didn't wash dishes. He rarely cleaned up after himself. He stayed out until all hours of the night. It felt like living with an irresponsible college student. Their patience, particularly Beth's, had started to run thin.

So they'd given the house to Rod. A few months after he moved in, Rod had his first date with Sarah. Not even a year later, they were married and living together—in Gary and Rod's childhood home.

Ten minutes after hanging up the phone, Gary brought his car to a stop in the driveway of Rod's house and texted him to let him know he'd arrived. He looked out the windshield as he waited for his brother. Rod had changed little about the house since moving in. It still had the same white aluminum siding, the same green garage door their father had installed years ago, the same rusted basketball hoop where Rod and Gary played countless games of H-O-R-S-E growing up. But there were subtle changes, too, little additions that were evidence that Rod and Sarah were starting to make the home their own. A new mailbox hung next to the front door. Clusters of pine bushes were planted near the sidewalk out front. A wooden yard decoration that read BLESS THIS LOVELY HOME was in the ground next to the driveway—Sarah's doing, Gary guessed, as he couldn't imagine Rod would put something like that up.

Rod appeared, jogging out of the house, his blond hair flopping around his ears like he was a shaggy dog. He opened the Corolla's front door and sat down.

"What's going on, Rod?" Gary asked. Rod had refused to go into any more detail on the phone. The moment the call ended, Gary had driven straight over.

"I was doing some thinking," Rod said. "You can't remember anything about the guy you met with, right?"

"Right. I've been thinking about the meeting I had with him in the park constantly. Trying to remember something, some sort of clue into who he is. But there's nothing."

"Did you ever think you're looking in the wrong place? That it's not the meeting you should be focusing on?"

"Meaning what?"

"You mentioned a locker."

"Yeah. The locker. He put the gun and the down payment in the locker. Said he was going to put the full payment in there once I . . . well, once it was over. But that was a lie."

"You ever rented a storage locker before?"

"No."

"I have. When you rent one, you have to provide a name, an address, a phone number. All that stuff. They need a way to contact you in case your rental runs out, there's a break-in and your items get stolen, something like that."

"Okay."

"So I was thinking, if we could get the guy's application from the storage company, we could find out who he is, where he lives—everything."

Gary felt a flutter of excitement in his stomach. "You're right," he said.

"Where's the storage facility?"

"Other side of the city."

"What are you waiting for?" Rod said. "Let's go."

MICHIGAN MINI STORAGE WAS TWENTY MINUTES AWAY. IT TOOK THEM TEN to get there.

Looking into the window of the front office, Gary could see the same lanky college-age clerk, Brian, behind the counter. Once again, his face was buried in his smartphone.

Gary and Rod exited the car and walked up to the front door. When the door opened, Brian looked up. "Hey, it's you," he said. "The guy from a few days ago."

"Right," Gary said.

They approached the counter, Rod a few steps behind Gary. Brian had swapped out the Led Zeppelin T-shirt for a Foo Fighters one today. Looked to be the same jeans as he'd worn the other day. He hadn't shaved; wispy hairs still sprouted from under his chin and on his cheeks.

"Listen, I have a question," Gary said. "If I wanted to rent a locker here, what would I have to do?"

Brian grabbed a pad of paper from behind the counter. "You want to rent a locker, all you gotta do is fill out one of these." He tore off a sheet from the pad and handed it to Gary. "And pay, of course. We take it all—checks, cards, cash."

Gary looked at the paper. It was a generic application form. There were three blank fields—NAME, ADDRESS, and PHONE NUMBER— above a half page of terms and conditions. A line for a signature and date was at the bottom.

"Does everyone who rents a locker have to provide this info?" Gary asked.

"Every single one."

"So the person who rented locker one fifty-one, he filled out one of these applications? The guy I was asking you about the other day?"

"If he rented a locker, then, yeah. He filled one out."

"I need to see that application."

Brian stared at Gary, looked over at Rod, back to Gary.

"I can't let you see someone else's application."

"Why not?"

"It's illegal. My boss would kill me. I would lose my job. All of the above."

"I won't tell anyone," Gary said.

"Doesn't matter."

"Listen, we need to see that form," Rod said, jumping into the conversation.

"I can't, man. No way. This place may look like a shithole, but it's the only job I got."

"Hold on," Gary said. He hurried back outside to the parking lot, threw open the Corolla's front door, and opened the glove compartment. Underneath a few folded-up road maps was the stack of hundred-dollar bills held together by an orange band. His down payment. The money had stayed hidden in the glove compartment since he'd picked it up earlier.

Gary pulled off five bills and put the rest of the stack in his pocket. He walked back into the front office and set down the five hundred-dollar bills on the counter.

"Five hundred dollars," Gary said to Brian. "It's yours. All I need is the name of the person who rented locker one fifty-one. He has something of mine, and I need it."

"Is that real money?" Brian said, staring at the bills.

"It's real. You give me a name and it's yours."

"You promise you won't tell anyone?"

"I promise. No one will ever find out."

Brian grabbed the bills off the counter and stuffed them into his jeans pocket. "Locker one fifty-one, you say?"

"Yes."

"Give me a second."

"Thank you," Gary said.

Brian opened a large filing cabinet behind the counter. He riffled around inside and pulled out a sheet of paper. He looked at it for a second, then set it onto the counter.

"Good luck finding this guy," he said.

Gary picked up the sheet of paper, Rod looking over his shoulder. The three fields at the top of the form were filled out in messy cursive handwriting.

NAME: *Elmer Fudd*

ADDRESS: *123 Bugs Bunny Lane*

PHONE NUMBER: *123-456-7890*

Gary threw the paper back onto the counter.

"This is all the information you have?" he said.

"Yeah."

"Why would you rent out a locker to someone using a fake address and name?"

"The owner doesn't care if they use a fake name—hell, he probably prefers it. They use a fake name or number, we have no way of contacting them when their rental runs out. We keep whatever's inside, auction it off."

Gary grabbed the form and looked at it again. In the corner of the application, APRIL 10 was stamped in red ink.

"This date stamped in the corner," Gary said. "What does that mean?"

"That's the date he rented it."

Just a few days ago.

"Were you working when he rented it? Do you remember the guy who rented it?"

"I don't."

"Think back. He has a rough, sandpapery voice. About six foot tall. Bald."

"I don't know, man. The owner's on vacation and he's got me working all day, every day. I see hundreds of people every shift."

"Think. Please."

"I have no idea," Brian said. "Sorry."

Gary shook his head. A dead end. The flicker of hope was extinguished, just like that. He turned to leave, but before he took a step toward the door, Rod's hand shot out and grabbed his wrist.

"Gary."

Gary turned toward him. Rod's arm was extended, pointing behind the counter.

"Check that out," he said.

A few feet above Brian, bolted to the wall, was a small security camera. A red light flashed on the front of the camera.

"Does that thing work?" Rod said.

"Does what work?" Brian asked.

"The security camera over your head."

"Yeah. It works."

"How long do you keep the tapes from the camera?"

"I don't know. A couple weeks, usually."

"So you'd still have the tape from April tenth, right?"

"Yeah."

The flicker of hope reignited.

"I want to see that footage," Gary said.

BRIAN PROTESTED. ANOTHER FIVE HUNDRED DOLLARS CHANGED HIS MIND.

"Okay, we gotta make this quick," he said.

Gary and Rod followed Brian into a small room with a laptop computer set up on a table. Brian sat down in front of the computer, clicked a folder icon, and scrolled through a list of dates. Gary recognized the system—it was similar to the one they had at Ascension Outerwear.

"April tenth, right?" Brian said.

"Yeah."

He clicked on a file and a video player showing a black-and-white isometric view of the front office opened up on-screen.

"What time do you want to look at?"

"Whatever time the guy who rented locker one fifty-one was here," Gary said.

"I don't know when that was."

"This place is open twenty-four hours, right?"

"Yes, but a clerk is only here from seven a.m. to ten at night."

"And he couldn't have rented a locker without a clerk here, right?"

"Yeah."

"So start at seven a.m."

"Okay," Brian said.

He moved a scroll bar at the bottom of the video player and clicked Play. On-screen, Brian sat at the front counter, the camera positioned behind him. A timer in the corner of the screen counted up, one second at a time.

"It will take us all day if we move at this pace. Should I speed it up?"

"Yeah," Gary said. "Not too fast, though."

Brian tapped a key on the keyboard. The minutes displayed in the corner ticked away like seconds. On-screen, Brian moved at a quicker pace, his thumbs flying over his smartphone screen as he sent off a text, his arm darting out to adjust something on the counter, his steps rushed as he walked across the room.

Seven turned to seven thirty. Seven thirty to eight. A man walked through the front door at 8:13. It wasn't Shamrock. Another hour passed by. Another. Six people visited at various times over the noon hour, their movements blurred and quick in the sped-up video.

"You see your guy yet?" Brian said.

"Not yet."

"Someone could've just rented the locker for him, you know."

Gary nodded. If that was the case, there'd be no way to tell which person had rented the locker. They weren't able to see what people were writing on the paperwork from the camera's viewpoint.

Two o'clock turned into three, the time passing in a snap. People came more frequently now, faster, scurrying in and out the door. Four o'clock came and went.

"Come on," Gary said.

At exactly 5:18 p.m., Shamrock walked through the front door.

"Stop it," Gary said.

Brian clicked Pause. Shamrock was on-screen, frozen in midstep, halfway to the front counter. A scowl was on his face. He wore jeans and a white T-shirt. The short sleeves showed off forearms covered in tattoos. A jumbled, random mess of them.

"That's him?" Rod said.

"Yeah," Gary said. "That's him. He looks different, though."

"How so?"

"The tattoos. When I met him in the park, he was bundled up in a heavy coat. It covered the tattoos on his arms."

Gary focused on the tattoos, zigzag ink patterns of all shapes and sizes. They really did make him look like a different person.

"Play the video," Gary said. "Normal speed."

Brian tapped a key on the keyboard. On-screen, Shamrock walked up to the counter. His lips started moving, but there was no audio on the surveillance footage. Brian slid a piece of paper—probably the application form—over the counter. Shamrock filled it out and handed it back. Brian said something and Shamrock grabbed a bill from his wallet and set it on the counter, then turned away and left the room.

The entire visit hadn't even lasted a minute.

"Play it again," Gary said.

Brian backed the video up. Gary focused on the image of Shamrock on the computer screen, looking for anything that stood out about him—something he did, some way he moved.

On-screen, the same sequence of events played.

He walked to the front counter.

Filled out the application form.

Set it and his money onto the counter.

And left.

Nothing distinguishing stood out.

"Play it again," Gary said. "Slower this time."

Brian played the video again at half speed.

"Pause it," Rod said, halfway through the video.

Brian clicked Pause. The image frozen on-screen was of Shamrock, hunched over the front counter, one hand holding a pen as he filled out the application.

Rod leaned in close, so the computer screen was only a few inches from his face.

"What are you looking at?" Gary said.

"When he leans over like that, the sleeve on his T-shirt rides up on his arm. The tattoo that it reveals looks like it says something. Some sort of word. Right there on his left bicep."

Gary focused on Shamrock's left arm. Rod was right. In the middle of the swirling, spiraling tattoos was a series of letters on his upper left arm. They were written in a jagged, hard-to-read script.

"What does it say?"

"Can't tell," Rod said.

Gary squinted, focused on the tattoo. "Neither can I."

"Can you print a copy of this image?" Rod asked Brian.

"Sure." Brian clicked an icon, and a printer on the other side of the room whirred to life. He grabbed the sheet of paper that printed and handed it to Rod, who folded it and put it in his pocket.

"Let's head out," Rod said to Gary.

"Where to?"

"I have a friend I want to talk with," Rod said. "I think he can help us."

21

"WE CAN DO THIS THE EASY WAY OR WE CAN DO THIS THE HARD WAY."
Otto's voice carried in the dim, dank basement of Solid Gold Pawn. He stood on the edge of the room, surrounded by the cardboard boxes of merchandise stacked against the walls. Champ was off to one side, his hulking frame perched in front of the room's only doorway. His massive forearms were folded across his chest.

In the middle of the room, Scotty sat at the metal table. Otto stared at him—the filthy goatee, the tattoos snaking up his arms, that dumb-shit tribal tattoo winding across the left half of his face.

"What's it gonna be?" Otto said.

"The hell are you talking about, O?" Scotty said.

The only light in the room came from the single lightbulb dangling from the ceiling directly above Scotty. The glow was hazy and faint, but it was enough for Otto to see the fear in Scotty's eyes. No matter how street-tough Scotty's voice sounded or how hard the scowl on his face was, his eyes didn't lie.

"The easy way or the hard way," Otto said. "What's it gonna be?"

"I got no idea what—"

"The easy way, you admit you squealed to the cops about me. The hard way, I make you admit it."

Scotty's eyes skittered over to the stairway, to the hulking monster standing in front of it. He looked back at Otto, shook his head.

"Squealin' to the cops?" Scotty said. "You out of your mind? O, man. I got no—"

"Last chance," Otto said. "Devon Peterson—he was shaking me down. You're the one who gave him my name. You told him all about me. Admit it."

"I'm telling you, man, I got no idea what you're talking about," Scotty said.

Otto looked over at Champ.

"Looks like it's the hard way," he said.

Champ nodded. He uncrossed his arms and picked up a cinder block resting on the ground near his feet. He held the cinder block in one hand, carrying it across the room with no effort or struggle at all, as if it were made of foam instead of forty pounds of solid concrete.

When he reached the table next to Scotty, Champ hefted the cinder block up and slammed it onto the steel tabletop. It landed with a loud metallic thud that echoed in the small room.

Scotty stared at the cinder block, only a few inches away on the table. He fidgeted in his chair.

"Put your hand on the table," Otto said. "Spread out your fingers."

"Wait a sec," Scotty said. The street-tough inflection in his voice wavered. "Hold on."

"Put your hand on the fucking table. The left one."

Scotty cautiously set his left hand on the table, a few inches away from the cinder block. He slowly spread out his fingers. His chest rose and fell with his nervous breathing. He looked away from the cinder block and hung his head.

"Okay," Scotty said. His voice was so low it was almost a whisper.

"What was that?" Otto said.

"I said, okay," Scotty said, still staring at the ground. "It was me. I gave your name to that cop."

"You fucker," Otto said. "You fucking piece of shit."

Scotty lifted his head and looked at Otto. The fear in his eyes was gone, replaced by a wide-eyed, maniacal desperation.

"I had to do it—you gotta believe me, O," Scotty said, the words spewing from his mouth in a frantic rush. "This cop was shaking me down. He'd come to my tattoo shop every two weeks. All my money was going to this bastard; I told him I couldn't pay no more, he threatened to plant drugs on me and arrest me."

Scotty paused a moment to catch his breath. He was breathing so heavily he was practically hyperventilating. The hand spread out on the table was trembling.

"I already got two strikes," Scotty said. "A third woulda ended me. Woulda been lookin' at the next two decades of my life in prison. So I told him about you, said you were who I bought from, the next man up on the food chain. I had to tell him. You gotta believe me, O, I wouldn't—"

"Do it," Otto interrupted. His eyes locked with Champ's.

With a lightning-fast movement, Champ raised the cinder block into the air and smashed it down onto Scotty's splayed-out hand. There was a sickening squishing sound as Scotty's hand was crushed between the block and the table. Bones snapped. Scotty screamed. Or cried.

Or just yelled. It was impossible to pinpoint the exact sound coming from his lips.

"Do it again," Otto said.

Champ lifted the cinder block and smashed it back down on the table before Scotty could move his hand out of the way, crushing Scotty's hand between the cinder block and the table again. More bones in Scotty's hand crunched, snapped like twigs. Scotty screamed even louder.

Otto walked over to Scotty and grabbed him by the throat, leaned in so their faces were only inches apart.

"I coulda broken your right hand, you piece of shit," Otto said. "I coulda messed your right hand up so bad that you'd never ink another tattoo for the rest of your worthless life."

Up this close, Scotty's blubbering cries were earsplitting. His breaths were short and choppy. Tears streamed down his face.

"But I didn't," Otto said, his hand still pressed against Scotty's throat. "Your right hand's fine. You can keep inking your tattoos. I'm a pretty nice guy, ain't I?"

"Yeah," Scotty said.

"What was that?"

"Yeah. You're a nice guy."

Otto gave Scotty's throat a final hard squeeze and shoved him backward.

"You remember this. You remember how nice I am. And if you ever think about pulling something like this again—"

"I won't! I promise!"

"You better not," Otto said. "Now get outta here."

Scotty stood up from the table. His hand was bloody, the skin bright pink. The hand hung from the end of his arm like a limp, deflated balloon. Scotty cradled his left hand with his right, keeping it steady.

Otto watched as Scotty ascended the stairs, his sobs and heavy breathing fading as he disappeared upstairs. Once he was gone, Otto turned to Champ. "Nice work."

Champ nodded.

Otto looked down. There was a bloody handprint on the table, a few smudges of blood streaking out from it. Otto grabbed an aerosol can of disinfectant and a rag from a shelf in the corner of the basement. He sprayed disinfectant all over the tabletop and wiped away the mess.

He could've killed Scotty—probably should've, too—but he'd made his point. And in some ways, hearing Scotty's screams, seeing the anguish on his face, was more satisfying than the tranquillity of a dead body. He'd keep a close eye on Scotty, but he was sure that the son of a bitch had learned his lesson. He wouldn't dare make another mistake like this.

Otto wiped the final streak of blood from the tabletop. He threw the bloody rag into a trash can, and the two men walked back upstairs.

———

"SO, WHO IS THIS GUY WE'RE MEETING?" GARY ASKED AS HE PULLED THE Corolla off the highway.

"He owns a bar I used to go to all the time," Rod said beside him. "Me and this guy, we had us some wild times."

"And why are we seeing him?"

"Because he owns a tattoo shop, too. I'm hoping he can identify one of those tattoos on the guy's arms."

"The guy owns a tattoo shop and a bar?"

"I know, right? They're right next to each other, too," Rod said.

"I've seen it lead to a bunch of bad decisions. Good for business, though."

Gary stopped at an intersection, then drove through it, the car's headlights cutting through the night. Not even an hour earlier, he'd been dead tired, ready for bed—but finding the security-camera footage at the storage-rental facility had energized him.

Ten minutes later, Gary pulled into an empty parking lot in front of two businesses. Dirty Dozen Tattoo was the business on the right. Magnificent Seven was the bar on the left.

Inside, the bar looked like the type of place Gary remembered Rod hanging out in before he met Sarah. It was old and dirty, with walls covered in cheap faux-wood paneling. Next to the bar was a seating area with roughly ten wooden tables and mismatched chairs. In the corner, by the hallway that led to the bathrooms, was a broken Ms. Pac-Man machine and a few shuffleboard tables.

Even though it was almost ten p.m., the man behind the bar was the only person inside. He was at least 250 pounds, some of it muscle, some of it bulk. He had a thick beard. Various tattoos littered his arms. An eagle on one wrist. A spiral design on the other. Curls of barbed wire around one forearm.

"Rod Foster," the man said. "Jesus, haven't seen you in a while."

"Hey, Lucas," Rod replied. They slapped hands in greeting, and Rod introduced Gary as his brother. Gary shook one of the big man's hands.

"Where the hell have you been, man?" Lucas asked Rod.

"Went and got myself married," Rod said.

"Now, why would you go and do a dumb thing like that?"

"I met a girl. She's amazing. Beautiful. Smart."

"Is she blind, too? What's a girl like that doing with a guy like you?"

Rod smiled. "I ask myself that question every day."

"God, I'm gonna puke," Lucas said. "Don't tell me you're here to get her name tattooed on your arm."

"No."

"Your ass?"

"Not there, either."

"So, what's up?"

"I came here because I got a few questions for you."

"Sure. Pull up a chair. Either of you guys want a beer?"

They both declined. They sat down on barstools across from Lucas. Rod pulled the security-camera still frame from his pocket and set it on the bar.

"We're wondering if you can help us identify any of the tattoos on this guy's arms," Rod said. "Anything at all. What the tattoos mean, who could've inked them—anything."

"Who is this guy?"

"Long story."

Lucas stared at the picture. "Well, a few of these are prison tattoos."

"How can you tell?"

"Edges aren't as refined. They use homemade guns, ink from urine and blood. They're sloppy."

Gary nodded. Though it didn't really help them, it was interesting. He stayed silent as Rod continued with questions.

"What else?" Rod asked.

"Most of these, they're just designs. Don't mean anything. No logic or reason behind them."

"What about the tattoo on his upper left arm?" Rod continued to prod. "It looks like a word or a bunch of letters."

Lucas squinted, focused on the tattoo. "Yeah, it is," he said. "It's a word, all right."

"What does it say?" Rod asked.

"Gimme a sec."

Lucas left the room and returned a moment later with a small cylindrical magnifying lens, the type Gary had seen jewelers use. He examined the picture with it.

"Edgewood," Lucas said after a few seconds.

"Edgewood?" Rod asked.

"It's a neighborhood in the southern part of the city. A lot of people get their neighborhood tattooed on their body. It's a pride thing."

Gary knew the Edgewood neighborhood. It was a small, nasty five-square-mile section of the city where carjackings, assaults, even murder were practically daily occurrences. Infested with drugs, crime, and people who took part in both.

"Do any other tattoos stand out?" Rod asked.

"Like I said, most of them are just random designs," Lucas said. "Could mean something significant, or could just mean that he thought it looked cool."

Gary grabbed the sheet of paper. "Thank you so much for your help," he said. "One final question: Do you have any idea which tattoo parlor did his tattoos? Do you recognize a style or design—something like that? We're trying to find the man in the picture, and we don't have much to go on."

"Find this guy? Jesus, why the hell would you want to find a guy like him?"

"We've got some questions for him," Rod said.

"Well, if he has Edgewood tattooed on his body, chances are that's where he lives, hangs out. Probably where he was born. And if he lives in Edgewood, I'd be willing to bet that's where he got most of his tattoos. I'd go to the neighborhood and show this picture to every tattoo artist I could find. A guy with this many tattoos, someone's bound to recognize him before long. The tattoo community is a close one."

"Thanks, man," Rod said.

"I'd watch out, though," Lucas said. "This guy doesn't exactly look like the type who's gonna invite you in for milk and cookies."

"SO," ROD SAID AS THEY WALKED TOWARD THE COROLLA. "EDGEWOOD."

"Yeah," Gary said.

"Can't say I spend a lot of time in that part of the city."

"You and me both."

Gary held the printed still frame from the security camera. As he walked across the parking lot, he stared at Shamrock's scowling face and his arms, covered in prison tattoos. Just looking at him, Gary had the feeling that taking him on would end badly. But if he had any doubts, all he had to do was think of Beth, think of how close he was to losing her.

"So, what's our plan?" Rod asked. "Are we just gonna drive around Edgewood, visit tattoo shops, show people this photograph, and see if anyone recognizes him?"

"That's as good of a plan as I can come up with."

"Think we have a chance at finding him?"

"Maybe. Edgewood's not that big."

"Probably too late to get started tonight," Rod said as he and Gary sat down in the Corolla. "I wouldn't want to be anywhere near that neighborhood this late."

"Tomorrow," Gary said. "We'll go then."

200

22

JUST BEFORE NINE THAT NEXT MORNING, GARY DROVE INTO A NEIGHBOR-
hood that looked like an unclaimed junkyard; pure urban blight.
Paint peeled from the sides of dilapidated buildings in huge barklike
strips. Gutters sagged off roofs. The streets were littered with trash and
debris—yellowed newspapers, smashed soda cans, fast-food containers.

"They've really cleaned up the neighborhood, haven't they?" Rod
said.

Gary didn't react to Rod's comment. He stared straight ahead at
the crumbling, rotting neighborhood around them. Most of the ram-
shackle buildings they passed had sheets of plywood nailed over door-
ways and windows, large Xs spray-painted on them. Houses that had
been abandoned. Whole city blocks almost entirely filled with them,
one right after another. The yards in front of these houses were nothing more than large plots of dirt strewn with litter.

"Where to, Rod?" Gary asked.

Rod looked at a sheet of paper—a list of tattoo shops Gary found on the Internet last night. There were nine of them. Tattoo shops seemed to be the only type of business that was thriving in the neighborhood.

"A place called Two Devils Tattoo looks closest," Rod said. "Take a left at the next turn. Drive for another mile and we should see it."

Gary drove on. A few homeless people pushing shopping carts and rummaging through trash cans were the only signs of life.

"We must stick out like a sore thumb here," Gary said.

"Not gonna lie: I'm a little scared," Rod said.

They passed more bombed-out buildings, cars on cement blocks. The scene reminded Gary of the setting for a postapocalyptic movie.

"Think anyone will help us?" Rod asked.

"Maybe. Your buddy said the tattoo community is a close one. Hopefully, someone recognizes him."

Five minutes later, they arrived at Two Devils Tattoo. It was a stand-alone shop in a graffiti-tagged brick building with bars over the windows.

"We both going in?" Rod asked.

"One of us should stay in the car. Last thing I need is for the car to get stolen."

"I'll take this one. You stay here," Rod said. He exited the car and disappeared inside the tattoo parlor.

Alone in the car, Gary pulled out his phone and texted Beth. **Awake yet? How's it going?**

A moment later, her response: **Just woke up. Slow period now. You coming in?**

Gary looked out the window, at the crumbling neighborhood surrounding him.

*Just got out of bed. Taking a shower soon. I'll be at
hospital in an hour.*

K

See you soon. Love you.

Love you, too, came her response.

He put his phone back in his pocket and cleared his mind. Tried
to, at least; it was difficult to ignore the questions floating around his
head. *What will the doctors find once they start testing? Has Beth's condition
worsened? Is Tyson okay?*

Less than a minute later, Rod returned to the car. "The dude
looked at me like I was crazy," he said. "He'd never seen the guy in
the picture before."

"What about his tattoos? Did he recognize any of them?"

"Nope. I asked him, but he just shook his head."

Rod took a pen and crossed off Two Devils Tattoo from their list.

IT DIDN'T SEEM POSSIBLE, BUT THE NEXT TATTOO SHOP WAS IN EVEN WORSE
condition than Two Devils Tattoo. Graffiti tags everywhere. Even
though the windows were behind iron bars, three of them were
smashed out, with cardboard raggedly patched over them.

"I'll take this one," Gary said.

He grabbed the security-camera still frame from Rod and walked
up to the entrance.

The only person inside was a tattooed Hispanic girl with a nose ring,
standing behind the counter. A door to her left was covered over with a
black curtain. The room was barely big enough for the two of them.

"I'm looking for the man in this picture," Gary said, setting the picture in front of her. "I'm hoping you might recognize him."

Nose Ring looked at the picture for a brief moment. She glanced back up at Gary. "Never seen him."

"What about his tattoos? Do you recognize any of them? Do you know where he could've had them done?"

She glanced at the picture a second time. Again, no longer than a second.

"No idea."

"Please. This is important."

She pushed the picture across the counter. "Look, you interested in getting a tattoo or not? If not, get the hell outta here."

THAT VISIT WAS MORE PRODUCTIVE THAN THE NEXT SIX SHOPS ON THE LIST. They visited each one in rapid succession. Two were closed; the buildings were so ruined that it was difficult to tell whether they were permanently closed or if it was just too early in the morning for them to be open. Of the remaining shops, Rod went into two and Gary went into the other two. Each interaction was brief. They showed the picture to whoever was working and asked if they knew the man in the photograph. No one recognized him. They asked about his tattoos. No one recognized those, either.

And just like that, there was only one shop left on their list.

Slouched in the Corolla's front seat, Gary dejectedly stared out at the battered, decaying buildings slowly passing by. The Edgewood neighborhood was small enough that it hadn't even taken an hour to visit the first eight shops. Even though they hadn't been in the car for long, Gary was worn down. He'd constantly felt tense and on edge as they'd driven through the neighborhood, certain that one wrong turn would bring them face-to-face with some strung-out maniac who'd rob them at gunpoint.

"What are we going to do if this last shop is a dead end?" Rod asked.

"If it is, it is," Gary said. "We'll figure out something." His voice was dry and detached. The hope, the anticipation, that he'd felt at the start of the day was nearly gone. If they didn't get any information from this next tattoo shop, he didn't know what they'd do.

After driving in silence for five minutes, Gary stopped in front of Silverside Tattoos. The building had the same dilapidated, graffiti-tagged exterior as every other building in the neighborhood.

"You wanna head inside? Want me to?" Rod said.

"I'll do it."

"Good luck."

Gary walked up to the tattoo shop's front door and entered a small shop with a collection of posters on the walls, each depicting various tattoos. An unsmiling man stood behind the counter. He had tattoos everywhere—all over his arms, his neck, even some sort of intricate tattoo covering half his face. He wore a backward Tigers hat, slightly tilted to the side. His left hand was covered in a monstrous plaster cast that extended up to his elbow.

"I'm looking for the man in this photograph," Gary said, setting down the photo. "I'm hoping you can help me."

Face Tattoo glanced down at the photo, then looked up at Gary, his hard eyes locked on him. "You a cop?" he asked.

"No."

"You gotta tell me if you're a cop, you know. It's a law."

"I'm not a cop," Gary said. "I just need to find this man."

Face Tattoo slowly shook his head. "Never seen him," he said.

"The tattoo on his arm—it says Edgewood. I'm hoping he lives in the neighborhood, is from here—something like that."

"Lotsa people have *Edgewood* tattooed on them."

"Do you recognize any of his other tattoos?"

"No."

"Please," Gary said. "Take a long look."

"I did. Don't know him. Never seen him. Don't recognize his tattoos, neither."

Gary picked up the sheet of paper. "Thanks for your time," he said, and exited the shop.

The moment Gary stepped outside, the man behind the counter walked over to the door and locked it. With the hand not covered in a cast, he grabbed his phone and made a call.

———

"FEEL LIKE GETTING YOUR OTHER HAND BROKEN, YOU PIECE OF SHIT?" Otto answered his phone.

When he saw Scotty's name pop up on-screen, he wanted to throw his phone across the room. Some nerve—the little bastard had some nerve, calling him up like nothing had gone on between them.

"Hold up—I come in peace," Scotty said. "You'll want to hear this."

"What?"

"Some guy stopped by my shop, was asking about you. Trying to track you down. Figured you'd appreciate a little heads-up."

Holding his phone to his ear with one hand, Otto barely paid attention to the statement. He looked out at the pawnshop floor.

"Who was it?" he said.

"I dunno. Some asshole."

"That don't narrow it down. Everyone I know is an asshole."

"This guy, whoever he was," Scotty said, "I think he was a cop."

That got Otto's attention. His grip tightened around the phone. "A cop?"

"Yeah. I think so, at least."

"Did he have a badge? Driving a cop car?"

"Nah. He didn't belong in this neighborhood, though. He was some white dude. Driving a shitty Corolla. I figure he was undercover."

"He was driving a Corolla?"

"Yeah. A blue one."

A blue Corolla. Otto thought about that for a moment. "This guy, did he have brown hair?" he asked. "About forty or so? Skinny?"

"Yeah, that's the guy."

Gary Foster. It had to be.

"Listen, if you got heat on you, I need to know," Scotty said. "I told you I got two strikes on me. I can't do another—"

"The guy ain't a cop."

"He looked like one."

"He ain't no motherfucking cop. He's no one. Ain't nothing to worry about."

"All right. Just figured you'd wanna know that there's some guy showing your picture around, asking about your tattoos, trying to find you."

"Hold up—what picture?"

"This guy had a black-and-white photo of you. Looked like it was from a security camera or something. He showed it to me, asked if I recognized you."

A security camera? Willow Park didn't have any security cameras. That was the only time they'd met. That was the only—

The locker. The storage-rental place. There must've been a camera there.

Shit.

"This guy, he sets foot in your shop again, you let me know," Otto said.

"Yeah, sure. This mean we're cool, O? Now that I helped you out, gave you a heads-up?"

Otto ended the call without responding. He tossed the phone onto the countertop. *Son of a bitch.* Silverside Tattoos wasn't more than a half mile away from Solid Gold Pawn. Right neighborhood and everything. And the photograph Gary had—Otto didn't like that at all.

He knew what he had to do. He picked up his phone and made a call.

"Yo," came Champ's deep baritone voice.

"Got a problem I need your help with."

"Start talkin'."

"Some guy is looking into me. I want you to follow him around. Tell me what he's up to."

Otto gave Champ Gary's name, address, and car description.

"I get a chance, you want me to rough him up, send a message?" Champ asked.

Otto gave it a moment's thought. "Nah, just follow him around—for now," Otto said. "Tell me where he goes. I wanna see what he's up to."

"Piece of cake," Champ said.

———

"MAYBE WE MISSED A TATTOO SHOP," ROD SAID AS THEY DROVE BACK through the Edgewood neighborhood, headed to the interstate.

"Yeah," Gary said. "Maybe."

"Like an underground place that doesn't have a storefront. If we drive around more, maybe we'll find a place not listed online. And those two places that weren't open—maybe if we come back at another time, later in the day, they could be open then."

"Right," Gary said. "There's a chance. We can head back here tomorrow. I have to get back to the hospital now."

They left Edgewood and Gary pulled back onto the interstate, motoring at an even sixty miles an hour. As frustrating as the trip had been, there was a part of him that was relieved to be out of the neighborhood.

"We're not just gonna give up," Rod said. "We'll keep plugging away."

"Of course," Gary said.

"Edgewood isn't that big. We keep driving around, we're bound to find the guy, find someone who knows him, find some sort of clue."

"As long as we don't get robbed first," Gary said. "Or shot." He forced himself to chuckle.

"We got this, Gary," Rod said. "We're gonna find this guy."

———

BACK TO THE HOSPITAL. ANOTHER LONG DAY OF TESTING. GARY HELD Beth's hand as they walked through the hospital hallways, off to various departments for different tests. He waited outside the room as

Beth had head scans done, and sat next to her as she performed some balance and coordination testing—standing on one foot, squeezing small foam balls.

More waiting. They played another game of Scrabble and grabbed lunch in the cafeteria.

Later in the afternoon, Dr. Narita entered the room, carrying a manila folder. He greeted them and sat down on a stool. He asked questions for a few minutes, then began talking about the test results.

"The first tests we performed today measured Beth's strength and reaction time," he said. "These are the same tests she's performed every week over the past month."

He pulled a sheet of paper from the folder and handed it to Beth. Gary leaned over and looked at the assortment of numbers and other figures on the sheet.

"This sheet compares the results of today's testing with the previous results," Dr. Narita said. "You'll see that today's results were lower in everything—strength, reaction time, balance."

Beth asked, "What does that mean?"

"It means the disease is progressing at a faster rate than we'd anticipated. We didn't expect to see a noticeable decline in your motor skills for at least another month. Instead, it's happened much sooner."

Gary stared at Dr. Narita, fully focused on him. The murder, Shamrock, everything else going on—it all vanished from his mind. "So what now?" he asked.

"We'll release Beth to go home. There's not much we can do for her here. But I want to stress how serious this is. At this rate of decline, it may only be a month before Beth starts having difficulty performing everyday activities—gripping a spoon, typing, simple actions like those. Earlier, I estimated her expectancy at eight to twelve months.

If her condition continues to decline at this rate, she might only have half that. I don't want to alarm you. I just want to set realistic expectations."

Gary and Beth were silent, speechless.

"How are things progressing with the GOSKA trial?" Dr. Narita asked.

"We're trying to raise the money," Gary said.

They'd looked at the fund-raising site earlier. Twenty-two thousand dollars raised. Combined with the donation from Rod and Sarah, they were still nowhere close to what they needed.

Dr. Narita began talking to Beth about symptoms to be on the lookout for over the next week—temporary loss of smell, drowsiness, short-term memory loss. Gary listened but nothing registered. All he could think about was the time bomb inside Beth's skull, the ticking time bomb that could go off at any moment.

Tick-tock. Tick-tock. Tick-tock.

23

AFTER LEAVING THE HOSPITAL, GARY HELD BETH'S HAND AS THEY ENTERED their home and walked into the kitchen.

"Take a seat," he said to her.

Gary pulled two burgers from a McDonald's bag they'd picked up from the drive-through on the way home. He unwrapped the burgers and placed them on separate plates.

"It's not much of a welcome-home dinner, but it'll have to do," Gary said, setting a plate in front of Beth. "At least it beats hospital food."

No reaction from Beth. She had said little at the hospital, even less on the drive back, and hadn't spoken since they'd arrived home.

They ate their hamburgers in silence. Just as they finished, Beth reached across the table, extending her hand toward Gary. "Hold my hand for a second," she said.

Gary placed his hand over hers.

"There's something I want to say to you," Beth said, her words slow and deliberate. "It's something I've been meaning to say for a while."

She paused for a few seconds. Then:

"If something happens to me, if I don't make it through this, I want you to promise that you'll move on with your life. Okay?"

"Don't talk like that, Beth," Gary said. "Losing you isn't an option."

"It is. It's very much an option. I hope I make it through this, but I might not. And if I don't, I want you to move on with your life, try to find someone else, do your best to be happy."

"Beth, please—"

"I want to make this very, very clear," she continued. "I love you too much to see your life ruined if something happens to me. It would break my heart if you turned into some grieving widower who shuts himself off from everyone and mopes around the house all day. It would crush me if you weren't able to move on. Earlier, when I was flipping through that picture album of all those memories we've shared over the years, seeing how happy we were . . . I'd want you to try to have something like that with someone else."

"I don't—"

"I'd want you to find someone who'd be perfect for Tyson. Someone who'd love him as her own son. Someone who'd be there for his soccer games, someone who'd stay up late to help him with homework, someone who'd do all those things that mothers do."

Gary let go of her hand and cupped his hand across her face, making her shut her eyes. He looked at her pale skin, her sandy brunette hair.

"Beth, I refuse to even think about a life without you," he said.

She moved his hand back onto the table and held it, squeezing hard.

"I don't want to think about this, either," she said. "But I'm sick of all this bad news. And I guess it would make me feel just a little better if I know that you'll do your best to move on if something happens to me. Maybe sleep will come just a bit easier if I know that you'd be happy without me, that Tyson would have a mother who'd love him as much as I would. So, please, can you promise me?"

Gary nodded. "Okay," he said.

"Okay what?"

"If I lose you, I'll do my best to move on. To try to find someone for Tyson. To try to be happy."

"Promise?"

He knew it was a lie, knew he'd never be able to move on without her—and, on some level, Beth probably knew it, too—but Gary said it, anyway.

"Yeah, Beth. I promise."

———

"WHAT ABOUT THE CHURCH?" BETH ASKED.

They sat at the kitchen table, eating breakfast. Chobani yogurt for them both. Yesterday, Beth had called Gloria from the community center, but they couldn't reschedule the fund-raiser for at least another two weeks, so they'd spent most of the evening brainstorming various people and organizations to reach out to for help with the money. They continued brainstorming the next morning.

"The church?" Gary said. "We haven't been to church in two years."

"I know. But sometimes they put the money they collect from the offering toward a cause. We could talk with the pastor. What's her name?"

"Karen."

"Right, Karen. We could talk to her, ask if they could put a week or two's worth of that money toward the Germany treatment."

Gary took a sip of coffee from his Tigers mug. "Ninety percent of the congregation doesn't even know who we are," he said.

"Still. It wouldn't hurt to try." Beth stood up from the table and walked over to the sink, throwing the empty container of yogurt in the trash on her way. She wore one of her favorite pieces of maternity clothing: a plain gray tank top she claimed was the most comfortable shirt she'd ever owned, so comfortable that she often joked that she'd continue to wear the tank top after she gave birth, no matter how oversized it was. In the past few weeks, her belly had grown so much that a small sliver of her baby bump peeked out from the bottom of the top.

"I almost forgot," she said, returning to Gary. She grabbed her phone off the table and tapped the screen a few times. "I recorded a video earlier while you were sleeping, posted it to the fund-raising site. Take a look."

She handed the phone to Gary. The video showed Beth, displayed from the waist up, looking into the camera.

"Hi. My name is Beth Foster, and this"—she reached down and placed her hand on her belly—"is Tyson. Maybe you know me; maybe you don't. But I need your help."

Beth gave a quick recap of everything that had happened thus far as the video continued on.

"If you've already donated, thank you," Beth said at the end of the video. "Thank you *so* much. If you're just now hearing about this, a donation would mean the world to me—and Tyson. Thank you for any help you can provide."

The thirty-second-long video ended. "That's nice," Gary said, handing Beth her phone.

"I figure it's a little more personal. Plus the video is easier for people to share on the Internet, forward to others. I don't know if it will make much of a difference. But it can't hurt, right?"

"Of course, Beth. It looks great."

The front doorbell rang. As Beth disappeared down the hallway to answer it, Gary looked out the window at their backyard. The drifts of snow leftover from winter had almost entirely melted away and the outside world was cast as a slushy, muddy mess. The grass was splotchy and discolored. Puddles of dirty water had formed in roads and on sidewalks.

Beth reappeared, standing in the kitchen doorway, looking in at him. She had a dazed, far-off expression on her face, almost like she was in shock.

"Who is it?" Gary asked.

"It's a police detective," she said. "He says he wants to talk with you."

A sledgehammer slammed against Gary's gut. It was impossible to breathe. "A police detective?" he choked out.

"Yes. Gary, what—"

"I have no idea."

He forced himself out of his chair and followed Beth to the hallway. Detective Whitley stood inside their front door, wearing a blazer and jeans, the blazer a slightly darker shade than the one he'd worn four days ago.

"I had a few questions for you, Gary," he said. As before, Whitley showed no emotion. Strictly matter-of-fact.

"Regarding what?" Gary said.

"I'll get into that later," Whitley said. "For now, I'd like you to come down to the station with me. We can talk there."

Gary felt his lower jaw tremble. He wondered if the detective noticed it. "Can't we do this here?" he asked.

"No," Whitley said. No elaboration beyond that. Just that one definitive word.

"I really have no—"

"Come on. Let's get going."

Beth stood on the edge of the interaction, a few feet to the side. She stared at Gary, wide-eyed. Confused. Concerned.

"I'll be back shortly," he said to her.

He had no idea whether that was the truth.

24

SEATED IN THE BACKSEAT OF AN UNMARKED POLICE CRUISER, GARY looked out the window at the passing city. Detective Whitley was on the other side of a metal grating that separated the front and back seats, one hand resting on the steering wheel, staring through the windshield, saying nothing at all.

Gary slowly breathed in through his nose, out through his mouth, in through his nose, out through his mouth. He had the increasing feeling that the battle was lost before it had even begun. This was going to be it. The end of the road.

After fifteen minutes, they arrived at the River Falls police station. The police station was a plain, older two-story building with a brick facade. An American flag swayed from a flagpole in the middle of the small front lawn.

The cruiser approached a chain-link gate at the side of the station. The gate automatically slid open as they pulled up and Whitley drove into the fenced-in area. Past the gate was a small parking lot filled with empty police cruisers and unmarked cars. Whitley parked in a vacant stall, walked around to the rear door, and opened it. Gary followed the detective up to a door on the side of the building. Whitley ran a key card in front of a small black reader and an LED light on the reader flashed green.

Inside, they walked down a hallway to a small, windowless room. The room contained a metal table, two chairs, and nothing else.

"Take a seat," Whitley said.

Instead of following him inside, Whitley shut the door behind Gary. Alone in the room, Gary waited. The room grew hotter and stuffier with each passing second. He wiped away a thin layer of perspiration from his forehead.

The dead bolt on the door clicked, sounding like a clap of thunder in the quiet room. Whitley entered, carrying a small tape recorder in one hand and a crisp manila folder in the other. He placed both items on the table in front of Gary. He asked Gary if he could record their conversation and Gary told him it was fine. Whitley switched on the small machine.

The detective's eyes remained on Gary as he stated his name and rank into the tape recorder, then asked Gary to confirm his name, address, and date of birth. Gary's voice wavered as he spoke.

"Where were you on the night of April twelfth?" Whitley asked.

The directness of the question hit Gary like a punch. He blinked his eyes, cleared his throat.

"The twelfth?" Gary said. "I have no idea."

"Think about it," Whitley said.

Gary paused for a moment. There was, of course, nothing to think about. He knew exactly where he was.

"I really can't remember," Gary said.

"It was a Thursday."

Gary shook his head.

"It was a cold, miserable night," Whitley said.

"I really have no idea," Gary said. "I'm sorry."

"If it helps jog your memory at all, the twelfth was the night Devon Peterson was murdered."

Gary stared at Whitley, holding his eye contact. It took every square inch of willpower inside of him to keep his expression blank, to show no reaction to the statement.

"Is that the police officer you were asking about the other day?" Gary asked.

"Right. We found the hat from your store at the scene of the murder."

The room fell silent. Whitley pulled a small pad of paper from the interior pocket of his jacket and wrote in it. Gary wondered if he should say something to break the silence—tell the detective that he'd be happy to help with the investigation in any way, dig deeper into the mystery of the missing hat, something like that. No, he decided. Better to keep his mouth shut, keep his words to a minimum.

Whitley looked up from the pad of paper.

"What kind of car do you drive?" he asked.

Gary squirmed in his seat. "My car?" he said. "Why do you ask?"

"Because I'd like to know the answer."

"A Corolla."

"Year?"

"It's a 2004."

"Color?"

"Blue."

"License plate?"

"KJY-two-three-oh."

Whitley nodded. He lifted the manila envelope, pulled a sheet of paper from inside, and slid it across the table to Gary. It was a black-and-white photograph of a Corolla on a highway, taken from a high angle. The photo was too grainy to see the person behind the wheel, but the KJY-230 license plate was clearly visible.

"This the car?" Whitley asked. Then, before Gary could answer: "Of course it's the car. This photo was taken from an I-Eighty-four highway-surveillance camera on the night Devon was shot, a few miles from his house. Around twenty minutes after the murder happened."

Whitley tapped the photograph with the end of his pen. "So it looks like we answered the question of what you were doing on the night of April twelfth. From this photo, it appears that you were out driving your car in the general vicinity of Devon Peterson's house."

So calm. Whitley was so calm, so collected, so cool. And somehow, his soft-spoken, composed demeanor was far more intimidating than if he'd been screaming and yelling in rage. There was a surety to his words, a quiet confidence in everything he said.

"That's not me behind the wheel," Gary said. He said it without thinking, with no idea what he would say next.

"This isn't you?"

"No."

"It's your car."

"Someone must've stolen it."

"Someone steals the hat from your store, and then they steal your car?"

"Yeah. Maybe."

"Was your car missing the next morning?"

"No."

"Does anyone else have a set of keys?"

"There's a spare set at the business. Sometimes we use my car to make deliveries and pick up packages."

"Were the keys missing last time you checked?"

"No."

"So someone steals your car, drives it around for a while, then just returns it to the same parking spot? And puts the keys back?"

"It's a possibility."

"If I'm going to steal a car to go for a joyride, it sure isn't going to be a beat-to-shit Corolla that's over a decade old. That doesn't make any sense."

Gary nervously looked around the room, at the blank concrete walls that surrounded him. A lawyer—he should ask for a lawyer. Wasn't that the smart thing to do, ask for a lawyer before he said something that would doom him for good? Perhaps, but requesting a lawyer would be an instant admission of guilt, a de facto confession that he had something to hide. Only guilty people asked for lawyers.

The detective stared across the table. Gary tried to hold his eye contact but withered under Whitley's penetrating gaze. He looked down at his hands.

"I brought you down here, Gary, because something seems a little fishy," Whitley said. "We found a hat from your store at the scene of the crime, covered in Devon's blood. Then there's the security footage from your business that's missing—you claimed the camera's battery ran out and it stopped recording. Conveniently, this happens on the night of the murder. Maybe that's the truth, and it was just a coincidence. Or maybe the footage was deleted because it showed something incriminating—someone grabbing an item from the store's shelves right before the murder, for example."

Gary's hands were slick with sweat. He dried them on the leg of his pants underneath the table.

"And now," Whitley continued, "you can't remember where you were the night of the murder—but highway-camera footage shows your car in the general area of the murder, right after it happened. Now, that's a busy stretch of highway—we printed a list of over two hundred cars that passed by the security camera in the half hour after the murder, and there's always the chance the killer drove away from the scene through a residential neighborhood. Or was on foot and ran away. But I recognized your name when I saw it on the list. It made me suspicious. This whole thing makes me suspicious. None of this proves anything, but there's some definite smoke here. And where there's smoke, there's usually fire. Nothing you've said so far has dumped water on that fire."

"I had nothing to do with this."

"Prove it, then. Give me an alibi for the night of the twelfth. Around eleven o'clock."

"I was working at my store at that time."

"Can anyone confirm that?"

"I was alone."

"So you don't have an alibi."

Gary was sweating even more heavily now. He could feel the perspiration soaking into the fabric of his sweatshirt, pooling under his armpits, turning his ass into a swamp.

"Ever since the investigation started, we've been searching for a suspect," Whitely said, his voice remaining even, steady, librarian-like. "We've interviewed hundreds of people. Every detective on staff has been putting in fourteen-, sixteen-hour days. And all that time, all those interviews, they didn't produce a single suspect. Every lead turned into a dead end.

"But now, after all this work, we finally have a suspect: you. Right now, you're the only person we're looking at for this. All those fourteen-hour days aren't going to be spent looking for other suspects. They're going to be spent looking into you. If you had nothing to do with this, there's no need to worry. But if you had some involvement in this murder, we'll take you down. There's no doubt in my mind. If you were careless enough to leave behind the hat, careless enough to drive right by a traffic camera after the murder, then you were careless enough to make other mistakes. And we will find those mistakes."

"I didn't do this," Gary said. It was a struggle to get the words out.

"I can help you, Gary," Whitley said. "I want you to know that. I can help you if you had something to do with this. Just by looking at you, there's no way this was premeditated—you're not a cold-blooded killer. Maybe it was an accident, a misunderstanding, an argument that got out of control. Maybe Devon was threatening you, shaking down your business, and you killed him in self-defense. He's done some pretty shady stuff in the past. Targeted plenty of small businesses and stolen money from them. It wouldn't surprise me if he was doing it again.

"Whatever happened, I want you to know that I'm your friend here. I mean that with one hundred percent honesty. No bullshit whatsoever. If you were involved in this murder, there had to be a reason. You confess right now, tell me what happened, I'm sure I could get the charges reduced to manslaughter. You behave, and you could be out of jail in ten years. Maybe less."

Gary stayed silent. *Keep your mouth shut,* he told himself. *Stay quiet and hope that Whitley will just give up for now.*

The silence lasted for only a second before Whitley continued.

"I want you to think of your child, Gary," he said. "Your wife looked like she was about eight months along—am I right?"

Gary didn't respond.

"Well?" Whitley said.

"Thirty-five weeks," Gary said. "She's thirty-five weeks pregnant."

"Boy or girl?"

"Boy."

"A baby boy. You keep denying, we'll lock you away and you'll miss out on your son's entire life. He'll be a grown man by the time you're released—and that's only if you're lucky enough to be released. But if you admit to this and we reduce the charge to manslaughter, you'll be out before he's even in middle school. He'll still be a kid. You'll have plenty of time to have a role in his life. And your wife—you cooperate, and we could work something out, let you visit her frequently, so she doesn't have to go through her sickness alone."

Gary slowly shook his head. He marveled that his heart had beat so fast for so long without simply giving way.

"I had nothing to do with this," Gary said. "You must believe me."

"I don't," Whitley said, his eyes staying on Gary. "The more I talk with you, the more I don't believe a word you've said."

THE QUESTIONS ENDED SHORTLY AFTER THAT, AND WHITLEY LED GARY OUT of the interrogation room. Directly outside the door were two uniformed officers, standing with their arms crossed. Gary avoided looking at them as he walked past, but he could feel them staring at him, eyeing him over.

He followed Whitley down the hallway and then outside. After having been in the dark interrogation room for more than an hour, the sunlight stung Gary's eyes. He squinted until he adjusted to the glare.

They crossed the parking lot in silence, side by side, passing parked police cruisers and empty parking stalls.

"We called a cab to give you a ride home," Whitley said. "Should be here in a few minutes."

"Thank you," Gary said.

"I'll wait with you until it arrives. There are a few more things I want to say to you off the record, away from the recorder."

Gary was silent. He didn't want to talk anymore. He just wanted to go home and get back to—to Beth. Jesus, what must she be thinking? She was probably out of her mind, wondering why a police detective had taken him down to the station.

When they reached the edge of the street, they stopped walking. Gary looked both ways. No cab in sight. Just an empty road with a few cars parked on the side.

"I've worked as a cop for twenty-seven years," Whitley said, glancing over his shoulder to confirm no one was behind them. "I've been a detective for sixteen of those years. In that time, I've interviewed thousands of suspects about thousands of crimes. And I can say, without question, that you are the worst liar I've ever interviewed."

"I didn't—"

"Save your breath. I've never seen someone so uncomfortable during an interrogation. You displayed every telltale sign of someone who's lying his tail off. Anyone watching your interview could tell that you're hiding something. I don't know if you pulled the trigger or were involved with Devon's murder on a smaller level. But you're hiding something."

Gary scanned the road, left, right, looking for the cab. Still nothing.

"What I want to tell you is that I meant every single word I said back there," Whitley said. "I'm your friend here. I think Devon was a piece of shit. A racist, corrupt piece of shit. It makes me sick that we hired someone who was accused of the things he was—between you and me, word is he had some dirt on our police chief from back when they worked together in Detroit, and he got the job by threatening to make it public. There's no doubt in my mind he was up to the same crooked tricks here as he was in Detroit. I'm sure whoever killed him had a very good reason."

Gary scanned the road again, looking, looking. Still no cab.

"Most people in the department don't feel the same way, though. They are out for blood. They don't take the murder of another cop lightly. Devon may have been a scumbag, but he was our scumbag—that's the mentality of most cops. I overheard a few of them talking about planting a ham sandwich on the person who killed Devon. You know what a ham sandwich is?"

"No."

"A ham sandwich is an untraceable gun. Some officers keep one hidden in their car. They ever kill someone by accident—or need a justification for killing someone they meant to—they plant the ham sandwich on the corpse. And suddenly, the cop has a reason for pulling the trigger. He claims the suspect threatened him with the gun, wouldn't drop it when asked, and was killed in self-defense."

At the end of the block, a cab turned onto the street. It headed in the direction of the police station. Gary stared at it, relieved.

"If we find that you had something to do with this murder, you're the one they will come after. You're the one who's getting a ham sandwich. There are some loose cannons on this force—guys who are even worse than the criminals we lock up. Guys who were friends with Devon. I can protect you from them if you confess right now. If you keep denying, you're fair game. There's no telling what could happen if they find you on the street."

When the cab reached them, it slowed to a stop. Gary pulled on the backseat door handle. Before the door swung open, Whitley stopped it with his hand.

"Last chance, Gary," he said, holding the door. "This is your last chance to confess. We're looking into every aspect of your life. Every detective on staff is homing in on you. Looking for one mistake that you could have made. When—not if, but when—we connect you to the murder, something bad's gonna happen to you out there on the street. I can guarantee it."

Gary looked into Whitley's eyes. For a brief, fleeting moment, he thought about confessing. Whitley was so straightforward, so convincing, that the idea flashed into Gary's mind for a millisecond: *Confess and end this. End it for good.*

"You're wrong—dead wrong," Gary said instead. He said it with total certainty. Total conviction.

"Fair enough," Whitley said. "We'll be in touch."

A BLOCK AWAY FROM THE POLICE STATION, CHAMP SAT IN THE FRONT SEAT of a newer-model midnight black Cadillac CTS. He had the seat reclined to make it easier to fit inside. Even with the seat pushed back as far as it would go, his knees still pressed against the car's dashboard.

He looked out the windshield at the two men standing on the side of the road in front of the police station. The black dude was a cop—a detective Champ had seen around his neighborhood before. The other guy was Gary Foster, the guy Otto told him to follow.

"Son of a bitch," he muttered.

Champ watched as a cab neared the two men and Gary sat down in the backseat. Once the cab disappeared down the street and the cop walked back into the police station, Champ picked up his phone and made a call.

"What's up?" Otto said.

"I've been following your little friend like you wanted me to."

"And?"

"You got a problem on your hands," Champ said.

————

OTTO TALKED TO CHAMP FOR TWO MINUTES, THOUGH HE DID MORE LIStening than talking.

When Champ finished, Otto told him to keep following Gary and to call him if he saw anything else.

Seated behind the counter of Solid Gold Pawn, Otto slammed down the phone so forcibly that he was surprised the glass counter didn't shatter. He kicked a chair next to him, hurting his toes and sending it rolling across the pawnshop floor, where it banged against the wall.

The police. Somehow the police had connected Gary to the murder. Otto could only imagine the scene inside the interrogation room—Gary frightened out of his mind, ready to shit his pants, a veteran homicide detective bombarding him with questions the entire time.

This was never supposed to happen. The police clearly knew something. They'd let Gary go this time, but did Otto trust him to keep his mouth shut? To remain calm if detectives put the screws to him again? Hell no.

Otto balled both hands into fists and walked over to the chair resting against the wall. He kicked it again, sending it hurtling back across the room.

Champ had been right—this was a problem. A big one. And now he needed to take care of it.

But first, there was someone he wanted to see.

———

GARY WAS FINALLY ABLE TO BREATHE ONCE HE ARRIVED HOME.
He stepped inside and shut the front door behind him. He'd hoped that being in the safety of his home would help alleviate the dull, constant pounding in his head, but it did nothing. He still felt like—

"My God, I've been worried sick." Beth poked her head out from the kitchen and hurried down the hallway toward him.

"What did that police detective want?" she said.

"Nothing."

"Nothing? You were gone for over an hour."

"It was a big misunderstanding."

"About what?"

"There've been a few break-ins close to Ascension Outerwear. Kids vandalizing businesses, stealing merchandise—that sort of thing. The detective had a few pictures to show me, wanted to see if I recognized anyone."

He'd barely been able to think straight on the cab ride home, but he managed to come up with a story to give Beth. He was surprised at how good it sounded.

"That's it?" she said. "It took over an hour to look at some photographs?"

"Yeah. I spent more time sitting around and waiting than I did looking at photographs, to be honest." He gave her a smile that he hoped looked normal and reassuring.

"You're sure everything's okay?"

Gary nodded.

"That police detective seemed so serious."

"That's just how police detectives are, I guess." He kicked off his shoes. "I'm going to hop in for a quick shower. Wash the smell of that police station off me."

As he walked past her, Beth stared at him. Again, that look of suspicion. That look he'd become so familiar with lately.

He disappeared into the bathroom before Beth could say anything more. In the shower, Gary tried to clear his mind, but it was no use. All he could focus on was the interrogation with Whitley. Gary tried to recall everything he said to the detective, every gesture and response, trying to remember any mistakes or subtle confessions of guilt he might have made.

One thing in particular that Whitley said stuck with Gary. He told Gary that there had to be other mistakes he made on the night of the murder. Gary had no doubt the detective was right. If he left behind the hat and drove past a highway camera on his way home, then there were undoubtedly other mistakes, probably plenty of them. And Gary feared it was only a matter of time before they, too, were discovered.

———

AN HOUR AFTER HIS PHONE CALL WITH CHAMP ENDED, OTTO VISITED the Bum.

Everything was falling apart and he was pissed off. He still couldn't believe what Champ told him. The police were now involved. The very thing he wanted to avoid was happening. The fucking police were sniffing around.

Now he needed a release.

"You ready?" Otto said to the Bum. They were in the same alley as their last meeting, the same alley where they always met.

The Bum nodded. The poor bastard's face was littered with the aftermath of Otto's visit last week. The skin around a just-healing cut on his forehead was red and puffy. One of his eyes was bloodshot and half-closed. His split lower lip had dried blood caked on it. The fucker was wearing the same ratty flannel; it had splotches of crimson stained on the collar from their last encounter.

Otto took off his shamrock ring and slipped on a pair of latex gloves. Now that everything was going to hell, now that the police were closing in, he knew he'd have to get involved personally. That pissed him off most of all. He wanted to stay far away, but there was no other option now.

Otto took a few steps forward, glared at the Bum's scraggly, dirty face. He cocked his fist back and threw his first punch.

Many followed.

25

GARY TOLD BETH HE HAD A HEADACHE AND WENT TO THEIR BEDROOM after his shower. He spent the afternoon lying in bed alone, staring at the ceiling.

He thought about how hopeless it all seemed. The face-off was a mismatch of epic proportions. The entire police force, with decades of experience investigating crimes, squaring off against him, Gary Foster, a man with plenty to hide and no confidence whatsoever that any of it would remain hidden. Even if they found the money for the GOSKA trial, would he be around to celebrate? Would he be locked away in prison while she was abroad, undergoing treatment? Would he miss out on Tyson's birth, his childhood, his entire life?

Despite the millions of things racing around in his mind, Gary somehow fell asleep. He woke up in the late afternoon and found Beth sitting on the living-room couch.

"Did I miss much while I was sleeping?"

"Yeah. You did." She stared at him. "The police were here again."

Gary clenched his jaw, tried to show no reaction, no outward sign of the tingling unease in his chest. "The police?"

"I was making some phone calls when the doorbell rang," Beth said, her eyes staying on him. "It was the same guy who was here earlier. Detective Whitley."

The feeling in Gary's chest was burning now, raging like a wildfire. "What did he want?"

"He kept asking me about the night of the twelfth. He wanted to know if I could verify that you were here around eleven o'clock."

"What did you tell him?"

"The truth—you were at the store and got back here around midnight," she said. "He had some really weird questions for me, too. He asked if you were ever violent toward me, if you lost your temper frequently. He wanted to know if we had any guns in the house."

Gary inhaled deeply through his nostrils, closed his eyes for a moment. "You should've woken me up, Beth."

"I was going to, but the detective said he didn't want you around when he was talking to me," Beth said. She nibbled on her lower lip and toyed with a strand of hair. She was nervous, Gary could tell. Concerned. "Gary, what is going on?"

"I have no idea."

"You better find out soon. The police are talking to our friends, too. People have been calling me nonstop, telling me the police were asking about you."

Gary thought back to what Whitley said during the interview. *We're looking into every aspect of your life. Every detective on staff is homing in on you.*

He remembered that he'd put his phone on silent when he was in the bedroom. He pulled it from his pocket.

Seven missed calls. Twice as many unread text messages.

Gary scrolled through the messages.

His old coworker Dave Stephens: *Police were here asking me about you . . . everything all right?!?*

Their neighbor Kenny Coleman: *You ok? Just had a cop ask some questions about you.*

More texts from friends, neighbors, others. All wondering why the police were asking about him.

"The detective told me it's an active investigation—an active investigation into what?" Beth said. Her voice was so high she was almost yelling.

"Just calm down, Beth," Gary said, starting slowly. He had no idea where he was heading with this, but he had to tell Beth something, had to at least attempt to put her at ease. "Do you remember that cop who was killed a few nights ago? The police found a hat at the scene of the crime. It turns out the hat went missing from our store last week. For some reason, this detective thinks there's something fishy about that, so he keeps badgering me. Asking me questions about the hat." Gary offered a small laugh. It sounded forced, even to him. He only hoped Beth didn't notice. "As if I gave the hat to the killer or something like that. As if I had something to do with this. It's ridiculous."

Beth stared at him, still working the strand of hair around her finger.

"They're asking you about a *murder*?" she said.

"Yes, but it's not that big of a deal," Gary said. He grabbed the hand toying with her hair and held it, lacing his fingers into hers. "Listen, honey. Don't worry about it. It's not just me this detective is looking at. He's talking to anyone who could've come in contact with the hat and eliminating them one by one. Hundreds of people. Thousands. He was even talking to Rod. Basically, he's just covering his bases."

Beth shook her head. "Why did he ask if you were ever violent toward me?" she asked. "Why did he ask if you own a gun? That seems like more than covering his bases."

"I'm sure he's asking those same questions to everyone he talks to. There's no need to worry. Seriously. Once the detective realizes I had nothing to do with this, he'll cross me off the list and move on. It'll probably happen tomorrow. Today, even."

Beth paused for a moment, absorbed it all. She stood up from the couch and walked over to the window that overlooked their backyard. "So, earlier, when you went down to the police station, it wasn't because the police wanted to ask about some break-ins that happened around Ascension?"

"No. I just said that. I'm sorry, but I didn't want to put you under any more stress." As before, Gary was surprised by how easily all of the lies came to him, how smoothly they blended together. "With everything you're going through, you didn't need another thing to worry about. I really figured this would be over by now. Figured I could tell you everything once it was done and we could have a laugh about it."

Beth sat back down on the couch. Gary put an arm around her and moved in close, just far enough away so he could still look her in the eye.

"I'm sorry I didn't tell you about this," he said. "I really am. Like I said, it's just a big misunderstanding. It will be over soon."

She tilted her head and looked back at him. Stared at him. And this time, there seemed to be more than suspicion in her eyes. Like she didn't just suspect he was lying to her. It was like she knew he was.

THEY ATE DINNER TOGETHER. IT WAS LONG AND MOSTLY SILENT. BETH SPENT almost all of it glancing between her food and the window that over-looked the backyard.

After dinner, Gary walked into the bathroom and grabbed the bottle of Tylenol from the medicine cabinet. He unscrewed the cap and dumped the tablets into the toilet, flushing it as the tablets began to dissolve in the water. He carried the empty bottle into the kitchen.

"I'm heading out to get some Tylenol," he said, shaking the empty bottle.

He had to get out of the house, but he couldn't simply disappear after their earlier conversation. Thankfully, Beth didn't question why the bottle of Tylenol they'd purchased just last week was already empty. Gary kissed her, grabbed his keys off the counter, and left.

With no destination in mind, he drove. Up one street, down another. Sometimes he drove fast, sometimes slow. Sometimes north, sometimes south.

There were a million things on his mind. The police. Beth. Tyson.

He drove more. Through downtown. On the interstate. He took an off-ramp and drove on through a silent, dark residential neighborhood.

He thought about the police as he drove the neighborhood streets. Right now, at this exact moment, what were they doing? Were they still talking to his friends, former employers? Carefully searching the crime scene for any missed evidence? Were they poring over printouts that covered everything about his life, every little detail? Were they—

In his rearview mirror, Gary saw a pair of headlights on his tail.

Two beams, shining out from an unseen, shadowy car. He wasn't even driving twenty-five miles an hour, but the headlights were so close that if he tapped his brakes he'd get rear-ended.

He turned left. The headlights followed.

He turned right. The headlights followed.

Gary gripped the steering wheel tighter. He focused on the mirror. It was too dark to tell the make of the car behind him, but Gary was suddenly sure that it was a cop car. He heard Whitley's voice in his head: *There are some loose cannons on this force—guys who are even worse than the criminals we lock up. Guys who were friends with Devon. There's no telling what could happen if they find you on the street.*

What was the term Whitley used? *A ham sandwich.* An untraceable gun. Kill someone, plant the gun on the corpse, and get away with it.

Gary felt his heart hiccup in his chest as he focused on those headlights in his mirror. Just as he was about to floor it and try to ditch the tail, he passed under a streetlight and the car behind him was briefly illuminated. A red midsize sedan; looked like an older Buick. Two teenagers in the front seat. At least two more in the backseat.

A few moments later, the car flashed its high beams and sped around Gary. As the car passed, one of the teenagers leaned out the backseat window and extended his middle finger; the rest of the teenagers in the car laughed.

Gary watched the car until it disappeared. He exhaled, only then aware he'd been holding his breath. He was safe. . . . But he didn't feel like it. Was this what his life would be like from now on? Constantly on edge. Paranoid. Unable to leave the house without the fear of something happening to him.

HE DROVE SO MUCH THAT HE HAD TO FILL THE CAR UP WITH GAS.

An hour passed. More driving.

Just as he was about to head home, his phone rang. He figured it was Beth, calling to see why he'd disappeared again. He had no idea what explanation he'd come up with this time. He'd have to think of some sort of excuse, an emergency at the store, something like that.

But when he glanced at the phone in the car's cup holder, it wasn't Beth's name he saw.

The screen read UNKNOWN.

Seeing that lone word, Gary felt a numb sensation spread throughout his body. Despite what the screen said, he knew exactly who was calling. Somehow, he knew.

He pulled the car to the side of the road and answered the phone.

"What did the police want?"

That voice. He recognized it immediately. That distinctive, scratchy voice. It was the first time Gary had heard Shamrock's voice since their last phone call, the brief call to confirm the murder was done. Hearing that voice again sparked something—anger, fury—to life inside of him.

"The money you cheated me out of," Gary said. "Where is it?"

"Why were you at the police station? What did they want?"

"We had a deal," Gary said, almost yelling. "Listen, you bastard—"

"No, you listen to me," Shamrock's voice roared back, so loud that Gary moved the phone away from his ear. "You don't tell me what the cops wanted in the next five seconds, I'll end this for good. Seven eighty-four Wayne Street—I could have someone there in ten minutes.

Put a bullet in your wife's skull, show you what happens when you fuck with me."

His address. Hearing Shamrock speak his address floored Gary, left him stunned.

"I got your attention?" Shamrock said.

"Yes."

"Good. Now, why were you at the police station earlier?"

"A detective had some questions for me."

"Questions about Devon Peterson?"

"Yes." There was no reason to lie.

Silence on the other end of the phone. Then:

"I want to meet with you. You know the Alpine Development?"

"I know it."

"Meet me there."

"Why?"

"To talk." There was a lot of topspin on the word *talk*.

"I want to meet somewhere more public," Gary said.

"No. Alpine Development. Thirty minutes. Don't try nothing funny. You don't show, you'll regret it. Your wife will, too."

The line went dead.

WHEN THE CALL ENDED, GARY RESTED HIS ELBOWS ON THE STEERING WHEEL and buried his head in his hands. He grabbed two fistfuls of hair and pulled as hard as he could.

It was over. There was no doubt in his mind. If Shamrock wanted to talk, they could've talked on the phone, at a restaurant. Instead, he wanted to meet at the Alpine Development, an abandoned housing project on the edge of town—isolated, out in the middle of nowhere.

There was no question in Gary's mind: if he showed up at the Alpine Development, he would be murdered.

Unless . . .

He had an idea, but he had to hurry. Gary pulled out onto the road and floored the accelerator. Ten minutes later, he approached the slanted street parking in front of Ascension Outerwear. There were no cars out front and the store was dark.

He parked his car and entered the store. Without flipping on the lights, he walked to the back room. He crouched down and pulled back the corner of the plywood wall. Reaching behind it, he moved some pillowy insulation to the side and felt around until his hands found the cold steel of the handgun he'd used to murder Devon Peterson. With every nearby body of water still frozen solid from the unseasonably late cold weather, the gun had remained hidden behind the wall, buried under the insulation, since the murder.

He pulled out the gun, carried it across the room, and placed it on top of the desk, right next to the computer. He stared at the gun, his expression blank. So this was what things had come to. More death. More bloodshed. Showing up at the Alpine Development and taking on Shamrock and anyone else who was waiting. A shoot-out in the middle of nowhere, like a scene from an action movie.

Just thinking about it, Gary felt a throbbing pulse in the center of his forehead. He massaged his temples, but it did nothing. Eyes focused on the gun, he realized how desperate and ridiculous this was. He wasn't Rambo. He wasn't Schwarzenegger. He was just a normal guy. Showing up with a gun and shooting up the place would be a death wish. He wouldn't stand a chance.

He felt the pulse in his head intensify, harder and faster, more of a pounding now. It circulated throughout his body—a burning in his chest, a trembling in his arms. He was like a pot that had reached its boiling point, a balloon that had finally popped. Everything, all of this—it was too much to keep bottled up inside.

He clenched his fist and smashed it down onto the keyboard. He gritted his teeth and smashed it down again—a second time, a third time, a fourth time. The last blow snapped off the Shift key.

His breaths were hot and heavy now; he was snorting like a bull in heat. Gary yanked the keyboard from the CPU and threw it across the room. It skidded across the floor and came to rest against the wall. He shoved the computer monitor; it toppled off the desk but didn't shatter when it hit the ground.

He jumped out from behind the desk, his eyes scanning the room, looking for something to throw, to break, to pound. He grabbed a few folders of invoices and wildly tossed them so the invoices scattered like snowflakes. He charged into a filing cabinet and rammed his shoulder into it, flipping it onto its side. He ran over to the wall and kicked it. The plywood cracked. Another kick, and the crack was louder. A third kick left a gaping hole.

Gary let loose, swinging and kicking at everything in sight—the desk, the wall, another filing cabinet. He tore into—

"What the hell?"

The voice startled Gary. He turned around. Rod stood next to the door, looking at the carnage in the room. The upturned filing cabinet. The destroyed plywood wall. The sheets of paper scattered everywhere.

"What's going on, Gary?"

Panting heavily, his thin cheeks almost purple, Gary stared at his brother.

"Why are you here, Rod?" Gary asked.

"I was gonna come in and get some things done," Rod said, still scanning the destroyed room. "I saw your car out front and figured I'd stop in, ask why you've been ignoring my texts and calls all day. Now, you answer me: What the hell is going on?" Rod stopped looking around the room when his eyes fell on the computer desk. "And why is there a gun on the desk?"

Gary walked across the room and slumped down into the desk chair. He waited until his breathing slowed before he spoke. "It's over, Rod," he said. "Everything's gone to hell."

"What do you mean?"

"The police came by the house this morning and took me down to the station. The same detective who was here. Whitley. He told me point-blank that he thinks I'm the one who committed the murder."

"What? How does he know?"

"A highway camera captured my car near the crime scene right after the murder. And Whitley knows I erased the security tape; he didn't buy the story about the battery running out. I tried to lie my way out of it but only dug the hole deeper."

Gary shook his head. He still couldn't believe how quickly everything had fallen apart. "Then Shamrock called me again. He knows I talked to the police. He must've been watching me. Now he wants to meet up. He said he just wants to talk, but . . ." Gary's voice cracked and he looked down at his feet. "I think . . . I think he's going to kill me, Rod. I'm the only link connecting him to the murder. He eliminates me, he'll be completely in the clear."

"Jesus. Where are you meeting him?"

"The Alpine Development."

"Right now?"

"Yeah. Right now. Late at night. All the way out there."

"Don't go."

"He said he'll kill Beth if I don't show up. He knows our address, said he could be there in ten minutes. I'm not putting her at risk. No matter what, I'm not putting her at risk."

"And the gun?"

Gary looked at the gun. It was the only item resting on top of the desk; everything else had been knocked off or thrown to the ground.

"I was going to bring the gun with me," Gary said. "I was going to shoot Shamrock. Blow him away, kill anyone who got in my way, and escape." He shook his head. "But that'd be suicide. I wouldn't stand a chance. No, the gun's staying here. I'm going to try to talk my way out of this. Somehow, I have to convince him that his secret is safe with me. Convince him that I'll never, ever confess anything to the police."

"Gary, you can't just meet this guy out in the middle of nowhere. You have to do something."

"There's nothing else to do. All I can do is try to convince him he has nothing to worry about. That's my only chance."

Just then, Gary's phone chimed with a text. He pulled the phone from his pocket and looked at the message. It was from Beth.

Hello? Get lost at the drugstore?

His thumbs hovered over the screen as he thought about how to respond. Instead of typing a message, he brought Beth's number up on-screen and called her.

"Beth," he said. "I'm sorry."

"Where are you?"

"I stopped by Ascension. I'm here with Rod. I didn't call because I thought I'd only be here a minute. But some stuff came up and . . ." He closed his eyes and felt a wave of emotion wash over him. He realized that this phone call might be the last time he ever spoke to his wife. "Oh, God, Beth."

"What's wrong?"

"Nothing," he said. He paused to compose himself. "It's nothing. I just wanted you to know I might be a while. This is going to take a little longer than I thought. I'm sorry I didn't call."

"Gary, your voice sounds different. What is it?"

"I told you, Beth. It's nothing."

Gary waited for her response, but there was just silence. The silence spoke volumes. Even through the phone, he could tell she didn't believe him. He didn't have to look into her eyes to know that.

Gary glanced at the clock on the wall. Time was running short. He had to get out of here.

"I really have to go right now, Beth. I'm sorry."

"Go ahead, then. We'll talk when you get home. You can't keep disappearing and wandering off like this without telling me anything. I don't like not knowing what's going on."

"I'm sorry." Gary took a deep breath. "Just remember I love you, okay? Never forget that. I love you more than anything in this world. I always have. I always will."

"You sound so dramatic," she said. There was no humor in her voice.

"I just felt like saying that. Wanted to make sure you know."

"Well, I love you, too."

The call ended, and he put the phone back in his pocket. He walked over to Rod and hugged his brother.

"Not a word of this to Beth," he said, squeezing Rod tight. "If something happens, never speak a word of this to Beth."

Gary pulled away from Rod and walked out of the store, stepping into the dark, peaceful night.

26

PERHAPS NO STRUCTURE IN TOWN REPRESENTED THE DOWNFALL OF RIVER Falls more than the Alpine housing development.

The project had been green-lighted twenty years earlier, envisioned as a cutting-edge community within a community, filled with residential buildings, retail stores, and more. Twenty acres of undeveloped land just past the western edge of the city were purchased for the development, the centerpiece of which was a thousand-unit, twenty-story high-rise housing structure—a grand, glass-covered building that would be the second-tallest building in the city.

But shortly after construction began, the local real estate market was hit hard. The Alpine Development was halted, with plans to resume construction once the market rebounded. The rebound never happened, and now, more than two decades later, the Alpine Development still stood on the edge of town—a massive plot of land a mile outside of the city, populated with half-finished structures and empty shells of buildings.

Fifteen minutes after leaving Ascension Outerwear, Gary turned onto the gravel road that led to the development. The beams from his headlights illuminated the area as he passed structures, some partially completed, some nothing more than concrete pilings planted in the ground.

Nature had started to reclaim much of the land. He passed a parking lot overcome with weeds and small sinkholes. An orange No Trespassing sign was covered in long, winding vines that crawled up from the ground.

He drove on for another minute, until his headlights shone on a person standing in the middle of the road, roughly a mile in.

He came into focus in parts. He was a mountain of a man with stubble on his head and cheeks, at least six foot four, with more than enough weight to match. He wore a T-shirt and Adidas track pants, the sleeves of the shirt hugging tight against enormous, muscular arms. He wore black gloves. In one hand, he held a roll of duct tape. In his other hand, he held a handgun. He made no effort to conceal the gun.

The big guy motioned to Gary. Gary pulled the Corolla to a stop roughly ten feet away. He turned the car off and opened the door, stepping outside.

"Move away from the car," the big guy said in a deep voice.

Gary did as instructed.

"Stand still."

The big guy walked over to Gary and worked free a length of duct tape from the roll. The tape was thick, with tough reinforcing threads baked into the silver plastic coating.

"Turn around and put your hands behind you."

Gary put his hands behind him, down by his lower back.

The big guy forced Gary's hands closer together and wrapped the duct tape around his wrists. Around and around. When he finished, the tape was so tight that Gary couldn't move his wrists at all. His left arm was wrenched at an awkward angle, causing a dull pain in his shoulder.

From behind him, Gary felt a hand push him in the back.

"Walk up the stairs to the door."

The stairs in question led up the outside of a salt-eroded, redbrick building. On the second floor was a door, next to a set of windows that were smashed out and open to the elements.

Gary slowly ascended the stairs. Once he reached the top, the big guy pushed open the door with one of his gloved hands.

Inside was a nearly empty room covered in a layer of cobwebs and dust. Two tables with chairs pushed under them rested in the corner, next to an empty and darkened vending machine. A dartboard with no darts hung from the wall. A row of cupboards ran along one wall, above a sink that was covered in filth. It looked to be a lounge area or some sort of large break room.

Sitting on a chair in the middle of the room was Shamrock. He wore a white T-shirt, the tattoos on his arms creeping out from under the sleeves. He stared at Gary, but his eyes gave away no emotion.

"Bring him in, Champ," he said.

Another hard shove to his back, and Gary walked forward. The floor was made up of long wooden boards nailed together. The boards creaked as Gary walked toward Shamrock. Suddenly, Gary felt the big guy behind him push down on his shoulders. Gary tumbled to the ground, landing on his rear. With his hands immobile behind his back, he was unable to brace his fall. The impact caused a jolt of pain in his lower back.

"Head back downstairs, Champ. Keep an eye out."

The big guy—Champ, Shamrock had called him—walked to the door they'd entered through and disappeared.

Shamrock sat in his chair like a statue, staring down at Gary. Like Champ, he also wore black gloves.

"The police don't have much," Gary said. The words echoed in the empty room.

"That ain't the point," came the response. "The point is that the police were never supposed to be involved, and now they are. What the hell happened?"

Total honesty—Gary was going to be completely honest, hide nothing.

"The hat I was wearing the night of the murder fell off when I was running away," he said. "And the police have a highway-camera photo of my car in the area after the murder."

"So they have evidence linking you to the crime."

"It can all be explained away," Gary said. He knew if he had any chance of leaving the room alive, he had to convince Shamrock that everything was under control. "The hat is from my store but it could belong to anyone. And the photograph doesn't show who's behind the wheel of my car. It's blurry."

Shamrock stared down at him, unblinking.

"You have to believe me: the police have nothing," Gary said. "If they had any incriminating evidence, they would've arrested me. If they had anything solid that linked me to the crime, there's no way I'd be a free man."

"The police could still find something else."

"They won't."

"What if they do?"

Gary's mind was spinning; he tried to sound calm. "Then they'll arrest me," he said. "And I will deny having anything to do with this until my last dying breath. I murdered a cop—if I go down for this, I'm in jail for the rest of my life. Even if I turn you in, I'm not getting out of that. There's no reason for me to mention anything about you to the police."

Shamrock got up from his chair and limped over to the empty vending machine. He stared at it, as if he were studying an invisible row of candy bars. "Right now, I got two options," he said, slowly walking back toward Gary. "The first option is that I believe everything you're telling me and I let you live. I trust you and hope that you're telling the truth, and I spend the rest of my life worrying that you'll get arrested. Spend every day worrying that you'll mention me to the cops and I'll have them on my ass, trying to find me."

He sat back down in the chair in the middle of the room.

"The second option is that I kill you now and have nothing to worry about."

He steepled his fingers, looked at Gary. "Two options," he said. "Letting you live leaves a lot of loose ends. Killing you takes care of everything."

"Killing me would be a mistake," Gary said. "Right now, I'm the prime suspect in the murder of Devon Peterson. If I'm suddenly murdered the day after the police interrogated me, the police will know someone killed me to keep me quiet. They will know that other people were involved in Devon's murder, and they will want to know who those people are. And if the police start sniffing around, there's no telling what they'll find."

Gary licked his lips and stared up at Shamrock. "But if you let me live and I'm arrested for Devon's murder, never in a million years will

I confess to the murder or mention you. Never. Not under any circumstances."

One side of Shamrock's mouth curled into a smile.

"You're a smart little fucker," he said. "Gotta hand it to you. You show up with a bullet in your skull a day after the police questioned you, they'll know something's up. They'll know someone killed you to keep you quiet. You're right about that."

"Then let me live," Gary said. He heard the desperate tone in his voice and tried to sound strong and confident instead. "Your secret is safe. You and I will be the only people who will ever know what happened. Believe me."

Shamrock looked away and stared past the shattered windows, out at the darkened night sky. He appeared to be a man in deep contemplation. Gary held his breath as he waited for a response.

Before that response came, the ringing of a phone pierced through the quiet room. Shamrock pulled his cell from his pants pocket and listened for fifteen seconds, twenty seconds. Finally, he spoke.

"Don't kill him," he said into the phone. "Not yet. Bring him inside."

"YOU ALMOST HAD ME CONVINCED," SHAMROCK SAID TO GARY AFTER ENDING the call. "I almost believed you."

"What—" Gary said.

"Don't talk."

The door to the room opened a few moments later. There were two people in the doorway, one behind the other. The man in the rear was the big guy from outside. Champ. He carried a baseball bat in one hand and held his gun in his other. The gun was aimed at the back of the person in front of him.

The second person, the one with the gun pointed at his back, was Rod. His fingers were interlocked above his head. There was a cut on his forehead. Blood was spread over the side of his face, matted into his blond hair.

"I found him outside, sneaking around," Champ said. "I dunno who he is, but I pistol-whipped him upside the head real good. He was carrying this." Champ held up the baseball bat with the hand not holding the gun. "Guess he thought he could take us on with it."

"Who is this asshole?" Shamrock asked Gary.

"I . . . I don't know," Gary said, light-headed, woozy, barely able to comprehend what he was seeing. "I've never—"

"I'm his brother," Rod said.

Shamrock's eyes didn't leave Gary. "Your brother? What's he doing here?"

"I don't—"

"Thought you just said you didn't tell anyone," Shamrock said.

Gary didn't respond. He watched in stunned silence as Champ led Rod to the middle of the room.

Rod looked over and made eye contact with Gary. "I followed you," Rod said. "I couldn't just stand by and wait—"

"Shut up," Champ said.

"I thought I could help you. I wanted to—"

"I said, shut the fuck up."

Champ swung the baseball bat with one hand and it connected with the back of Rod's knee. Rod yelled out, grabbed his knee with both hands, and collapsed onto the ground, grimacing in pain.

Champ stuffed the gun into the waistband of his Adidas pants. He tore loose a strand of tape and forced Rod's wrists together behind him, working the tape around, just as he had with Gary. Rod struggled but was no match for the massive man.

Champ dragged Rod next to Gary. The two men sat, side by side, looking up at Shamrock.

"So, the speech about keeping everything a secret was total bullshit, huh?" Shamrock said. "Just a way to distract me while your brother snuck up to ambush us."

"No," Gary said, looking at Rod, still floored that he was here. "I didn't know he was coming."

"I don't believe you."

"It's the truth. I had no—"

"Quiet," Shamrock said. He motioned to Champ, and they walked over to the bank of busted-out windows about twenty feet away from Rod and Gary. They began talking in low voices.

"Gary," Rod whispered from beside him.

"Jesus, Rod," Gary whispered back. "I can't believe it."

"I wasn't going to stand by and let you die. Listen to me—"

"Why—"

"Gary, listen to me," Rod said, leaning in closer. "I have the gun."

"What—"

"The gun you left behind at the store. It's tucked into the waist-band of my pants. The guy didn't search me. He took the bat and thought that was all I brought."

"Shut the fuck up over there," Champ said from across the room.

The gun, Gary thought. If they could somehow free their hands, the gun gave them a chance. He pulled his arms in opposite directions, trying to break loose of the duct tape. It was no use; the tape was so tight and strong, it was as good as a pair of handcuffs.

Champ and Shamrock were still talking over by the windows. Gary quickly scanned the room for something he could use to free his hands. He looked at the table in the corner, the dartboard above it, the ceiling. He glanced over at the shattered windows—grab a piece of glass to cut through the tape?—but the windows were too far away.

He looked at the floor, scanned it for something that might have fallen or been overlooked, but there was nothing. Just the scuffed, long wooden floorboards nailed into the ground—

A nail.

Thick nails were driven into the wooden floorboards every few inches, securing the boards into place. If he could work one of the nails free, there was a chance he could use the nail head to cut through the tape.

Gary blindly ran his fingers over the floor—searching, reaching, hoping to come across a nail. Back and forth, he felt along the wooden floor surface. Champ and Shamrock were still talking across the room but Gary's body shielded them from seeing his fingers searching the floorboards behind him.

Finally, the tip of his index finger slid over the rigid, uneven head of a nail in the floorboard directly behind him. It wasn't fully hammered into the floor; it stuck out roughly a quarter of an inch.

Gary pinched his fingers around the top of the nail and squeezed. He yanked upward. Sharp pain stabbed at his fingertips as the edge of the nail scraped against his thumb and finger, tearing away skin.

He pinched the nail head and yanked again. Again.

Across the room, Champ handed Shamrock the handgun. Shamrock walked over to them. Champ stayed on the other side of the room, watching with a blank expression.

More time. Gary needed more time.

"Please. If you let us go, we'll never tell anyone—"

"Shut up."

Behind him, Gary moved the loose nail around, yanked at it, pulled. Suddenly, the nail came free. Unable to see it, he ran his thumb and index finger over it to determine the size. The best he could figure, it was around two inches long.

Shamrock stopped walking a few feet in front of them. He looked at Gary, looked at Rod, back at Gary.

"I almost trusted you," he said. "I figured this thing could've been our little secret, just you and me. But if you told your brother about the murder, who else you gonna tell? What about him—he gonna tell anyone? Word gets out, it spreads quickly. Anyone could find out."

"Think of the police," Gary said. Behind him, he used the tip of the nail like a sword, frantically stabbing at the duct tape, puncturing hole after hole through the rough texture. "If I'm killed right after the police talked to me about Devon's murder, they will know that someone killed me to keep me quiet. They will know that—"

"I'll worry about that later. It's easier to end this now." Shamrock took a step toward them and pointed his gun at Rod. Gary gritted his teeth and pulled his arms in opposite directions. Still stuck.

Rod stared up at the gun, a few inches from his forehead. He was whimpering, lightly crying. "Please," he said.

And that's all he could get out before Shamrock pulled the trigger. A loud gunshot rang out and there was a wet sound, a nauseating liquid moan, as a bullet tore through Rod's forehead. Chunks of brain matter and fractured skull spurted from Rod's head like shrapnel from a grenade. Rod's lifeless body flopped to the ground. Blood pulsed out from the wound, pooling around his head like a halo.

It all happened so quickly that Gary could barely process it. Ears ringing from the gunshot, he looked at Rod's body, faceup on the floor, his arms still duct-taped behind his back, the puddle of blood around his head expanding and soaking into his blond hair. Rod's body twitched. Gary felt dizzy. His stomach lurched and he almost vomited.

Shamrock stood over Rod's body, staring down at it, holding the smoking gun in his hand. He looked over at Gary and took a step toward him.

Gary snapped out of his daze. He screamed and pulled as hard as he could against the duct tape, his arms shaking. The duct tape gave way with a rip and his arms swung out from his body in opposite directions. He tumbled forward and instantly sprang off the floor, jumping onto Shamrock as if he were on fire and Gary was trying to put out the flames. Shamrock tumbled backward, Gary on top of him. The gun flew out of his hand and slid away. It came to a stop roughly ten feet away, resting on the floor halfway between Gary and Champ.

From across the room, Champ raced to the gun. Getting to the gun before Champ was a fifty-fifty chance, so Gary jumped off Shamrock and sprinted away from the gun, away from the two men, away from Rod's body. He had no idea where he was going, but he spotted a door about thirty feet ahead. He didn't know where it led, didn't even know if it was unlocked, but Gary ran to it.

From behind him, a gunshot.

He reached the door in a panic and twisted the knob . . . and the door opened.

Another gunshot behind him.

Gary ran through the doorway into a long, dark hallway. On either side of the hallway were doors with numbers on them. Apartment numbers. It was an unfinished residential floor. At the end of the hallway Gary spotted an unlit Exit sign above a door.

Gary sprinted toward the sign, dodging cables and wires hanging from the ceiling. He reached the door and threw it open.

A stairwell. Two sets of stairs: one going up; one going down to the ground level. The ground stairway had wooden two-by-fours making an X that blocked it, so Gary sprinted up. He took the stairs two at a time as he ascended. He reached the next flight of stairs. Then the next.

Panting heavily, he kept running up, up, up. He scaled another flight of stairs and abruptly stopped when he heard a noise from outside the building.

The sound of an engine starting.

Gary crept over to a window in the stairwell and looked outside. Below, he saw a black Cadillac CTS, the taillights illuminated. Through the car's front window, he saw Champ and Shamrock. The car reversed a few feet before speeding away, kicking up gravel and dust.

Gary was safe, but he knew there was no time to waste. If someone had heard the gunshots, the police would arrive at any moment. Gary ran back down the flights of stairs and into the room he'd been in earlier. The break room.

The charred scent of gunpowder was still in the air. Rod's body lay on the ground in the middle of the room. Precious time was ticking away, but Gary couldn't leave. Not just yet. He went to Rod's body and leaned over it.

A hole was blown in the left half of his forehead. Blood, so much blood, covered the side of his face, his blond hair, the floor around his head. His wide, expressionless eyes blankly stared toward the ceiling. Both hands were still duct-taped behind his back.

"Rod," Gary said. Barely a whisper.

Gary looked at his brother's still body, at all of the blood. The bottom of Rod's shirt had gathered up around his chest as he'd fallen. Tucked into the waistband of his pants was a gun. Just as Rod had said. He'd brought the gun with him. The gun Gary had used to kill Devon.

"Oh, Jesus, Rod," Gary said, his voice a little louder. He fought back tears, refusing to let his emotions get to him. There was no time to mourn; he had to get out of there.

He turned to leave. And suddenly, out of the blue, a plan came to Gary.

He knew that if he gave himself any time to think it through, he'd talk himself out of it, so he sprang into action immediately. There were a million potential problems, but there was no time to think about any of them. Just act. Just act quickly, hope for the best, and get out of there.

Gary looked around the room and found a rag in the corner. He draped the rag around his hand and pulled the gun from Rod's waistband.

"I'm sorry, Rod," he whispered. "I'm so, so sorry."

With his free hand, Gary undid the duct tape that bound Rod's wrists together. He stuffed the tape into the pocket of his coat—he'd throw it away later, far away from here. He placed the gun in Rod's hand and manipulated Rod's fingers so his fingerprints and a palm print were on the gun. Using the rag, he picked up the gun and set it a few inches away from Rod's body.

The monstrous reality of what he was doing took firm shape in his mind.

He was framing his brother for the murder of Devon Peterson.

Gary saw no alternative. This was the only way that he could possibly escape this mess. There were no guarantees, but if everything fell into place, there was a chance he could end this for good.

Before leaving, he whispered a final apology to Rod. He didn't cry; he knew the tears would come eventually. There would be time later to mourn Rod, for the adrenaline to fade and be replaced by grief. But not now—now there was no time for a tearful good-bye.

He ran out to his car and sped away.

27

OTTO AND CHAMP SAT IN THE BACK OF A DARK, NEARLY EMPTY BAR NAMED the Griffin. A group of overweight guys in T-shirts and jeans played pool across from the booth where the two men sat. The sharp crack of pool balls was the only noise in the bar.

"At least we got the brother," Champ said. "His ass is dead."

"I don't give a shit about him," Otto said. "Gary's the one I'm worried about. He's the one the police are looking at. He's the one who can take my ass down for the murder."

"We shoulda stuck around and tracked him down."

"He coulda disappeared anywhere. We had to get the hell out of there before the cops showed up." Plus, he'd landed on his bad knee after Gary tackled him. The pain had been intense, made it damn near impossible to walk.

Otto picked up a glass tumbler off the table and took a drink. A gin and tonic made with shitty gin and flat tonic. He took a long, angry swig—the alcohol was helping dull the pain.

"Want me to go to his house?" Champ asked. "Take him out?"

"Not tonight. Enough action for one night. We were lucky to get outta there."

"So what're you gonna do?"

Otto took another drink from the glass tumbler. He set it back onto the table and looked at Champ.

"Ain't nothing to do but wait. His time'll come soon enough."

―――――

WHEN GARY ARRIVED HOME, HE STEPPED INSIDE AND QUIETLY SHUT THE front door. The lights remained off. He checked on Beth and, as expected, he found her in bed, asleep.

He sat down at the kitchen table and buried his head in his hands. Rod was dead.

An onslaught of bottled-up emotions hit Gary hard, leaving his mind frozen and numb. He sobbed hysterically into his hands. A muffled sound like an animal dying escaped his lips. The tears were uncontrollable, impossible to stop.

He thought about Rod and all the memories they shared, a lifetime of them. He thought of the early years—playing with Legos together, sneaking out of bed at night to watch TV shows forbidden by their parents, laughing uncontrollably when one of them farted or burped. He thought about how he'd grown tired of his younger brother when he'd discovered women in junior high and high school, how they'd argued and fought and been at each other's throats for what seemed like every day when they were teenagers. He remembered how Rod had cried, actually cried, when Gary moved away for college, and how much it affected him to see his younger brother so emotional. He remembered how, later in life, Rod would call on Sunday nights, at seven o'clock right on the dot every week, and tell Gary about whatever adventure he'd been on that week—some wild party he'd gone to when he was in college, a mountain he'd skied when he lived in Colorado, a failed audition he'd gone on while trying to break into acting in Los Angeles.

And now Rod was dead. There would be no more phone calls. No more entertaining stories. No more memories to share with one another.

Regardless of what happened next, nothing would change the fact that Rod was dead. Even if Gary were able to escape this nightmare and return to a normal life with Beth, Rod would still be gone. All because he'd come to save his older brother and gotten caught up in something that wasn't even his problem.

"Rod," Gary said, and uttered a long, trembling sigh.

Face buried in his hands, his tears continued. Every time he thought he was cried out, he recalled some other memory and the tears started up again.

Gary stayed hunched over the kitchen table for what seemed like an eternity. Once the tears finally stopped, he staggered down the hallway and showered in the bathroom. He felt numb and exhausted as the hot water rinsed over his body. After the shower, he walked into the bedroom and collapsed onto the bed. Beth didn't wake up beside him.

He fell asleep instantly.

28

THE NEXT MORNING, GARY WAS STARTLED AWAKE BY THE DOORBELL. HE lifted his head off his pillow. He peeked out the window that looked onto their lawn, and saw Detective Whitley outside the front door, alone, wearing a blazer over a light blue button-up shirt tucked into a pair of jeans.

Gary's grogginess disappeared in a flash.

The doorbell rang again. Beside him, Beth rustled awake.

"I'll get it, Beth. Go back to sleep," Gary said.

He threw on a shirt and jeans as he walked toward the front door. He thought back to last night, to how he'd hurriedly, haphazardly framed Rod for the murder of Devon Peterson. Had he made a mistake when he planted the murder weapon next to Rod? Any oversight or error? He didn't know. Everything was such a blur.

He opened the door just as Whitley rang the doorbell a third time.

"Hi, Gary," he said. The same steady, librarian-like tone. "Sorry for bothering you this early, but I need to talk with you."

"About what?"

"A few things," Whitley said. "No need to go to the station, though. Can I come in?"

Gary held open the front door and Whitley entered the house. They walked into the living room and sat down—Gary on the couch, Whitley in the recliner across from him.

"There's no easy way to say this," Whitley said. "We received a phone call late last night about gunshots at the Alpine Development, on the edge of town. After investigating, we found a dead body on the premises. I'm sorry to tell you this: the body was your brother, Rod."

Gary inhaled a sharp, sudden breath and brought a hand to his mouth. "Rod?"

"I'm sure this is difficult to hear," Whitley said. "I'm sorry."

"I don't understand. He's gone? What happened?"

"Gunshot. We're still sorting out the details, but foul play seems to have been involved. He was murdered."

"My God." Gary stood up from the couch and walked to the floor-length window on the edge of the room. He stared out at the back-yard for a moment, looking, he hoped, like a stunned, speechless man in the early stages of grief.

"I'm sure you want to be alone now," Whitley said. "But there are a few questions I need to ask you about Rod. It'd help us out in the investigation."

Gary turned away from the window and sat back down on the couch. He nodded.

"When was the last time you saw him?" Whitley asked.

"Last night."

"Where? What time?"

"We were at the store. He left around ten o'clock."

"Did he leave in his car or on foot?"

"He drove."

"Do you know where he went when he left?"

"I assumed he headed home."

"He didn't. We found his pickup parked a few hundred feet away from the Alpine Development, concealed by some trees. And his wife hasn't seen him since yesterday."

Sarah. In the frantic, madcap rush of the past twelve hours, Gary hadn't even thought about Sarah. She must be devastated. . . . But there was no time to think about her now.

Focus.

"You didn't talk with Rod after he left the store?" Whitley asked. "No text messages or anything like that?"

"No."

Whitley began tapping the end of his pen on the table in a steady, slow rhythm. Tap. Tap. Tap. "Your brother has a bit of a history with the law, correct?"

"He's been arrested a few times. But never anything too serious."

"I read over his record. Some tickets for public intoxication, bar fights that got out of control, possession of marijuana. Was he ever involved in anything bigger than that?"

"Meaning?"

"Something more than a nickel-and-dime offense."

"Not that I know of."

"Heavy drug usage? Something more than weed?"

"No. No, I don't think so."

"Reason I ask is, there had to be a reason your brother was out at a place like the Alpine Development late at night. Maybe he was selling drugs, buying them?"

Whitley went silent for a moment. The only sound in the room was the tap, tap, tapping of the pen against the table.

"There's more," he said. "We found a gun on Rod. Have you ever known your brother to own a handgun?"

"A gun? No. Never."

"We did a test on it. Ballistics confirmed that the gun was used in Devon Peterson's murder. I'm sure you remember: he was the cop I questioned you about."

"What does that mean?"

"It would appear Rod had something to do with the murder," Whitley said.

"Rod? No. No way." Gary slowly shook his head. His outward expression was one of confusion, total disbelief. But inside, he felt like a prisoner glimpsing sunlight for the first time in years.

"Best guess is that Rod was dealing drugs, mixed up with some bad people. Maybe he was using his product instead of selling it, suddenly finds himself owing them some serious money. Somehow, Devon Peterson enters into the equation. Maybe he discovered the drug ring and was shaking them down, taking a cut of their profits—I already mentioned he wasn't a saint. Drug dealers don't like giving up a portion of their profits, so they tell Rod his debt to them is taken care of if he kills Devon for them. He does it. Now Rod's a loose end, so they kill him to keep their secret a secret."

"I don't believe it. Not at all."

"I'm sure it's tough to hear," Whitley said. "But the evidence supports it. It tells us why we found that hat from your store at the scene of Devon's death—Rod probably grabbed it before heading out. He probably deleted the security footage of him taking it. It also explains why your car was in the area after Devon's death. You mentioned that you keep a set of spare keys at your business—he probably snagged those so he could take a car that wasn't his."

Whitley had made every connection Gary had hoped he would. The pieces snapped into place like a perfectly constructed jigsaw puzzle.

"Rod was wild, immature," Gary said. "He wasn't a hardened criminal. Are you sure about this?"

"Right now, everything points to a drug deal gone bad. We'll keep looking into it, of course, see if we learn anything to the contrary."

Whitley stopped tapping the end of his pen on the table. He stood up from his chair.

"I hate being the bearer of bad news," he said. "I truly hate it. Hardest part of my job, telling people that a loved one has died. You have my condolences."

"Thank you."

"Call me if you think of anything that might help us," Whitley said, setting a business card on the table. "Times that Rod acted differently, someone suspicious your brother hung out with, anything at all."

"I will," Gary said.

They walked back across the living room—Whitley leading, Gary following behind. Gary felt like he was stepping on eggshells, aware that just one slipup or mistake would bring everything down.

Whitley reached the front door. Before opening it, he turned back to Gary.

"I'm sorry for the mix-up earlier, when I brought you down to the station," he said. "I looked at the facts and made an educated guess. I took a shot, figured I'd put the screws to you, see if you were hiding anything. Sometimes it works out. Sometimes it doesn't. But I truly feel bad about how I questioned you earlier and bothered your neighbors and friends. I'm more than happy to speak to any of them, let them know it was just a big misunderstanding."

"Don't worry about it. You were only doing your job," Gary said. He just wanted the detective out of his house, out of his life.

"And I'm sorry about your brother. It looks like he was tangled up with some bad people, in way over his head. You have my word: we'll do everything we can to solve his murder."

"Thank you," Gary said.

"WHO WAS AT THE DOOR?" BETH ASKED, APPEARING IN THE KITCHEN MO-ments after Whitley left.

Gary hesitated. He knew the news about Rod would crush Beth. She'd always found Rod so charming and endearing, had grown so close to him over the years.

"Something happened last night, Beth," Gary said. "Something awful."

"What is it?"

They sat down at the kitchen table and he told her everything. Everything that he could, at least.

She listened to the whole story in stunned silence. When he finished, she finally spoke. "I don't believe it."

"I had the same reaction," Gary said.

"There has to be a mistake. Murder? Rod? No way."

"The police are sure of it. The evidence they have is rock solid."

"I thought you and Rod were together last night."

"He left the store around ten. He said he had something to do. But, God, I had no idea it was . . . something like this."

Beth blinked and a tear fell down her cheek. She grabbed a Kleenex from a box on the table and dabbed at her eyes. "I've known Rod almost as long as I've known you," she said. "I can't believe this; I *don't* believe this. Rod was wild, but he wouldn't have been involved in something this horrible. He's not a killer."

"I'm still in shock," Gary said. "I don't know how he could've kept something like this from everyone."

Lies. More lies. That's all the entire interaction was: just a series of lies, one right after another, right to Beth's face.

She stood up and threw her Kleenex into the small trash basket next to the counter. As she did, she winced and brought one hand to her forehead.

"Beth?" Gary said.

Her eyes remained closed, her hand resting against her temple. Gary's stomach tensed up.

"Beth, are you all right?"

Just as he was about to rush over to her, Beth opened her eyes. "I'm fine," she said.

"You're sure?" Gary said. For an instant, he'd really thought she was going to collapse again.

"I'm fine. I just . . . I can't believe this."

"We'll get through this, Beth. We'll get through everything."

He feared that, too, was another lie.

THEY CRIED SOME MORE, GRIEVED TOGETHER. AFTER AN HOUR, THEY GOT IN the car and drove a few miles in silence, pulling to a stop in front of the white two-story house Gary and Rod grew up in, the house Sarah and Rod were making their own.

He and Beth exited the car and walked up the small cement pathway. When they reached the front door, Gary rang the bell. The same familiar chime he'd heard countless times during childhood rang out.

A moment later, Sarah opened the door. Gary barely recognized her. Her bloodshot eyes were puffy and swollen, but the rest of her face was sunken, gaunt, stretched thin against her cheekbones and jaw. Her short black hair was uncombed. She wore baggy sweatpants and an oversized white T-shirt that limply hung over her body like a tent.

Sarah wordlessly motioned for them to step inside.

Beth hugged her, and both women began crying softly as they held each other. Next, Sarah hugged Gary. He felt her icy hands close around his back.

Sarah pulled away and looked at them both. Gary waited for her to speak, but no words came.

"We've called a few times," Beth said. "Did you get our voice mails?"

"My phone's off," Sarah said. Her voice was raspy; each word had jagged edges. "I haven't looked at it in hours. I don't feel like talking to anyone."

"We're here. You're not going through this alone."

"Alone, surrounded by friends—it doesn't matter."

They walked into the living room and sat down, Sarah and Beth next to each other on a couch, Gary a few feet away. A box of Kleenex rested in the middle of the coffee table between them. At least twenty wadded-up used tissues were scattered around the box.

"How did you find out?" Sarah asked.

"The police," Gary said. "A detective visited earlier. Whitley."

"He came by here, too," she said. "When a police detective woke me at six in the morning, I knew something was wrong. But this . . . I never imagined something like this."

Sarah grabbed a Kleenex from the box and blew her nose. She crumpled the tissue and threw it back onto the table.

"The detective said he thought it was a drug deal gone wrong," she said. "Did he tell you that?"

"Yeah," Gary said. "He did."

"There's no way. I told the detective, there's no way at all. Drugs? There has to be a mistake, right?"

"I don't know," Gary said. "This whole thing . . . It's just awful."

Beth put an arm around Sarah. She grabbed a Kleenex with her other hand and gave it to Sarah. Sarah didn't do anything with it. She held it in her hand and stared off into space, despondent.

"Don't hold back because of us," Beth said. "We'll be a shoulder to cry on."

"I've been crying nonstop for the past three hours," Sarah said. "I don't have any tears left." She stood up and walked across the room. She looked out a window into the small yard behind the house.

"The gun," she said. "Did they tell you about that? The gun they found on Rod?"

Gary nodded.

"That just doesn't make any sense. A gun? Rod? Have you ever known him to own a gun?"

"No," Gary said.

Sarah walked back to the couch and sat down.

"Drugs?" she said. "A gun? Telling me Rod murdered someone? I mean, this has to be a mistake."

"That's what I said," Beth said.

Sarah opened her mouth to say something, but closed it without uttering a word. She slowly, weakly shook her head. Her body collapsed forward and she covered her face in her hands.

She'd been wrong earlier—she wasn't out of tears. Face buried in her hands, she sobbed hysterically.

29

OTHER THAN A TWENTY-MINUTE TRIP TO GRAB TAKEOUT FOR LUNCH, THEY spent the entire day in the house with Sarah. Being secluded like that only made Gary feel worse. All day long, he'd notice little things that reminded him of Rod and their time growing up together. The hamper Rod used to hide in when they played hide-and-seek as kids—still at the top of the basement stairs, after all these years. The window by the basketball hoop that they shattered at least five times during games of one-on-one, always getting a strict reprimand from their father. The patched-over hole in the kitchen wall Rod and his friends had made by setting off a small firecracker in the house as teenagers.

Just after one in the afternoon, Gary received a text from a friend: *Can't be true—Rod?!?*

Gary pulled up a local news site on his phone. The lead story: the mysterious murder of police officer Devon Peterson had been solved. The article explained that local resident and small-business owner Rod Foster had been linked to the murder after Rod's body was discovered at the Alpine Development last night.

Underneath that, a picture of Rod. Gary recognized the photo instantly—it was taken at a local chamber of commerce reception when Ascension Outerwear first opened. Rod wore a suit and tie in the photo, and Gary remembered how they'd desperately raced around the city to buy the suit for him after finding out Rod didn't own one an hour before the ceremony began. He'd planned on wearing jeans and a T-shirt.

That first text from a friend soon turned into more. And more. Then came the phone calls. The calls came from well-wishers, friends, and others who were shocked at the news—both that Rod was dead and that he was behind the murder that had been the talk of the town for the past few days. Gary kept his words to a minimum, and each conversation lasted for no longer than a minute or two.

It was painful for Gary, agonizingly painful, to listen to people express their dismay over what Rod had done without being able to defend him. *You're wrong,* he wanted to tell them. *You're wrong about Rod. He was a good person. Wild and out of control at times, sure, but he was harmless. Never in a million years would he murder another human being.*

But Gary knew that he couldn't defend Rod; he couldn't tell anyone the truth about what happened. All he could do was hold the phone to his ear and listen as people expressed their condolences and disbelief.

———————

THEY HAD PLANNED ON SPENDING THE NIGHT WITH SARAH, BUT SHE INSISTED that she wanted to be alone, so Gary and Beth headed home around eight p.m.

The drive back across town seemed to take forever, as if the car were traveling at a fraction of the speed the speedometer read—five miles an hour instead of twenty-five. Gary stared out the windshield at the night sky above, at the dark road in front of them.

"You're doing all right?" Beth asked, placing a hand on his forearm.

"Yeah," Gary said. "This just doesn't seem real."

Two lies. He wasn't doing all right, and this whole thing did seem real, far too real.

Back home, Beth kicked off her shoes the moment she stepped past the front door. "I'm taking a shower," she said.

"I'll get one after you," Gary said. "Then I'm off to bed."

Instead of walking to the bathroom, Beth stayed in the foyer, staring at Gary.

"What happened last night, Gary? You really had no idea any of this was going on?"

"No. God, no."

"Rod wasn't acting differently last night? This week?"

"No. He was a little bothered by that police detective who was asking about the hat that went missing from our store. But I didn't think there was anything weird about that. I was freaked out by that detective, too."

Beth's eyes were so weary that he couldn't tell if she believed him or not. All he could see in her eyes was sadness. Any suspicions she had were buried under her grief.

"None of this makes sense," she said. "Rod was a clown, a jokester. He never took anything seriously; he cooked huevos rancheros in his underwear every morning when he lived with us, no matter how many times we told him to put some clothes on. He wasn't a bad person. He wasn't a murderer. He was just a lovable guy."

Gary nodded but stayed silent. He knew if they started reminiscing about Rod and sharing memories, they'd both be crying all night.

After Beth disappeared into the bathroom, Gary sat down in the living-room recliner and closed his eyes. The day had been such a struggle, but the most difficult part was seeing how completely devastated Sarah was. She was barely able to function most of the afternoon. She just walked around the house like a soulless ghost, speaking no more than a few words, showing little emotion other than a dazed, distant sadness.

Her grief, Gary knew, was different from his own. He had a lifetime of memories with Rod, but Sarah had a lifetime of memories waiting to be made with him. Dating for barely a year, married for six months—they'd still had the rest of their lives ahead of them. And now that had been taken from her. Gary himself had taken it away. Maybe he hadn't pulled the trigger, but he was the reason Rod was gone.

His phone chimed with a text message. A friend sending his condolences after seeing the news about Rod. It felt like the millionth message Gary had received during the day—calls, texts, social media messages.

Before he could text a response, Gary's phone rang. UNKNOWN appeared on the screen. Gary stared at that lone word. It could be anyone calling, he knew. Some long-lost friend reaching out to tell him how sorry he was to hear about Rod, how shocked he was by the news.

But he knew who was calling; of course he did.

He answered the phone.

"You weaseled your way out of it, huh?"

That rough, scratchy voice. The sound of it hit Gary like a shot of morphine.

"What do you want?" Gary said.

"I heard the news. Framing your brother for the murder? That takes stones. I gotta hand it to you."

Gary clenched his jaw. He was nearly trembling with righteous rage.

"You killed him, you bastard," he said.

"You're the one who dragged him into this."

"You shot him."

"My fault. Your fault. Don't really matter. He ain't coming back either way." Shamrock laughed, cold and humorless. "Look, I'm calling to tell you: this is over, okay? This thing between us—it ends now. The cops think they solved the case. So how's about you go your way, I go mine, and we never see each other again. Deal?"

Gary heard Beth turn off the shower and he lowered his voice so she wouldn't overhear him.

"The money," he said. "I want the money you owe me."

"You ain't getting the money, boy. You either agree to let this go or I end it myself—with a handgun pointed between your wife's pretty little eyes. As you saw last night, I'm a pretty good shot."

Gary swallowed. Clenched his jaw tighter.

"This is over," Shamrock said. "Deal?"

Gary's blood was hot, simmering for a fight. He wanted to say no and scream into the phone, vow to Shamrock that he'd make him pay. Pay the money to save Beth, pay for Rod's death, pay for getting Gary caught up in this horrible, horrific nightmare.

But he knew that would only put Beth's life at risk, his own life at risk. Even through his blind rage, he knew better than to start an all-out war.

"Fine," Gary said. "This is over."

"Good. Last thing I need is another couple dead bodies. I got enough headaches."

There was silence on the line. Then:

"Believe me when I say this—you do *not* wanna fuck with me," Shamrock said. "If I say it's over, it's over. I got eyes and ears all around this city—I find out you've been asking around about me, I'll destroy you. I'll come for you and your wife. You won't even know what hit you."

The line went dead.

Gary slammed his phone on the coffee table. He had experienced so many low points over the past week, but this point, right here, felt like the lowest. Before, no matter how low things seemed, there was always hope. Beth's diagnosis was crushing, but there was hope that chemo and radiation could help her. When they didn't, he had hope that they could find the money for the GOSKA treatment. And even when he was cheated out of the money, he had hope that he could track down Shamrock and make him pay.

Now the hope was gone.

He almost lost it again, just as he had at the store earlier. Almost went ballistic and started swinging at everything in sight. Instead, he buried the feeling and picked up his phone. He threw it across the room. It hit the wall and bounced off, landing faceup on the carpet by his feet, so he could see the shattered screen.

30

THE INTERIOR OF THE CAR WAS COMPLETELY SILENT AS GARY PULLED INTO a parking lot next to a tiny one-story building with a white stucco exterior. Floor-length windows looked out onto a small yard lined by a row of knee-high hedges. Next to the hedges was a sign: JONES FUNERAL HOME.

Gary parked the car, and he and Beth stepped out. A moment later, the rear door opened and Sarah exited. All three of them wore black—Gary in a suit, Sarah in a sleeveless dress, Beth in a maternity dress she'd borrowed from a friend. The dress stretched tightly over the bump of her stomach, looking as if it had been intended for someone who was four or five months pregnant, not eight.

Beth hooked her arm into Gary's and they walked across the parking lot, Sarah at their side. At the funeral-home entrance, Gary held open the door and followed the women inside. They stepped into a small room with a soft, prerecorded piano melody playing from a few speakers. Directly past the entrance was a table covered with a white cloth, an open sign-in book and a black ballpoint pen resting on top of the cloth. On the other side of the room was a rectangular casket with a light brown finish.

They approached it. Rod's embalmed body lay on the silver satin lining sewn into the interior. His eyes were closed and his skin was pale, not quite white, but much lighter than normal. He was dressed in a suit, his hands crossed over his chest, looking as if he'd fallen asleep midprayer. His hair was slicked down and brushed over his forehead, covering the entry wound from the bullet that took his life.

"Welcome."

Gary turned around. An older man with kind, weary eyes stood behind them. Gary recognized him as Mr. Jones, the director of the funeral home. They'd met with him yesterday to plan Rod's funeral.

"Do you have any questions?" Mr. Jones asked.

Beth shook her head. Sarah wasn't even looking at the funeral director. Her eyes were fixed on Rod's body.

"No questions right now," Gary said.

"Very well. I'll check on you from time to time, but I'll be in the room on the other side of those doors for most of the service," Mr. Jones said, pointing at a set of oak double doors. "Please come get me if there's anything you need." He gave them a brief, curt smile and excused himself.

"Are you two ready?" Gary asked, turning back to the women.

Beth nodded. Sarah didn't move. Her eyes remained focused on the casket, staring at Rod's body as if in a trance.

"Are you ready, Sarah?" Gary asked, as he lightly touched her forearm.

"Yeah," she said.

She didn't look like she was ready. Her skin was pallid, washed-out, a faded photograph. Her eyes were vacant and her mouth was a straight line; she looked like a smile would never cross her lips again. The skin under her nose was red, rubbed raw from blowing her nose over the past few days.

Gary guided Sarah to the entrance and Beth followed; they all stood next to the table with the sign-in book and waited for people to arrive.

Though it was taking place at a funeral home, Rod's funeral wouldn't be a service in the traditional sense. Instead, they'd decided to hold a small visitation to give people the chance to pay their respects and say their final good-byes. They'd spent the previous day planning it out, though there wasn't all that much to plan. There would be no speech from a pastor or singing of hymns. Considering the circumstances—that everyone in the city believed Rod murdered Devon Peterson—Gary, Beth, and Sarah agreed that a small private gathering would be best.

Once the funeral was over, Rod would be buried in a local cemetery, in a plot next to their parents' headstone.

TWELVE THIRTY—THE OFFICIAL START TIME OF THE FUNERAL—CAME AND went. They stood together next to the sign-in table as one o'clock passed, then one fifteen.

The first guests arrived just after that. Gary's high school English teacher and her husband. They offered their condolences. After they left, three people who said they knew Rod "from the bar" arrived, though Gary had no idea which bar they were referencing.

An hour in, Beth pulled over a chair and sat down. She slipped off her shoes and wiggled her toes a few times.

"You're doing all right?" Gary asked.

"Yeah," she said. "These shoes barely fit before the pregnancy. With the swelling, they're worse."

After stretching out her toes, Beth closed her eyes, ran a hand across her forehead, and massaged her temples.

"Is it a headache, Beth?" Gary asked.

"I'm fine. Just exhausted."

A few more people trickled in as time passed—some of Gary's former coworkers, a group of nurses who attended to Beth at the hospital, a few people who had gone to high school with Rod.

During a lull in the funeral, Gary turned to Sarah. "How are you doing?" he asked. "This isn't too much?"

"I'm fine."

"If you need to step away or take a break, you can."

"Gary, I'm fine. Don't worry about me."

There was a snappiness to her words. He'd noticed the same hard, bitter edge to everything she said yesterday, as they planned the funeral. Her heartbroken grief in the moments after Rod's death had given way to a cold, distant anger.

"Just let me know if you need anything, Sarah," Gary said.

She silently looked away from him.

More time passed. The guests arrived at the rate of a group or two every fifteen minutes, each staying for no longer than a few minutes. Most of Gary, Beth, and Sarah's time was spent together in the funeral home, just the three of them standing around with the light piano melody droning on from the speakers.

Guests continued to trickle in as another hour passed.

"I meant to tell you," Sarah said to Gary during a slow period. "You can have all his clothes."

"Clothes?"

"Rod's clothes. I have closets full of his clothes, and I have no idea what to do with them. Might as well just give them to you."

"We weren't even the same size. I don't—"

"Just take them, Gary. I don't want them in the house."

There it was again. That hard, bitter edge to her voice.

"You sure you're doing okay, Sarah?"

She didn't answer. She stared out at the funeral floor, as if the question hadn't registered.

"Sarah, are you—"

"I heard you the first time."

Her gaze wandered over to Rod's casket, on the other side of the room.

"No," she said. "I'm not doing all right. Not at all."

She locked eyes with Gary. To Gary, it seemed like something had changed—a crack in her steely expression, a hint of vulnerability behind her distant gaze.

"Everything's falling apart, Gary," she said. "Falling apart? No, everything's already fallen apart. My life has crumbled to the ground, and I don't know what to do."

She shook her head. "My phone wouldn't stop ringing last night," she said. "Someone must've found my number online, passed it around or something. All night long, people called and left harassing messages. Some of the things these people said . . . Just vile, horrible stuff. *Cop killer. Scumbag. Rot in hell.*"

Gary nodded. They'd received a few phone calls, too.

"You know what else happened?" Sarah said. "Somebody threw a brick through the front window of my yoga studio. Completely shattered the window. And fifteen people canceled their memberships yesterday. A few have family in the police force, and they told me they don't want to be around people like me. People like me—as if I'm involved in this, like I'm guilty by association. There were five more cancellations this morning. I'm going to have to close the studio. I put so much work into that business. Invested so much time, money, effort—everything. And now it's over."

"I know it's tough now, but things will get better with time," Gary said, putting an arm around her shoulder.

"They won't," she said. She took a step away to slip out of his embrace.

"They will, Sarah," he said, but he knew she was right. Time could only do so much. This wound was far too deep for the mere passage of time to heal it. This wound was permanent, one that would affect them all for the rest of their lives.

Sarah's eyes drifted over to the casket. She stared at it for a long moment.

"You know, I still don't believe the story," she said. "The story about Rod being involved in drugs. Killing the police officer. The whole thing just doesn't add up."

"It's tough to hear, I know," Gary said. He hoped Sarah would stop there, but she didn't.

"It just doesn't make any sense," she continued. "Rod had some second life? A life he kept secret from me, from you, from everyone? If Rod was up to something, I would've known about it. You would've known about it. He would've mentioned something. Or acted differently. But there was nothing."

Sarah went silent, her eyes staying on the casket. Then she turned back to Gary. "I don't know," she said. "I'm sure I sound ridiculous, don't I? Like the police framed Rod or someone set him up. Like there was some big conspiracy or something."

"It's best not to think about it too much, Sarah," Gary said. "Just try to move on."

Beth rose from the chair a few feet away and walked over to them, barefoot. The light, low piano melody played on through the speakers.

"You'll be able to get through this," Beth said to Sarah.

"I don't know. I really don't."

"You have to remember the good times with Rod. The happy memories."

"I'm too busy figuring out how to put my life back together to remember the good times."

"We'll be here for you," Beth said. "You know that. Together we can get through this."

"Maybe someday I'll be able to piece everything together. But right now, my business is sunk. My reputation is ruined. It feels like my life is over."

She slowly shook her head, as if she couldn't believe any of it.

NO GUESTS SHOWED UP FOR THE FINAL HALF HOUR OF THE FUNERAL. AT three thirty, the soft piano music abruptly cut out. Mr. Jones returned and made small talk for a minute. After handing them a pamphlet titled "Moving On: The Next Steps," he led them toward the exit.

Before they walked outside, Gary looked back at Rod's casket. From the other side of the room, he could just barely see Rod's body inside.

"Do you mind if I get some time alone with him before we go?" Gary asked.

"Of course," Beth said.

Sarah nodded. The women exited, Mr. Jones with them, leaving Gary by himself. He walked across the silent room. When he reached the casket, he looked down at Rod's body. Rod looked so distinguished, so serious in his suit.

"I'm sorry, Rod," Gary said, his voice barely above a whisper. "I'm so, so sorry."

Gary placed his hand on the edge of the casket and left it there. Rod's death was a tragedy; using any other word to describe it seemed insufficient. Gary had lost his younger brother, his best friend. Sarah had lost her husband, her soul mate.

"I'm sorry, Rod," he whispered again. His final apology.

He stared down at his brother's still body. He had so much more to say, but if he kept talking he didn't know if he'd ever stop.

Gary felt emotion flood throughout his body but the tears didn't come. He was too drained for tears.

"KNOW WHY I'M CALLING?"

Standing in the basement of Solid Gold Pawn, Otto held his phone to his ear. He hadn't recognized the number on his phone, but he recognized Carlos's voice immediately; must've been calling from a burner. The last time Carlos phoned, the call had ended with Otto watching a video of a man about to be decapitated by a chainsaw.

He hoped this call would end on a more positive note.

"Yeah," Otto said into the phone. "I got a pretty good idea of why you're calling. The money, right?"

"Nah, I'm calling to get some financial advice. I'm thinking about buying some Apple stock, wanted to get your thoughts." Carlos scoffed. "Of course I'm calling about the money," he said. "What you owe De La Fuente. The two hundred large you bitched out on last time we met."

"I remember."

"You said you couldn't pay 'cause of some problem going on."

"The problem's been taken care of."

"So you got the money?"

"Yeah. I got it."

"You ain't fucking with me, right? 'Cause I'm gonna be up in your area in three days. If you don't have the money, De La Fuente will—"

"Gimme a second."

Otto put the call on hold and walked over to a safe pushed against the basement wall, nearly hidden by the cardboard boxes and merchandise piled around it. He spun the combination and pulled open the door.

Inside the safe was $270,000 cash. All one-hundred dollar bills in small bundles of ten thousand dollars, stacked in the safe like a small foothill.

Otto grabbed twenty of the bundles and carried them over to the table in the middle of the room. He threw the bundles of money on it and snapped a picture with his phone. He messaged the picture to Carlos.

"See the picture I just sent?" Otto said, returning to the call.

"I saw it."

"Show that to De La Fuente. Let him know there ain't nothing to worry about."

"Have the cash waiting for me. I'll see you in three days." Carlos ended the call.

Otto slid his phone into his pocket. He grabbed the bundles of money off the table and threw them back inside the safe. Before closing the door, he stared at the pile of money.

There it was. Two hundred seventy thousand dollars. Damn near every last cent to his name, right inside that safe. It was a lot of money, but the expression on his face remained impassive; the sight of large sums of money had long ago ceased to impress him.

Over the past few days, Otto collected on all the debts dealers had with him, emptied out his bank accounts, and liquidated some of the higher-dollar items in the pawnshop. He took all the money he'd rounded up—about seventy thousand dollars—and added it to the two hundred grand already stored in the safe.

It was time to end it all.

Time to give up this life and get out while he could. This mess with Devon Peterson had been too close for comfort. It was time to leave the drug game behind, get away from this decaying piece-of-shit city, and start over somewhere else. Somewhere warm.

Otto closed the safe door and spun the combination. He walked over to a shelf and grabbed a large jug of paint thinner nestled among the stacks of cardboard boxes. After taking care of his debt with De La Fuente, he'd have seventy thousand dollars left. Not bad, but not enough to begin a new life. To fix that, Otto planned on dousing Solid Gold Pawn in paint thinner and burning the place to the ground. Like any good business owner, he was insured. He'd be looking at a settlement well into the six figures. Add that to the leftover cash in the safe, and it was more than enough to start over.

He set the jug of paint thinner on the table and returned to the pawnshop's first floor. He looked out the window at another cold, dreary day. Yep, moving somewhere warm sounded nice. As soon as

Carlos arrived to pick up the money for De La Fuente, he'd torch this place and leave this city for good.

"THAT WAS SAD," BETH SAID THE MOMENT THEY ARRIVED HOME AFTER Rod's funeral.

Gary kicked his dress shoes onto the rug inside the front door. Beth stepped out of her flats. They carried their shoes down the hallway to the bedroom.

"I don't know which was worse: the funeral or the fact that barely forty people showed up," Gary said.

"A lot of people were busy, I'm sure. We only gave them a day's notice."

Gary didn't respond. He knew they could've given plenty of advance notice and the turnout would've been the same. In the eyes of most people, Rod wasn't some poor, innocent civilian who'd unfairly lost his life. Rod was caught up with some bad people; he was a cop killer. And his poor decisions ultimately led to his death.

It was amazing to Gary how many people had blindly believed that. How few of them questioned the story, or challenged the idea that Rod could do something so horrible. Everyone had abandoned Rod, distanced themselves from him. Everyone except Sarah—on the drive home, she'd mentioned again that she thought there was more to Rod's death. It unnerved Gary, hearing her talk about her suspicions, but he was too sad to worry about it now.

In the bedroom, Beth set her flats in her closet and turned her back toward Gary. "Unzip me?" she said. She bunched her hair in her hands, exposing the back of her neck. Once out of the dress, Beth slipped into an orange sweatshirt and a pair of yoga pants, her belly hanging low and heavy over the waistband.

Gary set his shoes onto the ground in his closet. He loosened the tie around his neck and slipped it off. One by one, he took off the rest of his funeral attire: his suit, his socks, his button-up shirt. He moved sluggishly, every action slow and deliberate. There was a huge block of pain lodged beneath his chest. Was it the weight of guilt causing the pain? The stress from everything that had happened?

Or perhaps it was just a broken heart. That seemed the most likely explanation. His throat tightened as he thought back to the funeral; he nearly started crying. The entire funeral felt like one giant mistake, like something they shouldn't have even bothered with. It wasn't a beautiful celebration of Rod's life, a remembrance of the joy he'd brought to others. Instead, it was just a sad affair that few people showed up to.

Rod deserved so much better.

"I'm going to take a nap," Beth said. She walked over to the bed and lay down, pulling up the sheet over her belly. She closed her eyes and leaned her head back onto the pillow.

From across the bedroom, Gary stared at her. Beth had spent nearly all of the funeral sitting in a chair, only standing when a visitor arrived. She claimed her feet were sore, but Gary wasn't sure if that was the whole story. He'd caught her grabbing her forehead and wincing a few times, but each time he asked her about it, she insisted she was fine.

He walked over to the bed and sat down next to Beth. She opened her eyes.

"Are you feeling okay?" Gary asked. He reached down and brushed a strand of hair away from her forehead.

"I'm just tired," she said. "It's been an exhausting day."

"It's more than exhaustion, Beth. I can tell you have a headache. If it's bad, we should go to the hospital, get you checked out."

"If I went to the hospital every time I had a headache, I'd be there a few times a day." She smiled a barely-there smile, closed her eyes, and turned to the side.

Gary remained sitting on the bed, staring down at her.

Beth.

So much had happened, so much tragedy, and it had all been for Beth. And yet even with everything that had occurred, her life still hung in the balance. At any time, he could lose her. Just as quick as a light switch being flipped off, she could be gone.

If Rod's death had crushed him, losing Beth would annihilate him, blow him away. Grief would consume him for the rest of his life. The emptiness would be too much to bear.

Gary stared at the back of Beth's head. He thought about the time bomb inside her skull, the time bomb that continued to tick away.

Tick-tock. Tick-tock. Tick-tock.

31

THAT NEXT MORNING, GARY SAT ALONE AT THE KITCHEN TABLE. A BOWL of instant oatmeal and a cup of lukewarm coffee rested on the table in front of him, but he wasn't looking at his breakfast. He was turned away from the table, staring down the hallway at their closed bedroom door.

The door was closed because Beth was in bed, the same place she'd been for almost every one of the sixteen hours since Rod's funeral. The only time she'd gotten out of bed was to eat a brief breakfast with Gary earlier. She'd said little during breakfast and promptly walked back to the bedroom, closing the door behind her.

Something was wrong. Gary could feel it, sense it, like a change in air pressure. Beth hadn't spent almost an entire day in bed because of exhaustion or the pregnancy or grief from Rod's funeral. No, it was the tumor. Her headaches were getting worse.

Gary pulled out his phone and typed a Web site address. His screen was partially shattered from when he'd thrown it against the wall, but the phone still worked. Once the site loaded, he stared through the cracked screen at the fund-raiser page that Beth had set up last week.

The thermometer stick at the bottom of the page was just past twenty-five thousand dollars. If they factored in other donations and the money they could scrape together themselves, they'd hardly crack forty thousand. Just a fraction of the money they needed.

He let out a long, heavy sigh. Since Beth's very first collapse, everything had been so frantic and desperate, but now he was just tired. Weary. Beat down. He felt like a man drowning in a sea of grief, endless waves crashing around him, soon to swallow him whole.

What was he going to do? Piece together the money from friends? Beth had already pleaded with every single person they knew. Keep plugging away with the fund-raising site? It would take years to raise the money they needed at this rate. Pray for a miracle or—

The doorbell rang, interrupting his thoughts. He walked down the hallway and looked out the small window next to the front door.

His heart caught in his chest when he saw who was standing outside.

"I WAS IN THE NEIGHBORHOOD, WANTED TO STOP BY," DETECTIVE WHITLEY said after Gary opened the door.

Gary was too shocked to do anything but silently stare at the detective. Whitley wore a button-down shirt, blazer, and jeans, which seemed to be the only type of clothing he ever wore. He had a serious, no-nonsense look on his face. That expression seemed to be the only look he ever wore, too.

"I wanted to check in with you regarding the investigation into Rod's death," Whitley said. "Can I come in?"

He's found something, Gary thought as he moved aside so Whitley could enter the house. Whitley was visiting because he'd found something at the scene of Rod's death. One of Gary's fingerprints, an eyewitness who saw his car, some bit of evidence that linked him to the scene. This was going to be it. Whitley knew he was hiding something.

"What have you found?" Gary asked.

"Well, nothing, actually. We haven't found a thing—no fingerprints at the scene, no eyewitnesses, no nothing. If we're going to solve this, we're gonna need one of two things: a miracle or some sort of lead. That's why I'm here. It's been a few days. Have you been able to think of anyone Rod knew who might've done this?"

Gary stared at Whitley. The detective wasn't here to arrest him, but Gary felt no elation or joy. Not even relief. All he felt was the same old weariness.

"I know I already asked you this question earlier," Whitley said. "But I thought a few days might've helped you remember something or someone. A friend, an enemy, someone Rod argued with? Anyone who could've played a part in this?"

Gary shook his head.

"What about the funeral yesterday? Did anyone show up who seemed suspicious? Someone you didn't recognize?"

"No."

"No one at all?"

"The turnout was pretty small," Gary said. "There weren't more than forty people in attendance."

"We heard the same thing from his wife when we talked to her.

Sarah. She wasn't much help—she spent most of the time talking about how she thought there was more to the story, like there's some conspiracy."

Whitley walked back toward the front door and stepped outside. "I wish I had better news to report," he said. "We'll keep looking into it, do everything we can to find whoever did this. Obviously."

"Thank you."

"You've got my card—don't hesitate to call if you think of anything."

"I will."

Gary grabbed the door handle to shut the door behind Whitley. Before it closed, he stopped. "Wait a second."

An idea had flashed into Gary's mind, an idea of how to end everything. Before he even had a chance to think it through or talk himself out of it, he had called out to Whitley with those three words: "Wait a second."

"Gary?" Whitley said.

He could still back out. Gary knew he could just tell Whitley that it was nothing and the detective would leave. And there was a voice in his mind telling him to do just that, telling him that it was foolish to turn this thought into action. It was a logical voice. . . . But Gary realized that he wasn't operating on the basis of logic anymore. He was tired and broken and, above all, willing to risk everything to end this. He just wanted it to be over.

"I thought of someone," Gary said.

"Go on."

"It might be nothing, but around a week ago, Rod met a man outside of our business," Gary said. He was making up the story on the fly, freewheeling it. "They had a really intense, heated discussion in the parking lot. This guy was yelling at Rod, gesturing wildly. Rod was screaming back at him. At one point, I thought there was going to be a fight. When Rod came back into the office, he was really shaken up. Distracted. He claimed he was fine, but I could tell he wasn't."

"Why didn't you mention this earlier?"

"I'd forgotten all about it, with everything that's happened. It just popped into my mind. Like I said, maybe it's nothing."

"Do you know who this guy was?"

"No, but I remember what he looked like."

"Describe him."

"He was bald. Medium height. These piercing, intense eyes. A scowl on his face. And tattoos. He had tattoos everywhere, all over his arms."

"White guy?"

"Yeah. He looked Irish."

"What did the tattoos look like?"

"Most of them were just random lines and designs. He had the word *Edgewood* tattooed on one arm—I remember that."

"Edgewood, as in the neighborhood in the south part of town? You're sure that's what it said?"

"Positive."

"Okay," Whitley said. A bit more of a reaction—moderate intrigue. "What else do you remember?"

"Nothing, really. It's not much, I know. But I still remember what the guy looked like. If I saw a picture of him, I'd recognize him."

"Might be a long shot, but it's worth looking into," Whitley said, nodding. "If the guy has a connection to Edgewood, I can pretty much guarantee he's in our system. I'll do a search, see what comes up. You got an hour to come down to the station with me, take a look at a few mug shots?"

"Of course," Gary said.

DETECTIVE WHITLEY AND GARY SAT ON OPPOSITE SIDES OF A DESK, IN A ROOM that was some sort of wide-open communal office area. Approximately twenty desks littered the area, a handful of which were occupied by plainclothes detectives and uniformed officers. The room's walls were covered in maps of the city, Post-it notes, sheets of paper with random scrawlings. Commotion and activity were everywhere—phones ringing, murmured conversations, the tapping of fingers on keyboards.

Whitley rummaged through a few desk drawers until he found a small key chain.

"I'm gonna run the description you gave me through our system," he said. "For a few years now, we've photographed the tattoos of people we arrest, kept a log of them. An Edgewood tattoo'll be pretty common, but maybe we'll get lucky. Maybe you'll recognize one of the results."

Whitley walked away. Alone at the desk, Gary blocked out the chatter and activity surrounding him. He concentrated, focused, cleared his mind.

Twenty minutes earlier, he'd scrawled out a note for Beth, left the house, and followed Whitley's cruiser to the police station. His heart beat heavily in his chest for the entire drive. Being inside the police station only made him more nervous. This haphazard plan that he'd put together on the fly was a risk. If he slipped up at any point and Whitley suspected something, everything could go terribly, horribly wrong.

But he had no other options. And if everything worked out, there was a chance he could get Shamrock's name from the police. That was all he wanted. A name.

When Whitley returned to the desk, he carried two items: a can of soda and a stack of papers roughly thirty sheets high.

"Brought you a Coke," Whitley said, setting it down.

"Thanks." Gary popped the top and took a sip.

"I ran a search in our system for anyone with an Edgewood tattoo on their arm who matched your description," Whitley said. "Got thirty-four names. I figured there'd be more. I sometimes feel we've arrested every single resident of Edgewood at some point in their lives."

Whitley spread out the sheets of paper on the desk in front of Gary. "Now, there are no guarantees here. No guarantee this guy's been arrested before. Even if he's in our system, there's no guarantee he had the Edgewood tattoo when he was arrested—maybe it's a recent tattoo, something he got after he was arrested. And there's obviously no guarantee the guy Rod was talking with had anything to do with his murder."

"Right," Gary said.

"Guarantees or not, take a look at these mug shots and tell me if you recognize anyone."

Gary looked at the thirty-odd mug shots spread out on the desk. Scowling, angry faces stared up at him. Each mug shot was taken from the neck up, in front of a white backdrop. Fat, skinny, young, old. Some white; some looked Eastern European; some looked to be lighter-skinned Hispanic.

Gary scanned past the depressing collection of mug shots, his eyes darting from picture to picture, eliminating them one by one.

The one in the upper left—the guy was too young.

The one next to that—the face was too full.

In the picture underneath that, the man had a teardrop tattoo underneath one eye, something Gary didn't remember seeing on Shamrock. Another had a Mexican flag tattooed on one cheek. Another had two gleaming gold teeth for his front teeth. Gary scanned the pictures, eliminating a few more because of weight, age, tattoos or other marks he didn't remember seeing.

And then Gary spotted him. On the right side of the desk was the mug shot he was searching for. Shamrock. He had a street-tough scowl on his face and was staring into the camera with those cold, dead eyes.

Gary knew he had to proceed carefully. He reached down and picked out five of the mug shots—Shamrock's and those of four others who looked somewhat similar to him.

"These five kind of look familiar," Gary said.

"Okay."

"Do you know their names? Maybe I'll recognize one, remember Rod mentioning a name," Gary said.

Whitley looked down at the five mug shots Gary picked out. He moved the mouse on his desk and the computer screen came to life. Whitley clicked the mouse a few times and then typed something.

"The one on the left there is Miguel Sanchez—Dirty Sanchez is his nickname," Whitley said.

More typing.

"Next one is Mike Smith," Whitley said. "No known nickname."

More typing. The third mug shot, the one in the middle, was Shamrock.

"Next one is Otto Brennan, no known nickname."

Whitley mentioned a name for the other two mug shots, but Gary wasn't paying attention.

Otto Brennan. Otto. That was Shamrock's name.

"Any of those names sound familiar?" Whitley said.

"Sanchez," Gary said. He wanted to steer them away from Otto. "Yeah. I think I remember Rod mentioning the name Sanchez into the phone. Maybe it's nothing, but it sounds familiar."

"It's worth looking into," Whitley said. "Common last name, but it could be something."

BACK IN HIS CAR, IT TOOK GARY TEN MINUTES OF SEARCHING ON HIS SMART-phone to find that Otto Brennan owned a pawnshop named Solid Gold Pawn. Looking at the address, Gary realized that he and Rod had passed within a few blocks of the pawnshop when they'd been in Edgewood earlier.

Gary started up his car and backed out of the stall.

He had a name and an address. He needed only one more thing.

————

" NEED A GUN."

Brian stared at Gary from behind the counter of Michigan Mini Storage. Gary had driven straight to the storage facility after leaving the police station. He'd walked up to the counter and gotten straight to the point—no small talk, not even a greeting.

"Excuse me?" Brian said.

"I want to buy a gun from you," Gary said. "You mentioned that you keep the contents of lockers when people fall behind on their payments, auction off the items if they don't claim them. Do you ever find guns?"

"Sometimes. People aren't supposed to store firearms in the lockers, but they do."

"I want to buy one from you."

"You want me to sell you a gun?" Brian said.

"Yes."

"Are you serious?"

"I am."

"Man, I can't do—"

Gary reached into his pocket and set a small stack of hundred-dollar bills on the counter—money from his "down payment."

"How mu—"

"Two thousand dollars," Gary said.

Brian looked up at Gary.

"Two grand?"

"It's yours. All I need is a gun."

"That's a ton of money to pay for a handgun, you know."

"I don't have time to deal with the paperwork and applications. I need the gun now. That's why I'm willing to pay so much."

Brian stared at the stack of hundred-dollar bills. "What's the gun for?"

"Does it matter?" Gary said.

"Kinda. Yeah. I mean, if you're gonna, like, kill someone, I could get in trouble."

"I'm not going to kill someone," Gary said. "I need the gun for home protection. There've been some break-ins in my neighborhood recently and they haven't caught anyone yet. I want the gun for protection. Just in case."

Brian's eyes remained fixed on the stack of money.

"Please," Gary said. "My wife is pregnant with our first child, and I don't feel safe right now. I'm sure I won't even need it, but I have to be able to protect her if something happens."

Brian nodded. "All right," he said. "Take the money out to your car. I'll bring the gun out to you. So we're not caught on camera."

Gary grabbed the stack of bills and walked out to his car. A minute later, Brian exited the office and sat down in the passenger's seat. Gary handed him the money and Brian set a handgun on the armrest between them. It was the same compact size as the gun Gary used in the murder. This gun had a two-tone finish, all black except for a stainless-steel barrel.

"If anyone asks, you didn't get this from me," Brian said.

"Of course."

"It's not loaded, so you gotta—"

"It's not loaded?"

"Nah, we empty out the clips when we store the guns."

"It's useless to me if it's not loaded."

"There's a couple boxes of ammo inside. I know how to load a gun, so I could do it for you." Brian smiled. "But that'll cost you extra."

Gary handed another hundred-dollar bill to Brian, who took the gun and walked back inside. Reappeared after a few seconds. Gave the gun back to Gary.

"It's loaded," Brian said.

"Thank you." Gary grabbed the gun and slid it into the front pocket of his jacket. "Not a word of this to anyone."

"Right," Brian said. "Same to you. Not a word to anyone."

———

H E HAD A NAME, AN ADDRESS, AND A GUN. ALL THAT WAS LEFT WAS TO wait for night to arrive.

Gary placed the gun in the Corolla's glove compartment and left.

Back home, he walked down the hallway and lightly pushed open the bedroom door. Beth was up and out of bed, standing next to her dresser.

"You're awake," Gary said as he walked into the bedroom.

"I am," she said. "Bonnie Jacobs called and woke me up. She said her husband sold off his old set of golf clubs and they're giving us the proceeds. Almost four hundred dollars."

"That's great."

Beth grabbed a pair of white socks from a dresser drawer. She tossed the socks and a T-shirt onto a pair of pants laid out on the bed.

"How are you feeling?" he asked.

"I'm fine."

"Is your headache—"

"I'm fine, Gary. I just needed to lie down."

But Gary knew there was more to the story. She'd spent most of the past day in bed, yet she still looked worn-out. She was moving sluggishly. Even if she said she was fine, he could tell she wasn't.

Beth grabbed the small stack of clothes from the bed and gave Gary a peck on the cheek as she passed him. "I'm taking a shower," she said.

"I'll warm up some lunch. You have any preference?"

"I'm starving—anything sounds good," she said as she headed toward the bathroom.

"Hold on," Gary said.

Beth turned around and looked at him. "Yes?"

"Come here for a second. There's something I want to say."

"Can this wait until I'm done with my shower?"

"This'll only take a minute."

"What is it?" she asked.

"Do you remember what you said to me earlier?" Gary said. "It was when you returned from the hospital, right after you collapsed the second time. You made me promise that I'd move on if something happened to you. You said you didn't want me to be consumed by grief if I lost you. Remember?"

Beth nodded.

"I want you to know that I feel the same way. If something happened to me, I'd want you to move on if you survive. If I wasn't around any longer, I'd want you to find someone else. Someone who makes you happy, someone who would be a good father to Tyson. Okay?"

"Why are you saying this to me?" Beth asked.

"I don't know. Maybe it was Rod's funeral. Something like that puts things into perspective. Makes you think." He reached over and squeezed her hand.

"But I mean it. Promise me you'll move on if something happens to me." She stared at him. That same familiar look of suspicion. Like she was trying to read him. Trying to understand if he was being totally honest with her.

"Okay," Beth finally said. "I will."

"Good."

And he added, right after that:

"I love you."

He reached out and hugged her, holding her in his arms. Behind Beth was a small mirror hanging from the wall. Gary looked at his reflection, stared into his eyes. He'd aged a decade since Rod's death, it seemed. His complexion was ashen and pale. His hairline looked like it had thinned even more; the hair that remained was unkempt. His eyes were shadowed and dark.

But there was no recklessness in those eyes. There was just clear, lucid intensity staring back at him. The moment was almost here.

Earlier, he'd felt like a man drowning at sea, waves of anguish and grief crashing all around him, pulling him under.

But now he thought he might just have one final kick left in him. One last desperate kick before the current swallowed him whole.

32

AN HOUR AFTER BETH WENT TO BED THAT NIGHT, GARY STOPPED HIS CAR a half block away from Solid Gold Pawn, on the opposite side of the street. The pawnshop was located in a battered, decaying building, the type of place that had probably looked depressing the moment it was built. The lights inside the pawnshop were on, but the front window was so crammed with merchandise, it was impossible to see inside the store from this distance.

Gary removed the key from the ignition and grabbed the gun from the glove compartment. He waited in his car for five minutes. No vehicles passed through the street intersection beside Solid Gold Pawn. No people walked past the pawnshop. He was alone.

He opened the car door and stepped out into the chilly night, his trembling hand clenched tightly around the gun. He quickly walked across the empty parking lot and crouched down in front of Solid Gold Pawn. He peeked past the merchandise stacked in the window.

It looked like a regular pawnshop, nothing out of the ordinary. Otto stood behind the counter, roughly thirty feet away from the front door. The big man from the Alpine Development—Champ—stood next to him. Neither man noticed Gary looking in at them through the window.

Gary swallowed. This was it. The tension was so great that he felt like his body could simply cease functioning at any moment.

He opened the door with one hand and held the gun out from his body with his other hand. The movement caught the men's attention and they looked over. Neither man uttered a word.

Gary moved the gun from Otto, to Champ, back to Otto, going back and forth between the two men. He took another step into the pawnshop.

"Nobody move," he said.

NOBODY MOVED.

Otto stood behind the counter, frozen in place, staring across the room at Gary Foster—more accurately, staring at the gun in his hand. The barrel was pointed at Otto's chest, not point-blank range but close enough. Less than twenty feet. If Gary started firing, it'd be over. His life would end at the hands of Gary Foster. Of all the hardened criminals and thugs he'd squared off against over the years, this pissant would be the one to end it all.

That wasn't going to happen.

"Just calm down," Otto said.

"I am calm," Gary said. His voice was soulless, detached. There was a dead, cold confidence in Gary's eyes. He wasn't fucking around.

Otto put his hands up in the air, palms out. "We can work something out," he said.

"I want the money," Gary said. He took a step toward them. Fifteen feet away now.

"Just calm d—"

"Where the hell is the money?"

The gun remained pointed at Otto's chest. One squeeze of the trigger—that's all it would take to end everything. Somehow he had to buy himself some time. "The money's downstairs," Otto said. "All of it. You can have it."

"Downstairs?" Gary said.

"There's a fake door built into the wall. Right underneath those guitars to your left. A staircase is behind it. There's a safe with the money down there."

"You're lying."

"I'm not. This is no bullshit. I'm the only one who knows the combination to the safe. You kill me, the money stays there. You let me live, it's yours."

The silence in the room dragged on. Gary stared across the room, looking far different from the timid, desperate man Otto had met with before.

"Lift up your shirt," he said. "Show me you're not carrying a weapon."

Otto lifted the hem of his white T-shirt, revealing his ink-covered stomach. He slowly spun around. When he was facing Gary again, he bent over and patted down the legs of his pants. "No gun," Otto said. "See? I'm not armed. I'm not gonna try nothing."

"What about you?" Gary said. He gestured at Champ. "Lift up your shirt."

Champ lifted his shirt and slowly spun around. He patted down his legs. "No gun," he said.

"Okay," Gary said. "Walk over to the door. Either of you try anything, I'll pull the trigger."

GARY KEPT THE GUN POINTED AT CHAMP AND OTTO AS THEY WALKED ACROSS the pawnshop floor. When they reached the display of electric guitars hanging from the wall, Otto nudged the gray wainscoting underneath the guitars. The wall moved inward, opening on hinges that made a low, barely audible squeaking noise.

Behind the door, Gary saw a darkened stairway. A set of around fifteen wooden stairs descended down to a pitch-black room. "The money's down there?" Gary said.

"Yeah. The light switch is right over there, to my left. I'm gonna hit it," Otto said. He flipped the switch and a light at the base of the stairs flickered on.

"Start walking," Gary said.

They took the stairs one by one. Otto in front, struggling to navigate the stairs with his bad leg. Champ in the middle. Gary in the rear, the gun pointed at their backs. Gary was in total control of the situation but that did little to calm his racing heart.

Once they reached the final step, Gary looked around the small shadowy room. The floor was made up of scuffed panels of driftwood. The room was packed with metal storage racks pushed up against the walls. Cardboard boxes marked with their contents were stacked on the shelves: LAPTOP COMPUTERS, DVDS, PAPERBACK BOOKS. A dim lightbulb hung in the middle of the room, directly above a large metal table with various items strewn on top of it.

"Where's the money?" Gary asked.

"The safe's right there," Otto said. "To your left. On the floor."

Gary's eyes scanned past the cardboard boxes stacked on top of one another. Below them, a metal safe rested on the floor.

"You," Gary said, gesturing at Champ with the gun. "Stand in the corner of the room."

Champ walked over to the corner.

Gary turned to Otto. "Now unlock the safe."

OTTO CROUCHED DOWN IN FRONT OF THE SAFE, WINCING AT THE DULL PAIN in his bad knee. He spun the dial until it came to rest on the notch directly above the 15. He took his time, trying to think of some sort of escape plan, some way to get out of this mess. Something. Anything.

Gary would blow his ass away the moment he handed the money over. Of that, Otto was positive. This sure as shit wasn't going to end with them sharing a laugh over the misunderstanding and happily going their separate ways.

But even if he somehow convinced Gary to let him live, he'd have no way to pay off his debt to De La Fuente without the money in the safe. He'd be a dead man walking.

Otto turned the safe dial to the right. He thought about the contents of the boxes stacked against the wall. Was there a gun in one of them? Probably, but there was no time to search for it. Gary would pull the trigger and end him long before he could rummage around in the boxes.

"Unlock the safe," Gary said. "Get to it."

Otto stopped the dial on the 21. He slowly spun the dial back to the left and stopped on the notch above the 25. There was a clicking noise from inside the safe as the lock disengaged.

"Don't open it," Gary said. "Leave it unlocked and walk five steps to your left."

Otto stepped away from the safe, counting off five steps in his mind. He came to a stop just in front of the table in the middle of the room. Champ was a few feet away.

"Stay there and put your hands up," Gary said.

Otto raised his hands over his head. His mind was racing. He had to think of something—some sort of weapon or distraction. He focused on Gary, but through his peripheral vision, he scanned the items on the table in front of him.

There were a few rags and some assorted junk he'd purchased over the past week. The small toolbox resting on the edge of the table intrigued him—he knew there were some scissors and a hammer inside—but Gary was almost ten feet away, too far for either item to be useful.

He glanced at Champ, a few feet away in the corner of the room. Could Champ save him? Doubtful. The big man wasn't even armed. Champ had come to talk, nothing more. Otto was going to hire Champ to burn down Solid Gold Pawn once his debt with De La Fuente was squared away. He planned on being halfway across the city when Champ doused the place in paint thinner and—

Paint thinner.

His eyes skittered back to the table in front of him.

Next to the toolbox was the tin container of paint thinner.

When Otto saw the book of matches on the table beside the paint thinner, he suddenly knew his next move.

GARY TOOK A STEP TOWARD THE SAFE. HE HELD OUT THE GUN FROM HIS BODY with one hand, fingers clenched tightly around the grip, moving the gun back and forth between Otto and Champ.

"It's all inside that safe," Otto said. "The money. It's yours."

Gary was silent. He took another step, passing a storage rack filled with five smaller cardboard boxes sealed with duct tape, each with JEWELRY written on the side. Another step, and he passed two large cardboard boxes—LAPTOP COMPUTERS and DVDS.

Gary finally reached the safe but his eyes and the gun remained fixed on Otto and Champ. With his free hand, he reached behind him and ran his fingers over the front of the safe until he found the latch next to the combination dial. He pulled on the latch and the safe opened.

He glanced away from Otto and looked in the safe. Inside were bundles upon bundles of hundred-dollar bills with orange bands holding them together, an enormous mound of money.

OTTO WATCHED GARY GLANCE AWAY FROM HIM AND LOOK INTO THE SAFE. The money provided a brief distraction, but it was just enough of a window of opportunity. This was his chance. Otto lunged forward and knocked over the can of paint thinner. It glugged out of the container and poured across the table. He immediately grabbed the book of matches and struck one. The flame caught on the first try; he threw the match into the expanding pool of paint thinner.

When the match's flame hit the liquid, there was an instant explosion.

BY THE TIME GARY NOTICED OTTO'S MOVEMENT, IT WAS TOO LATE. BEFORE he could pull the trigger, a whirlwind of orange and yellow flames jumped off the table, shooting nearly to the room's ceiling, rushing toward him like a blast from a flamethrower. The burst of fire hit him before he could turn away. The flames stung Gary's eyes like acid, singed his skin. He instantly fell backward, away from the flames, landing on his back.

He dropped the gun and furiously rubbed his hands into his stinging eyes, unable to see anything but total blackness. Gary coughed, dry heaved. The filthy, scorched smell of smoke was spreading throughout the room. Bent over on his hands and knees, Gary blinked open his eyes. His vision was blurred, eyes watery. Through the blurriness, he saw three things.

First, the flames; they were everywhere. The fire had spread onto the dusty, dry cardboard boxes that lined the room. The flames jumped from box to box, quickly scattering throughout the room.

The second was a person covered in thick flames, flailing his arms in the corner of the basement as the fire roared all over him.

The third thing Gary saw was a shape charging toward him through the smoke billowing throughout the room.

Otto.

Gary tried to stand, but before he could get to his feet, Otto kicked him in the ribs. The tip of Otto's boot felt like an ice pick stabbing into the side of his body.

Gary let out a grunt and collapsed onto his stomach. He gasped for air and inhaled a lungful of smoke. He coughed. His vision clouded with tears.

Flames roared around them. From the other side of the room, Gary heard screams coming from the body on fire. He recognized Champ's deep voice. Champ continued to scream and yell and flail his burning body around on the ground.

Gary felt Otto's boot smash against his ribs again, in nearly the same spot. The impact made him roll onto his back. Another vicious kick from Otto forced Gary back onto his stomach.

"You motherfucker, you almost had me," Otto said.

Another kick from Otto. The pain in Gary's ribs was so intense that it hurt to breathe. He felt like he was on the verge of passing out. He inhaled another lungful of smoke and instantly coughed it back out—a whooping, powerful cough that rocked his entire frame.

Suddenly, through his blurred vision, he spotted it. The handgun. He'd dropped it when he fell to the ground, but there it was, on the scuffed wooden floor, just a few feet out of reach. Gary stretched for the gun, but before he could grab it Otto's boot streaked past his hand and kicked it away. The gun slid across the floor and disappeared into the flames.

END THIS. OTTO KNEW HE HAD TO END THIS AND GET THE HELL OUT OF THE basement before it was too late. The storage racks of cardboard boxes were quickly turning into a giant, roaring wall of fire. Some of the flames were jumping so high that they reached a section of the ceiling. It was only a matter of time before the first floor collapsed right on top of them. This shitbox building was old. It wouldn't withstand much more.

He didn't know how much longer he'd be able to hold up, either. He was kicking Gary with his good leg, but with every kick, he felt his bad knee buckle. It could give out at any time.

End this, grab the money, and get out of here—that was what he had to do. Otto limped toward Gary's writhing body and kicked him in the ribs again.

Through the corner of his eye, Otto saw Champ. He was no longer moving, no longer screaming. Flames danced all over his motionless body.

Otto looked around the room and tried to spot the gun. Where the hell had it gone after he kicked it?

Fuck it. He didn't need a gun to kill someone.

———

BLACKNESS CREPT IN AROUND THE CORNERS OF GARY'S EYES. HE FELT woozy, dazed. He inhaled another lungful of smoke and he coughed, wheezed, nearly vomited.

Another kick or two and he'd pass out for good. Somehow he had to fight back. He forced himself onto his knees. The room spun around him, moving in and out of focus. He felt the tip of Otto's boot kick him in his lower back, right by his kidney. The impact propelled Gary forward. He slammed against the metal table, upturning it and sending the scattered items on top crashing to the ground around him.

Gary could barely see or breathe, but in the mess of items on the ground he spotted an overturned red toolbox. Small wrenches, a couple of hammers, and a pair of scissors littered the ground.

He mustered up every last bit of willpower and stretched out his arm. He closed his fingers around the first item he could reach: the scissors.

He spun onto his back. Otto kicked toward him again, but this time Gary was ready for him. He reached out with the hand not holding the scissors and blocked the kick. Gary wrapped his arm around

Otto's leg and squeezed it against his body, as if holding on for his life. With his other hand, he stabbed the scissors into Otto's left knee socket, the same leg he'd been limping around on. Otto screamed out in pain. Gary forced the scissors in farther, leaning in and putting his full body weight behind them. He twisted his wrist and felt the scissors scrape against bone, sever through tissue. Otto screamed again. Gary let go of the leg and Otto fell to the ground, holding his knee.

OTTO YANKED THE HANDLE BURIED IN HIS KNEE, TRYING TO PULL THE SCIS-sors loose. He grimaced and screamed. The bullet shattering this knee-cap years ago had been excruciating, but this pain was far worse, unlike anything he'd ever felt.

He clenched his jaw. Yanked the handle again. He felt the blade inch out of his knee, the pain so intense he nearly passed out.

GARY STOOD UPRIGHT, ALMOST FALLING BACK DOWN BEFORE CATCHING HIS balance. The air was heavy with heat and smoke and both were rapidly intensifying.

He looked over at Otto, sprawled on the ground a few feet away, grabbing the scissors in his knee. Directly to Otto's side, towering above him, was a large metal storage rack, its shelves filled with cardboard boxes and assorted merchandise, all of it on fire.

Gary hobbled over to the storage rack. He grabbed a rag from the ground and wrapped it around his hand. Without hesitating, he thrust the hand into the flames and grabbed a diagonal cross brace on the side of the rack. Holding on to it, he leaned backward and pulled as hard as he could.

The rack tipped over. Gary rolled to the side, moving out of the way just as the burning boxes of merchandise all tumbled off the shelf, falling onto Otto, covering his body in flaming boxes. The storage rack toppled, too, trapping Otto underneath the flames.

Gary unwrapped the fiery rag and threw it to the side. Under the flaming pile of boxes, he could see Otto thrashing on the ground. Otto's hand shot up from the flames, moving wildly from side to side, pounding feebly against the large storage rack, rocking it in place but barely moving it at all.

And then the hand went limp, motionless. It fell back to the ground and was swallowed whole by the raging flames. Gary stared at it, waiting to make sure it didn't move again, but it remained lifelessly flopped on top of a burning cardboard box, the skin charring to a deep black as the flames consumed it.

Gary scanned the room.

Champ's body was a motionless heap in the corner, completely covered in flames.

All around Gary were stacks of burning cardboard boxes.

To his left was the safe.

The safe's door was still open, lightly swaying on its hinges. Flames were dancing around it, but they hadn't yet spread to the bundles of money inside.

He ran to the safe. A black duffel bag resting on top of the safe was also untouched by the fire. Gary grabbed the bag and held it open in front of the safe. In one sweeping motion, he shoveled the stacks of money into it. A few bundles landed inside, but most spilled out onto the floor. Gary grabbed them and threw the handfuls of money into the bag as quickly as he could.

He heard a loud snap, followed by a tremendous boom that shook the floor. He glanced behind him and saw that a four-foot-wide section of burning ceiling had caved into the basement, leaving an open hole above him. Flames danced through the hole, reaching the pawnshop's first floor.

Gary grabbed the final stack of money from the floor and threw it into the bag. Shielding his eyes from the smoke, Gary ran to the staircase and hurried up the steps. Behind him, he heard another boom and a loud crash. The entire building shook.

He reached the top of the stairs. The floor of the pawnshop was covered with holes, some no more than a few feet wide, some larger. Gary sucked in a deep breath and held it as he ran across the pawnshop floor, avoiding the flames that leapt from the holes. He could hear the fire roaring in the basement below, could feel the heat spewing up like blasts from a furnace.

Gary reached the front door and kicked it open. He stepped out into the night and immediately collapsed to the ground, inhaling deep lungful after deep lungful of the fresh, cold night air.

He huddled on the ground for a few seconds. The fire hadn't consumed enough of the pawnshop's ground floor to attract attention yet, but it would be only minutes until it did. The fire department and police would be showing up soon.

Gary stood up and looked both ways down the block. No people, no cars—nothing but abandoned and boarded-up buildings in either direction.

He hurried across the street to his car and threw the duffel bag onto the passenger's seat.

He started the engine and drove away from Solid Gold Pawn.

33

GARY'S FIRST STOP WAS ASCENSION OUTERWEAR.
With the black duffel bag slung over his shoulder, he headed
into the bathroom in the rear of the store. He flipped on the lights
and looked at his reflection in the mirror.

He'd expected worse. He'd expected to see some mangled, charred,
unrecognizable mess staring back at him. But he didn't look terrible.
Black soot and ashes covered his clothes and face, and there was dried
blood caked around a cut on his forehead, but the soot could be washed
away and the cut was small, less than an inch long. The skin on the
hand he'd thrust into the fire was pink but not terribly burned—the
rag he'd wrapped around kept it protected.

He threw the duffel bag on the ground and lifted up his shirt.
Purple bruises covered his rib cage and stomach. He let his shirt fall
back into place and turned on the faucet. He cupped his hands un-

derneath it and splashed water onto his face, washing a darkened mixture of soot and blood down the drain. He dried his face on his shirt and looked in the mirror. Better.

He changed into fresh clothes taken from the store shelves and carried the duffel bag into the back office. The room still hadn't been cleaned from his earlier outburst, and papers and various items were scattered all over the floor. He watched his step as he walked over to the desk. He flipped the duffel bag upside down and half-inch-thick bundles of money scattered onto the desktop. Gary counted each bundle as he arranged them into two stacks. When he finished stacking them, he'd counted exactly twenty-seven bundles in total: fourteen bundles in one stack; thirteen bundles in the other.

Two hundred seventy thousand dollars, right in front of him.

Strangely, the sight was a little underwhelming. Two hundred seventy thousand dollars seemed like such an enormous amount of money, such an inconceivable figure, but it looked like nothing special when it was arranged like this. Just two small stacks, each barely six inches thick.

Gary placed the money back into the bag. He zipped it shut and set it down by his feet. He leaned back in the chair. The rush had dulled but it wasn't entirely gone; his body still hummed like a low-voltage electrical wire.

"Jesus Christ," he said, staring at the ceiling. "That just happened."

———

"BETH, I HAVE SOMETHING AMAZING TO TELL YOU."

Beth turned over in bed, squinting her eyes as she adjusted to the light in their bedroom.

"Gary, what—"

"Just listen to me, Beth."

In one hand, he held a nondescript plastic shopping bag. Inside was the money and a note he'd printed off at the store. The note was nearly identical to the one he'd typed earlier—the message explaining the money was from an anonymous donor.

He handed the shopping bag to Beth.

"What is this?"

"Look inside."

She set the bag on the bed beside her and glanced inside. No reaction. Not at first. She turned the bag upside down and stacks of money fell out onto their bedsheets.

"What . . ." she whispered.

"Read the note, Beth."

The note had fallen on top of the money. Beth picked it up and read it. Still no reaction. "I don't understand," she said.

"An anonymous donor came through with the money. We have enough to pay for the trial, the Germany trip. Everything."

"Gary, what . . ." Again, the word trailed off. She looked at the pile of money, back at the note, at Gary. "Who was it?"

"I have no idea," he said. "I was at the store, and there was a knock at the door. When I answered it, this bag was right out front. Inside, I found the note and the money."

Beth's eyes went back to the stacks of money. Her jaw started to tremble.

"Someone gave us the money?" she said.

"Yeah. Someone came through. There's two hundred seventy thousand there. I counted it. Everything we need, plus extra."

"I don't believe it." She placed a hand over her mouth. Still in disbelief, but sheer joy was starting to creep into her expression, too.

"I didn't believe it, either. Not at first. When it finally sank in, I came straight here. I had to wake you up to tell you."

Tears welled in Beth's eyes. She sat up from the bed and wrapped her arms around Gary, hugging him tight. Gary winced from the pain that flared up when the bump of Beth's belly pushed up against his ribs.

She had more questions for Gary, mostly about the identity of the anonymous donor. Had he seen anyone in the area? Did he have any idea who it could be? Gary told her he had no clue.

"This can't be real," Beth said.

"It's real, Beth. Believe it."

———

DEPOSITING THE MONEY WAS A PAINLESS PROCESS.

After staying up almost all night, their first stop was the bank that next morning. The bank officer barely even reacted when Gary told him he wanted to deposit $270,000 cash. He didn't ask where the money came from, and Gary or Beth didn't volunteer that information. After having Gary present two forms of identification, the bank officer led them to a room in the back, where the money was counted. And then they were done.

The entire process took less than fifteen minutes.

THAT AFTERNOON, THEY HAD A SKYPE CALL WITH A REPRESENTATIVE FROM GOSKA. Pages of paperwork were e-mailed to them. Gary and Beth filled them out.

As they waited to hear back, they posted an update to the fund-raising site that told people about the anonymous donation. Beth and Gary offered to repay everyone who'd donated through the site, as the money was no longer needed. It seemed like the right thing to do, but many insisted that Gary and Beth keep the money.

A few days after they sent their information to GOSKA, they received the e-mail they'd been waiting for: Beth had been approved for treatment.

It would begin on June 4. Two weeks after Beth's due date.

Barely a month away.

34

LATER IN THE WEEK, BETH WAS OUT GROCERY SHOPPING, SO GARY HAD the house to himself. It was one of the first times he'd been truly alone since that night at Solid Gold Pawn.

He sat down at the kitchen table. The days had been so busy. They'd planned out their move to Germany. Booked plane tickets. Found a cute Airbnb place to rent. It was ironic that the exotic move abroad they'd always talked about over the years would finally happen—under circumstances that neither of them could have ever foreseen.

As the days had passed, Gary had constantly searched for any information about the pawnshop fire. Thus far, there was nothing. It wasn't so surprising—the pawnshop was a run-down business in a rough neighborhood, a neighborhood where crime happened so frequently the local media barely even covered it.

But as he pulled his smartphone from his pocket and looked at it now, Gary found an article: the police had discovered two dead bodies buried in the rubble of a pawnshop fire that occurred days ago in the Edgewood neighborhood. Drug paraphernalia was found in the rubble, and authorities suspected a drug deal gone bad. The fire wasn't newsworthy, but apparently the discovery of two dead bodies was enough to necessitate a two-paragraph article.

Accompanying the story was a picture of the pawnshop. Rather, the large, smoldering hole in the ground where Solid Gold Pawn once stood. Looking at the charred remains, Gary knew the fire had destroyed any evidence that could have linked him to the crime.

AFTER HE PUT HIS PHONE BACK IN HIS POCKET, IT HIT HIM.

Sitting in the kitchen, all alone, Gary's emotions got the best of him. He buried his face in his hands and cried. He'd held it in over the past few days but the tears came now, overpowering and uncontrollable, messy and hot. His deep sobs echoed in the empty house.

It was impossible to pin down the exact reason for his tears. Were they tears of remorse? Tears of grief? Tears of relief, knowing that they had a shot at saving Beth?

He'd done exactly what he'd wanted to: given Beth a chance at life. He'd accomplished his one goal, the reason for everything that had happened.

So why did he feel like a boxer who'd won on a technicality? There was still so much uncertainty with Beth, but it was more than that. The cost had been so great. So much tragedy. So much heartbreak. He'd done things he never thought himself capable of, seen things he'd never be able to forget.

Gary continued to cry, sobbing into his hands. He inhaled deep, sloppy breaths that racked his entire body. When he thought the tears were over, they started again, even more intensely than before.

―――――

A FEW DAYS LATER, GARY PULLED HIS CAR INTO SARAH'S DRIVEWAY. BETH sat beside him, holding a plain white envelope.

They walked up to the front door and Gary rang the doorbell. Sarah answered a moment later. She was pale and a little shaky, but she looked better, like she was slowly recovering from the flu. There was some life to her eyes. A bit of color had returned to her complexion.

"Hi, Sarah," Gary said. "Can we come in?"

"Of course."

They walked into the living room and sat down on couches across from one another. Beth kept the envelope in her hand.

"I'm sorry I haven't visited," Sarah said. "I wanted to. But . . . well, just look at me."

"You look great," Gary said.

"Thank you. It's not true, but I appreciate the kind words."

"I mean it. I really do."

She briefly smiled. "Well, I'm trying. I don't even know how to begin to move on, but I'm trying. I had the front window to my yoga studio replaced and held a class yesterday—the first one I've held since . . . since Rod died. Only a few people showed up, but it felt nice."

"That's great."

"I'm not sure if I can keep the studio open. Probably not. I don't even know if I want to. The more I think about it, the more I just feel like getting away. Getting away from all the memories here. I just got back from a short trip to Cincinnati, visiting a friend. It was nice."

She turned to Beth.

"Enough about me. How are you?"

"A nervous wreck." A wry smile.

Sarah glanced at Beth's belly. "Three weeks?"

"Unless he comes early. Then a few weeks of rest, for both me and Tyson. And then it's off to Germany."

"That's great. I want to hear all about it."

Gary glanced at the envelope in Beth's hand. He looked back at Sarah.

"There's a reason we're visiting," he said. "We want to talk to you about something."

"Sure."

"As you know, an anonymous donor saw the newspaper article about Beth's situation and came through with the money for the treatment in Germany," he said.

"Yeah. I still can't believe that."

"They gave us about two hundred seventy thousand dollars. With everything taken into account, we'll need about two hundred grand. So we have some money left over. Quite a bit, actually."

"Good. You two deserve it."

"I'm going to use some of the money to close the store. There are bills that need to be paid, fees for breaking our lease—things like that."

"You're closing Ascension?"

Gary nodded. "Keeping it open would just be too difficult."

"I'm sorry. I know how much work you and Rod put into it. He loved the store."

"I can't keep the place open without him. And I wouldn't want to take on another partner. I wouldn't want to do it with anyone but Rod."

"I'm sorry, Gary. I really am."

"There's going to be some money remaining after I tie up all the loose ends. Fifty thousand dollars or so. A pretty decent amount." Gary nodded to Beth. She set the envelope on the coffee table between them.

"What's that?" Sarah asked.

"Open it."

Sarah opened the envelope and pulled out a small piece of paper. A check. She held the check in her hand, staring at it as if it were a foreign object.

"What is this?"

"Exactly what it looks like," Beth said. "A check for sixty-two thousand dollars. We're paying back the twelve thousand you gave us earlier, and we're giving you the money we have left over. All fifty thousand dollars. We want you to have it. You deserve it."

"I . . ." she began, the word trailing off.

"The money's yours, Sarah," Gary said. "Do whatever with it. Use it to move somewhere, if you feel like starting over. Keep your yoga studio open with it if you want to. After everything you've been through, we want you to have it. We talked about it and agreed that this money should go to you."

"I . . . I can't," Sarah said. Her voice was little more than a whisper.

"Of course you can. We insist."

Tears filled her eyes. "Gary . . . Beth . . . this is unbelievable."

Sarah's eyes stayed on the money for a long moment. "Thank you. Thank you so much," she said.

"It was Gary's idea," Beth said. "You should be thanking him."

"Gary," Sarah said. "You're my hero."

Hero. It stung Gary, hearing the word. He wasn't a hero. The heroic thing to do would be to tell Sarah everything. Tell her that Rod had died trying to save him. Tell her that he'd framed Rod for the murder of Devon Peterson. Tell her that Rod was innocent, that he was a good person, that the goofy kid trapped in a man's body that she'd fallen in love with was the real Rod, the true Rod. The Rod she deserved to remember.

That's what a real hero would do: make sure her lasting memory of Rod was an untarnished one, a happy one.

But Gary's secret had to remain a secret. He simply couldn't tell Sarah, couldn't tell anyone. It was unfair to Sarah, so horribly unfair to her, but nothing about any of this was fair. The money didn't make it fair, either, but it was something.

Sarah stood up and hugged Beth. She walked over to Gary and wrapped her arms around him.

"I'm not a hero, Sarah," Gary said. "Not at all. I just did what anyone would've done."

35

"THIS LOOKS GREAT, GARY. ALL OF IT."

Seated at the kitchen table, Gary stared down at the setup in front of them. Plates of chicken carbonara. Sides of roasted asparagus. A vase of roses in the middle of the table next to a bottle of Pinot Grigio. A few candles.

"You deserve it," he said.

"We both do."

The five weeks in Germany had been long and draining. Adjusting to a foreign country. Surrounded by unfamiliarity. Relying on a translation app for most interactions. GOSKA's facility was nearly ten miles from the small apartment they'd rented, and even though they made the trip on a near-daily basis, they repeatedly got lost—the wrong stop, the wrong train, the wrong transfer. As before, Beth had good days and bad days. Some days she hardly got out of bed, and some days she seemed like the same old Beth.

At the end of the five weeks, they'd met with Dr. Tobin, the doctor they'd had their very first Skype call with. She couldn't contain a smile as she gave them the news.

There was no evidence of Beth's tumor.

She was cancer-free.

The moment was pure joy. Gary was so overcome with emotion that, looking back on it, he could hardly recall exactly how they'd reacted. They'd hugged. They might've kissed. He thought they cried but he couldn't remember.

Once they were done celebrating, Dr. Tobin laid out what they could expect going forward. Beth would have to get regular screenings. The cancer could return at any time. Chances were, it probably would, and there was no telling when. A year from now. A decade from now. Or never.

They'd returned to Michigan a week ago. A group of friends waited for them at the airport. In the days that followed, more friends visited.

Their first few days back in the States had been more exhausting than their time abroad. Exhausting in a good way, but they'd longed for a quiet evening to themselves. They'd blocked off their calendars for tonight. It took Gary all afternoon to get everything into place—the grocery shopping, the cooking, the setup.

He grabbed the bottle of wine and filled their wineglasses.

"What should we toast to?" Beth asked, grabbing her glass.

"Your call."

She thought about it for a second.

"The future," she said. "Here's to the future."

They clinked their glasses and took a drink.

Right as they were about to start eating, they were interrupted by a low, barely audible sound from just down the hallway.

The sound of a baby, lightly crying.

IN THE NURSERY, TYSON LAY IN HIS CRIB, FLAILING HIS ARMS AND KICKING his legs. He wore a blue onesie with a baseball bat and the words ALL-STAR on the chest. His pudgy face was scrunched up.

Beth picked him up.

"Bad dream, little guy?" she said, patting his back. He stopped crying almost instantly. She held him in her arms.

"I think he's up for good," she said to Gary. She smiled. "So much for our quiet night alone."

They returned to the kitchen, Tyson strapped to Beth's chest in his carrier. As they started to eat, Gary looked across the table at them both.

A healthy wife.

A beautiful baby boy.

Everything he could ever want.

So why did he feel so sad?

There'd been happy moments over the past month—Tyson's birth, the meeting with Dr. Tobin, other moments with Tyson—but for a majority of the time, all Gary had felt was an inescapable and all-encompassing sadness. It followed him around at all hours of the day. Sometimes there was nothing crushing or overwhelming about it; it was more of a constant, dull sadness, a gloominess that was always there, steady like a flatlining heart rate monitor.

But there were the times, too, when the monitor would suddenly spike. That was when the memory of everything became especially fresh, the times when the sadness would get too big to keep inside of him and the tears came. It didn't happen often, but when it did the breakdown was paralyzing, left him unable to do anything but find a secluded place (usually the shower) and cry until the tears stopped.

He had no one he could talk to about his sadness, about his guilt, about everything that still plagued him. When the tears came, there was no shoulder to cry on. The irony, of course, was that he had murdered Devon Peterson and gotten involved in this mess because he wanted to save Beth, wanted to avoid the crushing sadness he'd feel without her. Instead, he felt as sad as he'd ever felt.

———

THE NEXT DAY, GARY WALKED THROUGH THE AISLES OF ASCENSION OUTerwear.

Up near the entrance were two piles. One was filled with hats, jackets, shoes, and office supplies such as unused printer ink cartridges and a few bar-code scanners. This was the Save pile, the items Gary hoped to resell. Next to this was a slightly smaller Junk pile, the items that would go straight to the garbage—catalogs, promotional posters, some filing cabinets and storage bins that might be worth a little but were too big to hassle with.

Since returning from Germany, he'd spent some time emptying out the store, in preparation for permanently closing it. He still had a long way to go. It sometimes seemed like closing the store was more work than opening it.

He grabbed a few Windbreakers from a rack and carried them over to the Save pile. As he walked back across the store, his eyes caught one of the items still hanging from the wall: the picture of him and Rod on the first day of business. He stared at their smiling, naive faces.

He missed Rod. Missed him so much. That was a huge part of his sadness. Rod had always been so dependent on him—for money, for a place to live, for advice or a steady, helping hand—but Gary had never realized how much he depended on Rod, too. For a quick laugh. For a smile. For a little silliness. For the very things he could use most right now.

With each passing day, it seemed like there was less and less to remember Rod by. And now Ascension Outerwear would soon be closed, gone forever, taking with it all of the late nights and early mornings Gary and Rod had spent together, all of the times they'd shared, just the two of them.

WHEN HE RETURNED HOME, HE FOUND BETH IN THE LIVING ROOM WITH A guest who hadn't visited in a while.

"Sarah," he said. "This is a surprise."

She sat on the couch next to Beth. Gary hadn't seen her since they'd been back from Germany, but she still had that same sad, somber look on her face that he remembered. Frail. So different from the confident, lively woman Rod had fallen in love with.

"It's great to see you," he said. "Come over to see Tyson?"

"Actually, I came to see you," she said. "I had a few questions."

"YOU KNOW, I NEVER BELIEVED THE STORY ABOUT ROD," SARAH SAID. "THE drugs. That he murdered the cop. I never believed any of it."

Gary sat in a recliner, a few feet away from Sarah and Beth. He tried to appear casual despite the tightness in his gut. Something about Sarah's presence left him feeling uneasy.

"I had so many questions," Sarah said. "So much didn't add up. I hated not knowing what happened—I mean, the police still haven't even arrested anyone for the murder. Do you know what that feels like? Your husband is murdered, you're given this explanation that he was involved in drugs, told that he killed someone, and then no one is even arrested for his murder. The uncertainty, the not knowing—it's been horrible. So I decided to do something about it."

"What do you mean?" Gary said. He didn't like where this was heading.

"That money you gave me, the fifty thousand dollars—I used some of it to hire a private investigator," Sarah said. "I told him to look into everything about Rod, everything about the night he was killed. See if Rod really was hiding some secret life. See if all those things the police claimed were true. Just so I could get an answer. Just so I could find out what happened. I had to know."

Gary glanced over at Beth. She stared back, her face a blank slate. Had she and Sarah been talking before he arrived back? Had Beth already heard all of this?

"This private investigator, he talked to all of Rod's friends," Sarah said. "Everyone, even people Rod knew before he met me. One of the people he talked with was the owner of a bar Rod used to go to. A guy named Lucas. He said Rod showed up to his bar the night before he was killed. He showed Lucas a picture of someone he was trying to find. A guy with tattoos all over his arms. Prison tattoos, Lucas said. An Edgewood tattoo. For some reason, Rod was trying to track this person down. The very next night, Rod was killed."

Gary cleared his throat. Coughed once. That feeling of discomfort was eating away at his insides like a virus.

"When the private investigator told me all of this, something didn't seem right. Rod's looking for this person, a guy covered in prison tattoos, and then Rod is murdered the very next night? That's suspicious. But the most suspicious part about the whole thing was Rod wasn't alone when he visited Lucas. Lucas said that Rod was with someone: his brother, Gary. You were there with Rod, looking for this person."

Gary shifted in his seat. Sarah's eyes were locked on him.

"What is going on?" Sarah asked. "Who was this guy you and Rod were trying to find? Why was Rod dead a day after you were searching for him? I want some answers."

Gary's stomach lurched. He couldn't believe what he'd just heard.

"It was nothing, Sarah," he began.

"What do you mean?" Sarah said.

Gary's mind raced. One more lie. That's all he needed. Come up with one more lie, explain everything away, and keep it all a secret. He'd told so many lies that one more shouldn't be a problem.

"Rod came to me and said he needed help finding someone. He wouldn't tell me who the guy was. He wouldn't tell me why. All he said was that he needed to find this person."

Both women stared back at him. Gary felt like he was under interrogation.

"I said I'd help. Rod had this picture: a guy covered in tattoos. We went to a few people to try to identify any of the tattoos. Lucas was one of them. He was able to read that one of the tattoos said *Edgewood*. Like the neighborhood."

"And then?"

"That was it. Rod said, 'That's all I needed to know.' Something like that. And we both went home."

"And Rod was killed a day after this happens? A day after he's trying to find this person?" Sarah said. "You didn't think that was suspicious?"

"I did. And I told the police about it. Said that Rod was looking for a guy, this guy covered in tattoos. Nothing ever came of it."

Sarah stared off for a moment.

"Edgewood. Why was Rod looking for someone from Edgewood, of all places? Who do you think it was?"

"A drug dealer? Some criminal? I don't know. I don't really want to know, to be honest. If the police weren't able to find anything, I'm not sure if any of us would be. It's best to just let it go. Try to move on."

More silence from Sarah. She shook her head.

"Maybe you're right," she said.

Sarah stood up from the couch, and they walked her to the door. She left without saying anything. Gary and Beth watched out the window as Sarah walked down their driveway.

"I feel so bad for her," Beth said.

"I know."

"You really don't know who the guy in the picture was?"

"No clue."

"No idea why Rod was trying to find him?"

"Not at all."

Beth turned away from the window. She stared at Gary for a moment. Waited.

"Can I ask you one more question?" she said.

"Sure."

"Why are you lying?"

—————

GARY COULDN'T KEEP THE LOOK OF SHOCK OFF HIS FACE. BY THE TIME HE clenched his jaw and tried to hide his reaction, it was too late. Beth had already seen it.

"I'm not—"

"You are, Gary," Beth said. Her mouth was slightly open, her eyes narrowed. That look of distrust, skepticism. That look he'd seen so often.

"Please don't deny it," she said. "Your face. Your reactions. They give it away. Why did you lie to Sarah?"

Gary opened his mouth but stopped before saying anything. Staring at Beth, he suddenly felt incredibly exhausted. A heavy weight behind his eyes. A stiffness in his chest. His legs felt so weak that he nearly collapsed.

He was sick of the lies. Sick of keeping everything bottled up inside. Sick of it all.

He just wanted this to be over. Wanted it all to end. And he knew it never would be over while he still had this secret, this secret that he dragged with him like an invisible weight.

It was time to come clean. Time for the truth.

It was time for closure.

"I'm going to tell you something, Beth," he said. "No matter how unbelievable what I'm about to say seems, I want you to let me finish. Okay?"

She nodded. Still that same skeptical look on her face, but her features had changed just a little. Curiosity. Like she wasn't quite sure where this was heading.

"Let's sit down for this," he said.

He led her into the living room and they sat down on the couch. Gary breathed in deeply and turned to her.

"Right after we started trying to raise money for your treatment, a man approached me. He made me an offer. . . ."

THE WORDS CAME OUT IN A RUSH AS HE TOLD THE ENTIRE STORY. THE WHOLE truth, leaving nothing out. He'd wanted someone to talk to for so long, and now that he finally had that, it was therapeutic to let it all out.

Beth sat on the couch and listened to it all. No reaction. No words. Gary didn't see her blink even once.

When Gary finally finished, he slowly shook his head.

"So, that's the story," he said. "I killed a man to save you. I was cheated out of the money. Rod was helping track the guy down. And things got out of control. Rod's dead all because of me. It's weighed on me ever since it happened. Losing him was hard enough, but knowing that I'm the reason he's not around anymore . . . It's been awful."

Beth stared back at him blankly. Gary searched her face, searched for any sort of reaction. But there was nothing.

He waited for her to speak. Or cry. Or storm out of the room. Waited for any kind of response. Finally, the waiting became too much.

"Can you talk, Beth?"

Silence.

"Beth?"

"You killed a man, Gary."

He nodded.

"You framed Rod for the murder."

Another nod.

"And the police detective who visited . . ."

"He almost put it together. Pinning it on Rod was the only way out of it."

"This is too much," Beth said, standing up from the couch. She stumbled a little, like she was about to fall back down, but caught her balance. She walked across the room.

"I knew something was going on," she said. "The way you kept disappearing. Kept acting so distant. I knew something was going on." She shook her head. "But this . . ."

"I had to do it. I wasn't going to lose you."

Beth bit her lower lip. Trying not to cry.

"You kept this from me, from everyone, the entire time it was happening?" she asked.

"Yeah. I did."

"Why did you finally decide to tell me?"

"I'm sick of lying. Sick of keeping it bottled up inside."

Beth slowly paced around the living room. Walking a little wobbly, still looking like she might tumble to the ground at any moment.

"I don't know what to do with this information," she said.

"Do whatever you want with it."

"Should I just pretend like you never told me? Thank you for saving my life? Turn you in to the police?"

"If you think I deserve to be punished, I'll accept that. If you want me to confess to the police or tell Sarah everything, I will."

"No," she said. "I don't want that."

Beth walked back over to the couch and sat down next to him. She asked more questions. Asked about Devon Peterson. Asked about the night Rod was killed. Asked about that night at Solid Gold Pawn. Gary mechanically recited every detail, repeating much of what he'd already told her. Beth listened to it all—still not reacting much, mostly just asking questions.

When she finally finished with her questions, Gary placed his hand on her thigh.

"It's unbelievable, I know," he said. "All of it is. Just know that I did it all for you. You and Tyson."

———

DAYS PASSED. WEEKS. MONTHS. GARY FINISHED CLOSING ASCENSION Outerwear. Started looking for a new job. Beth found a full-time teaching position for the upcoming school year. They spent countless hours with Tyson.

Confessing to Beth changed something between them. Altered their relationship—just slightly, but enough for Gary to notice. At times, it felt as if they were two people on a first date, conscious of every word and mannerism, not a couple who'd been married for nearly twenty years. Long stretches of silence. Conversations that seemed forced. An uncomfortable feeling when they embraced.

Occasionally, Gary would catch Beth looking at him with a far-off, empty gaze in her eyes. Like she was staring through him, not at him. Whenever he saw that look, Gary knew. Beth was thinking about what he'd told her. Thinking about the fact that her husband was a murderer.

They still played Scrabble most nights, still watched Netflix whenever they could. They were still in love—at least, Gary thought they were. It just felt different. He'd hoped that confessing to Beth would be the first step toward moving on. Putting everything behind him. Instead, it all still lingered—the sadness, the guilt.

He told himself that someday it would end. Told himself that the memory of what he'd done would fade, that he'd remember the happy times with Rod, that his relationship with Beth would return to normal. *Someday,* he told himself, *it will all get better.*

But he wondered if he was only lying to himself.

ACKNOWLEDGMENTS

I'll begin by thanking my agent, Laney Katz Becker at Massie & McQuilkin. She's absolutely incredible. Her knowledge, insight, and patience helped me improve this book tremendously. Plus, she sold the book to an amazing editor.

That amazing editor is Danielle Perez at Berkley. I can't put into words how fortunate I am to have such a diligent, talented, and over-all fun editor to work with. Danielle was enthusiastic about *Killer Choice* from the start, and I'm forever indebted to her for everything— including taking a chance on a new author.

I also want to thank my copy editor, Robin Catalano, who did a phenomenal job, especially when it came to ironing out all the details. Also, a big thanks to the art director, Emily Osborne, for designing this cover, which I absolutely love. And a huge thank-you to all the amazing people on the team at Berkley—you all helped make my dream come true.

Jordan Redwood, Dr. Richard Mabry, and Dr. Joshua Sasine helped with the medical details in this novel. Jordan and Richard are also thriller authors, so check out their books. And just remember: if

ACKNOWLEDGMENTS

there are any errors in the medical scenes in *Killer Choice*, I'm the one to blame.

I wrote a majority of this novel at Y Cafe on Twelfth and B in New York City. Thanks to Gloria and the rest of the staff for giving me a great place to write, hang out, and grab a bite; they're the best. Order the catfish curry if you go.

Lastly, thanks to you, the reader. There are so many good books out there, and I'm honored you chose *Killer Choice*. I hope you enjoyed it.

ENJOYED *A KILLER CHOICE*?

DON'T MISS TOM HUNT'S THRILLING NEXT NOVEL:

ONE FATAL MISTAKE.

'Full of shocks and twists you won't see coming'

LEE CHILD

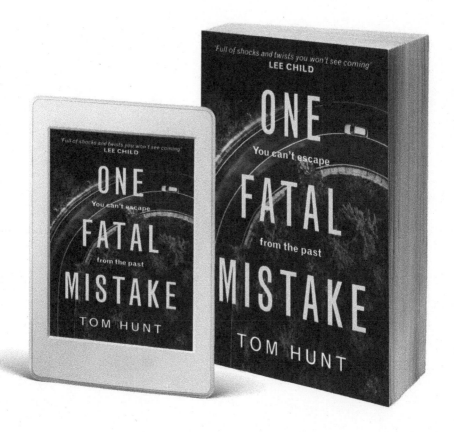